Without a T.....

The chronicles of Hugh de Singleton, surgeon

The Unquiet Bones
A Corpse at St Andrew's Chapel
A Trail of Ink
Unhallowed Ground
The Tainted Coin
Rest Not in Peace
The Abbot's Agreement
Ashes to Ashes
Lucifer's Harvest
Deeds of Darkness
Prince Edward's Warrant
Without a Trace

Without a Trace

**The twelfth chronicle of
Hugh de Singleton, surgeon**

MEL STARR

LION FICTION

Published by
Lion Hudson Limited
Wilkinson House, Jordan Hill Business Park,
Banbury Road, Oxford OX2 8DR, England
www.lionhudson.com

ISBN 978 1 78264 267 1
e-ISBN 978 1 78264 268 8

First edition 2019

A catalogue record for this book is available from the British Library

Printed and bound in the UK, June 2019, LH26

For Russell Clark Starr
(1904–2000)

and Mabel Osborne Starr
(1899–1966)

Acknowledgments

Several years ago when Dr Dan Runyon, professor of English at Spring Arbor University, learned that I had written an as yet unpublished medieval mystery, he invited me to speak to his fiction-writing class about the trials of a rookie writer seeking a publisher. He sent chapters of Hugh de Singleton's first chronicle, *The Unquiet Bones*, to his friend Tony Collins at Lion Hudson. Thanks, Dan.

Tony has since retired, but many thanks to him and all those at Lion Hudson who saw Hugh de Singleton's potential. Thanks also to my editors – Jan Greenough for the first nine books, and Penelope Wilcock for the most recent – who know Sir Hugh well and excel at asking such questions as "Do you really want to say it that way?" and "Wouldn't Hugh do it like this?"

Dr John Blair, of Queen's College, Oxford, has written several papers about Bampton history. These have been valuable in creating an accurate time and place for Hugh.

In the summer of 1990 Susan and I found a delightful B&B in a medieval village north of Lichfield named Mavesyn Ridware. Proprietors Tony and Lis Page became friends, and when they moved to Bampton some years later they invited us to visit them there. Tony and Lis introduced me to Bampton and became a great source of information about the village. Tony died in March 2015, only a few months after being diagnosed with cancer. He is greatly missed.

Ms Malgorzata Deron, of Poznan, Poland, offered to update and maintain my website. She has done a marvelous job. To see her work visit www.melstarr.net.

Glossary

Almoner: official of castle or monastery charged with dispensing alms – food or money – to the poor.

Ambler: an easy-riding horse, because it moved both right legs together, then both left legs.

Angelus: the church bell was rung three times each day – dawn, noon, and dusk – announcing the time for the Angelus Devotional.

Bailiff: a lord's chief manorial representative. He oversaw all operations, collected rents and fines, and enforced labor service. Not a popular fellow.

Banneret: a military rank superior to a knight.

Beadle: a manor official in charge of fences, enclosures, and curfew. He served under the bailiff and reeve. Also called a hayward.

Beans yfryed: beans first simmered, then fried in oil with onions and/or garlic.

Beaulieu: Cistercian abbey near Southampton.

Bruit: a sauce of white wine, breadcrumbs, onions, and spices.

Candlemas: February 2. Marked the purification of Mary. Women traditionally paraded to the village church carrying lighted candles. Tillage of fields resumed this day.

Capon: a castrated male chicken.

Chauces: tight-fitting trousers, often particolored, having different colors for each leg.

Coney: rabbit.

Coppice: to cut back a tree so that a thicket of saplings will grow from the stump. These shoots were used for everything from arrows to rafters, depending upon how long they were permitted to grow.

Corn: a kernel of any grain. Maize – American corn – was unknown in Europe at the time.

Cotehardie: the primary medieval outer garment. Women's were floor-length; men's ranged from thigh to ankle.

Cotter: a poor villager, usually holding five acres or less. He often had to labor for wealthy villagers to make ends meet.

Crécy: French village where, in 1346, Edward III defeated the French army.

Cresset: a bowl that could be filled with oil and with a floating wick used for lighting.

Cyueles: deep-fried fritters made of a paste of breadcrumbs, ground almonds, eggs, sugar, and salt, then fried.

Daub: a clay and plaster mix, reinforced with straw and/or horse hair, used to plaster the exterior of a house.

Demesne: land directly exploited by a lord and worked by his villeins, as opposed to land a lord might rent to tenants.

Dexter: a war horse, larger than pack horses and palfreys. Also the right-hand direction.

Dowry: a gift from the bride's family to the groom, intended for her support during marriage and during widowhood, should her husband predecease her.

Dredge: mixed grains planted together in a field – often barley and oats.

Eels in bruit: eels served in bruit sauce.

Farrier: a smith who shoes horses.

Farthing: one-fourth of a penny. The smallest silver coin.

Gathering: eight leaves of parchment made by folding the prepared hide three times.

Gentleman: a nobleman. The term had nothing to do with character or behavior.

Glebe: land belonging to or providing revenue for a parish church.

Grange: a farm associated with and providing food and revenue for an abbey.

Groat: a silver coin worth four pence.

Groom: a household servant to a lord, ranking above a page and below a valet.

Grope Lane: street in Oxford now known as Magpie Lane.

Hallmote: the manorial court. Royal courts judged free tenants accused of murder and felony; manorial courts had jurisdiction over legal matters concerning villagers.

Hanoney: eggs scrambled with onions and fried.

Hosteller: monastic official in charge of providing for abbey guests. Also called "guest master."

Hue and cry: alarm call raised by the person who discovered a crime. All who heard were expected to go to the scene of the crime and, if possible, pursue the felon.

Infangenthef: the right of a lord of a manor to try and execute a thief caught in the act.

King's Eyre: a royal circuit court, presided over by a traveling judge.

Kirtle: a medieval undershirt.

Lady: a title of rank for a female. As with "gentleman" it had nothing to do with character or behavior.

Lammastide: August 1, when thanks was given for a successful wheat harvest. From Old English "loaf mass."

Leech Lombard: a dish of ground pork, eggs, raisins, currants, and dates, with added spices. The mixture was boiled in a sack until set, then sliced for serving.

Liripipe: a fashionably long tail attached to a man's cap and usually coiled on top of the head.

Lych gate: a roofed gate at the entry to a churchyard under which the deceased would rest during the initial part of a medieval funeral.

Marshal: a high-ranking official having charge of a lord's stables, military resources, and ceremonies.

Marshalsea: the stables and their associated accoutrements.

Martinmas: November 11, the traditional date to slaughter animals for winter food.

Maslin: bread made with a mixture of grains, commonly wheat and rye or barley.

Meselade: a dish of beaten eggs and bread, sprinkled with sugar.

Michaelmas: September 29. The feast signaled the end of the harvest. Last rents and tithes were due.

Michaelmas Term: the academic term from September to Christmas.

Midsummer's Eve: June 23/24. (By the fourteenth century the Julian calendar was about ten days off.)

Palfrey: a riding horse with a comfortable gait.

Parchment: animal skin, usually sheep or goat, prepared for writing.

Pardoner: religious official who raised money by selling indulgences.

Porre of peas: a thick pea soup made with onions, spices, and sugar.

Portcullis: a grating of iron or wood hung over a passage and lowered between grooves to prevent access.

Pottage: anything cooked in one pot, from the meanest oatmeal to a savory stew.

Pottage of whelks: whelks boiled and served in a stock of almond milk, breadcrumbs, and spices.

Pound: there was no one pound coin in the fourteenth century. The term represented twenty shillings or 240 pence.

Quarter noble: a coin worth one shilling and eight pence.

Radcot Bridge: assumed to be the oldest bridge over the River Thames. Built in about 1200, and still in use for light vehicles on the A4095 between Clanfield and Faringdon.

Reeve: an important manor official, although he did not outrank the bailiff. Elected by tenants from among themselves, he had responsibility for fields, structures, and enforcing labor service.

Refectory: the abbey dining hall.

Rice moyle: a dish of rice simmered in almond milk, saffron, and sugar.

Runcie: a small common horse of lower grade than a palfrey.

St. Beornwald's Church: today called the Church of St Mary the Virgin, in the fourteenth century it was named for an obscure Saxon saint.

Shilling: twelve pence. Twenty shillings made a pound, although there were no shilling or pound coins.

Solar: a small room in a castle, more easily heated than the great hall, where lords preferred to spend time, especially in winter. Usually on an upper floor.

Statute of Laborers: following the first attack of plague in 1348–49 laborers realized that because so many workers had died, their labor was in demand and so required higher wages. In 1351 parliament set wages at the 1347 level. Like most attempts to legislate against the law of supply and demand, the statute was generally a failure.

Stewed herrings: herring stuffed with a mixture of breadcrumbs, parsley, thyme, black pepper, currants, sugar, and onions, all chopped finely, then boiled.

Stockfish: the cheapest salted fish, usually cod or haddock.

Stone (weight): fourteen pounds.

Tenant: a free manor resident who rented land from his lord. He could pay his rent in labor or, more likely in the fourteenth century, in cash. Or a combination of both.

Toft: land surrounding a villager's house, often used for growing vegetables and keeping chickens.

Trinity Term: the third term of the academic year, from mid-April to the end of June.

Twelfth Night: the evening of January 5, preceding Epiphany.

Valet: the highest-ranking servant to a lord.

Verderer: the forester in charge of a lord's woodlands.

Vicar: a priest serving a parish church but not entitled to its tithes.

Villein: a non-free peasant. He could not leave his land or service to his lord, or sell animals without permission. But if he could escape his manor for a year and a day he would be free.

Void: dessert – often sugared fruit and sweetened wine.

Wattle: interlacing sticks used as a foundation and support for daub in forming the wall of a house.

Weald (the): a "suburb" to the southwest of Bampton, its inhabitants were tenants of the Bishop of Exeter.

Week-work: the two or three days of labor per week (more during harvest) that a villein owed his lord.

Whitsunday: "white Sunday," ten days after Ascension Day, seven weeks after Easter.

Wimple: a cloth covering worn over the head and around the neck.

Yardland: about thirty acres. Also called a virgate and, in northern England, an oxgang.

Bampton to Oxford; fourteenth century

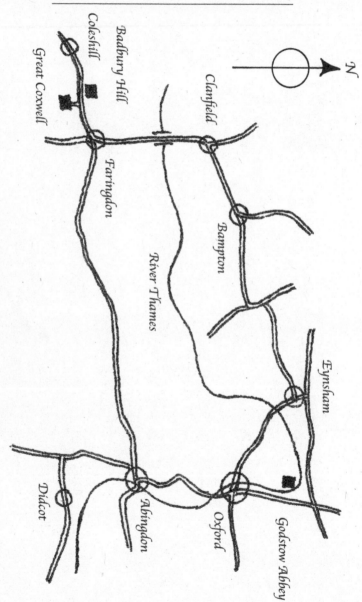

Chapter 1

June and July are hungry months. Hogs slaughtered and smoked and salted at Martinmas have been consumed, and unless a man is adept at setting snares to poach his lord's coneys and hares, he and his family will go without flesh upon their trenchers.

In the June of 1373 corn was also in short supply. The harvest was not bountiful last year, so in June of 1373 most folk of Bampton village lived with hollow bellies and prayed for an abundant harvest this year.

Two of my Kate's hens had gone missing since Whitsunday so we were without their eggs to feed ourselves and Bessie and John, and Kate's father. I was angry that some villager had made off with the fowls, but what would I do if my babes were crying from hunger? Would I steal to spare them? Or to keep them alive? I pray I must never be brought to such a pass.

Men sometimes wonder how they might conduct themselves in a crisis. Such a question can only be answered when a crisis visits. Better, perhaps, to never know the answer to such a question, for to know means that evil has come.

No man had made off with Kate's rooster, so the creature awoke me as he greeted the dawn on the twenty-first day of June – a Tuesday. I remember the day well, for before the sun dropped below Lord Gilbert's wood to the west of Bampton Castle my employer, Lord Gilbert Talbot, assigned me the most vexing task I had yet undertaken in his service.

I am Hugh de Singleton – Sir Hugh, since Prince Edward saw fit to award me a knighthood for my service to him some months past – surgeon and bailiff to Lord Gilbert Talbot at his manor of Bampton. My post often requires of me that I seek out miscreants who trouble the peace of Lord Gilbert's villeins and tenants. Because I have had success in such duty Lord Gilbert has sometimes seen fit to instruct me to assist friends who require the services of a sleuth to unravel some knotty trouble.

I broke my fast with a fragment of stale maslin loaf and a cup of ale, then set off for John Prudhomme's house. John has been chosen reeve of Bampton Manor for several years, and this day we must divide our duty – one to oversee haying, the other the ploughing of a fallow field of Lord Gilbert's demesne. I sent John to watch over the ploughing, to make sure the ploughmen turned the sod deeply so the roots of weeds were exposed, and went to observe the haying.

Ten of Lord Gilbert's villeins, with their wives and older children, arrived at the meadow shortly after the sun had dried the dew. The men set off with their scythes while the women and children followed, turning the hay to ensure that it dried evenly. My presence as observer of this labor was not really required. A successful hay crop means more animals can be kept over the next winter – for fresh meat, or breeding stock, or sale. So the men at their scythes swung them close to the ground and the women and children were careful to leave no clumps which would molder if the weather turned wet.

The day grew so warm that the haymakers had stripped to their kirtles by the fourth hour, and sweat mingled with dust upon their brows when the Angelus Bell rang from the tower of the Church of St. Beornwald, signaling noon and a break for dinner. The work was arduous, but the laborers grinned as they went to their meals. The hay crop was good.

As I turned from Bridge Street to Church View Street on the way to my own dinner, I saw Adela walking ahead, returning to Galen House from the baker with three loaves in her arms. Adela's father is a poor cotter of the Bishop of Exeter's lands in the Weald. My service to Prince Edward last year included discovering who had slain Sir Giles Cheyne, the prince's companion at the Battle of Crécy. For this labor I had been made Sir Hugh, and also awarded a sixth part of the revenues of the murdered knight's lands – prosperity enough for me to hire a servant to assist my Kate, who was now Lady Katherine to the folk of Bampton and the Weald.

Dinner this day at Galen House was a porre of peas, and the loaves yet warm from the baker's oven. Thrifty Kate had eked out the gammon, so we still had some scraps of it to flavor the pottage.

"Have Lord Gilbert's guests arrived?" my father-in-law asked as we ate.

"Nay, but Coleshill is not far distant and the roads are dry. Sir Aymer should arrive before supper."

The care and feeding of guests at Bampton Castle is not a part of my duties to Lord Gilbert, but his instructions for his cook, chamberlain, valets, and grooms regarding any forthcoming visit of guests were soon known to me and most others of the village.

Sir Aymer Molyns, the expected guest, was wed to Philippa Felbridge, cousin once removed to Lady Petronilla, Lord Gilbert's wife. Lady Petronilla had succumbed to plague when the disease reappeared four years past. Lady Philippa was Sir Aymer's second wife, his first bride, Lady Alyce, having also perished in the return of plague in 1369.

As we enjoyed our repast with its welcome flavor of pork added to the peas, we speculated about the mealtime conversations at the castle when Sir Aymer came to stay. Did the memory of old sorrow and the specter of plague stand in the shadows? Or were present friendship and married felicity cheer enough? Bittersweet, mayhap. We chewed it over along with our meal, then at last I must wipe my mouth, lay aside my napkin, and return to the tasks of the day.

A man with a scythe is expected to mow an acre of hay in a day. As there were ten men at work in the hayfield – which measured little more than half a yardland in size – they had nearly completed when, at the ninth hour, I saw riders, two carts, and an elaborately painted wagon approach the castle from Cowleys Corner. Here, I thought, are Sir Aymer and Lady Philippa.

A painted canvas stretched over hoops covered the wagon. As this had been a day of bright sun I assumed Lady Philippa traveled under the canvas so as to keep her complexion pale. Most gentlefolk think this a mark of beauty. And status. A tanned visage is the mark of a woman of the commons, who must labor in the sun. My Kate is usually tanned by Michaelmas. This does not diminish her beauty. Not to me. Why is it, I wonder, that the summer sun will cause skin to grow darker and hair to become lighter? Here is another question for my mystery bag, to be opened when the Lord Christ welcomes me to His kingdom. Surely He will know.

When I first came to Bampton in Lord Gilbert's employ I was surprised to learn of a practice I had not seen before. At the end of a day's haying, men are permitted to take for their own as much of the lord's hay as they can carry from the field upon their scythe. But they must not be over-greedy. If any hay falls before they carry it from the field, all they have piled upon their scythe is forfeit.

I watched as the villeins stacked remarkable mounds of hay upon their scythes and carried the fodder away, then I left the hayfield and walked to Bampton Castle's forecourt. Lord Gilbert's visitors had but moments before passed under the portcullis and into the castle yard. Arthur and Uctred, two of Lord Gilbert's grooms who had in the past been of service to me in seeking felons, were among the servants taking Sir Aymer's beasts in hand as he, his squire, and a dozen or so grooms and valets dismounted.

I had no business at the castle, no reason to greet Lord Gilbert's guests, but I passed into the castle yard to admire Sir Aymer's horse, a fine chestnut destrier. I was about to retrace my steps to the forecourt when I heard raised voices. I did not at first comprehend the words, but turned to see whence the din came, and heard Sir Aymer roar, "Empty, by heavens! Where is she? She entered the wagon this morn. Why is she not within now?"

The knight addressed these shouted questions to an elderly wispy-haired man who had, until a moment earlier, been mounted upon the first of the three runcies which drew the wagon. The fellow was frail, and glanced from Sir Aymer to the wagon with an open mouth and startled expression.

Lord Gilbert drew aside the canvas enclosing the rear of the wagon and as I watched he peered inside. The roads were dry.

The wagon was closed front and back to keep out dust. When my employer withdrew his head his bluff features registered puzzlement. Apparently Sir Aymer's wife – who else would travel in such a conveyance? – was not to be found.

This disappearance soon set tongues wagging. Sir Aymer's grooms and valets put their heads together, and Lord Gilbert's servants did likewise. Meanwhile Lord Gilbert stood, arms akimbo, studying the wagon, and Sir Aymer continued to berate the dejected postilion rider.

The curious spectacle caught my eye. I stood near the castle gatehouse to watch and listen. How could a lady disappear between Coleshill and Bampton, a distance of but nine miles? This question was about to be assigned to me, for as I watched Sir Aymer berate the wagon driver Lord Gilbert's eye fell upon me. A moment later he beckoned vigorously and I approached him.

"Here is a puzzle," Lord Gilbert said over the clamor of competing voices pronouncing opinions regarding the vanished lady. "The Lady Philippa and her maid went into the wagon this morning at Coleshill, but are not within now. I fear some evil has befallen the lady."

Sir Aymer, meanwhile, left off castigating the hapless postilion and stalked to where Lord Gilbert and I stood. "My wife has been taken," he concluded. "I and my men will ride back along the way we came to see if Lady Philippa may be found."

"I will join you," Lord Gilbert said at once. Then, to me, "You come also, Hugh. Arthur! Uctred! Saddle my ambler and three palfreys! We four will accompany Sir Aymer."

Arthur and Uctred hurried to the stables to do Lord Gilbert's bidding, while my employer hastened to his hall. He returned a moment later buckling a sword to his belt.

"If there are felons about who stole the lady 'twill be well to be armed. Have you your dagger?"

I touched the hilt of my weapon in reply.

Sir Aymer, his squire, five of his grooms and valets, along with Lord Gilbert, Arthur, Uctred, and me clattered across the castle drawbridge a few moments later. We rode past Cowleys Corner, across Radcot Bridge, beyond Clanfield, out all the way to Faringdon, but we saw no trace of the missing lady, nor any sign that some felony had taken place along the road. Sir Aymer often called Lady Philippa's name. Silence was the only reply.

We occasionally saw men working late in the fields along the road, and once passed two travelers afoot. None of these had seen a lady and her maid. At Clanfield we questioned several folk. A woman of the village recalled seeing Sir Aymer and his party pass earlier in the day – Lady Philippa's colorful wagon would be remembered. Since then, she said, only a cart and men afoot had traveled the road before her house.

'Twas near to Midsummer's Eve, so we had ample light to inspect the road and verge. Nothing was amiss. Lady Philippa and the maid had vanished.

Even on this longest day, the sun had set when we returned to Bampton Castle. For six hours we had sought Lady Philippa without success. But the search was not ended.

As he dismounted, Lord Gilbert turned to me and spoke. "Hugh, I wish for you to discover what has befallen Lady Philippa. It may be that she was taken whilst upon my lands, near to Bampton. If so, I'll not have a guest so ill-used. Come to the castle early tomorrow and we will consider what must be done."

Chapter 2

Kate, the children, and my father-in-law were abed when I stumbled, exhausted, in the dark to Galen House. After much thumping upon the door I roused Caxton from his bed and he lifted the bar to admit me.

I had also awakened Kate, and when I ascended the stairs to our chamber she insisted I tell her the reason for my tardy return. She had an opinion.

"Either the lady was taken by felons, or she conspired in her own disappearance," she said. "Either way, some man will be involved."

"Aye, a lady and her maid will not purpose to vanish into the country with no man to protect them... if they are willingly gone away."

"If men have stolen her," Kate said, "Sir Aymer will soon receive a ransom demand."

"Aye, he will. But how could such fellows take two women from a wagon and not be seen or heard at the business?"

"How could the lady have fled the wagon of her own will, with her maid, without being seen or heard?" Kate replied. "Either is unlikely."

"But one is necessarily true, else the Lord Christ took the women to Him. I do not know Lady Philippa, but it seems unlikely she would be so holy as to escape death."

Kate made no reply, but sank back to her pillow and soon her regular breathing indicated sleep. I, however, stared at the rafters and considered what I might do to bring Lady Philippa back to her husband. The wagon driver seemed most likely to know what may have happened along the road, yet he could shed but little light upon the matter – and for sufficient reasons. So I thought.

I hurried to the castle as the morning Angelus Bell sounded, eager to set about solving this mystery. Sir Aymer was breaking his fast with Lord Gilbert when I arrived, and told me the postilion had made his bed for the night with Lord Gilbert's grooms. I found the man rubbing sleep from his eyes, his back toward.

Sir Aymer said the man's name was John. I spoke the name and received no reply. Uctred was near, and spoke.

"Deaf as a stump, that one. You'll need to shout."

I did, but a third and even louder call was required before the man turned his head to me. He blinked his eyes and I saw they were white with cataracts. I could deal with this malady, but had other, more pressing matters for my attention.

I managed to make myself understood, and asked the fellow of what he had seen and heard as he guided Lady Philippa's wagon to Bampton. I was not surprised to learn he had seen and heard nothing. "Three beasts hitched to wagon," he said. "I was ridin' first." I would need information from someone who had not lost vision and hearing.

The hoary fellow seemed genuinely grieved that his mistress had disappeared from under his nose and he could offer no help in finding her. I saw a tear upon his red, wrinkled cheek as I left him.

"The rooks," he croaked. I turned to the man. "Sir Aymer said sky was full of 'em. Hundreds of rooks. Evil sign, when rooks assemble. Evil."

Lord Gilbert and Sir Aymer had retired to the solar to discuss matters privily. I found them with heads together, trying explanations for Lady Philippa's disappearance, discounting one possibility after another.

"Have you learned anything from John... anything more than I, which was little enough?" Sir Aymer asked when I entered the solar. "Told me last eve he'd not seen or heard anything untoward. Of course, he'd not likely do either."

"The carter's vision is clouded and he suffers the disease of the ears," I replied. "He will be of little help in finding your wife, I fear."

"True enough. John served my father before me, and my grandfather before him. I'll not turn him out, and even if I would Lady Philippa would not hear of it. I thought he'd do no harm, riding

24

postilion, with so many other eyes and ears in our party. Normally I'd have a younger man as wagoner, but he's been taken ill."

"Where were you and your other servants placed as you traveled?" I asked.

"I rode ahead, with Giles and most of my men."

"Giles?"

"My squire."

"Did any man ride behind the wagon?"

"Aye. Much of the time Maurice and Brom rode with the wagon."

"Much of the time? When did they not?"

"There is a hill leading to Faringdon, and another leaving Clanfield. The runcies on Lady Philippa's wagon had a struggle. The wagon fell behind for a time."

"Have you spoken to the grooms about this?" I asked.

"Aye. Said this morning they were with the wagon all the journey but for the hills near to Faringdon and Clanfield."

"Then that is where your wife was taken," Lord Gilbert said. "One of those places."

"Likely. But why did she not cry out? Maurice and Brom would have heard her, even if John could not. They had not gone that far ahead of the wagon, I think."

I wondered why the grooms had ridden on ahead of the slowed wagon. Why not hold back?

"We will begin this day's search at Clanfield," I said, "if this meets with your approval. Mayhap, if Lady Philippa or her maid struggled with those who seized her, there will be some sign. I wish your grooms had spoken of this yesterday, when we passed the place in our search. The trail, if there is one, would have been fresh."

If Maurice and Brom had been assigned to remain with Lady Philippa on the journey, had not done so, and feared Sir Aymer's wrath, there would be reason enough for them to hold their tongues.

"I intend to return to Coleshill," Sir Aymer said. "If felons have my wife they will soon demand a ransom for her return. They will expect me to be there, not here."

"We will accompany you as far as Clanfield," Lord Gilbert said, bidding me to ready the horses. "Do you wish your servants and squire to accompany you to Coleshill, or remain here to assist in the search?"

Sir Aymer considered the question. I spoke.

"I would like the grooms Maurice and Brom to remain at Bampton. Perhaps your squire also. They may assist in the search, and if we find a lady they may tell me if 'tis Lady Philippa or not. I would not know your wife. And should we find her she will need escort back to Coleshill."

Sir Aymer shrugged. "As you wish. They'll do no good in Coleshill, waiting."

Lord Gilbert's solar may be entered from within the castle or without. The door to the castle yard leads to stone steps which descend to the ground. I departed the solar through this door, and as I closed it behind me looked out over the castle yard to a sea of upturned faces. Sir Aymer's servants and Lord Gilbert's grooms and valets gazed up at me. They knew decisions were being made within the solar and wondered what these might be.

Again I told Arthur and Uctred to see to the preparation of horses, then found Maurice, Brom, and Giles and told them that after this day's search they would return to Bampton – unless Lady Philippa was found – while Sir Aymer and his other servants returned to Coleshill.

John, the postilion, accompanied the search this day. I was unsure what he could offer to the quest, but seated him upon Lord Gilbert's gentlest runcie and brought him along.

We wasted no time calling for Lady Philippa or examining the verge, but hastened to the hill east of Clanfield, beyond Black Bourton Brook. 'Tis not much of a hill, traveling in either direction, but enough that three beasts would struggle to lift a heavy wagon to the summit.

Our party dismounted at the top of the rise, tied the horses to saplings, and left John and another of Sir Aymer's grooms to watch them. Sir Aymer assigned me, with Arthur, Uctred, and Brom, to walk the verge on one side of the road while he and Lord Gilbert with Maurice, the squire, and three of his servants examined the other.

There had been no rain for several days, for which the haymakers were pleased, but this meant the road was firm and dusty. No mud gave away footprints, or cart tracks in some place they should not have been.

Our two parties descended to the village, finding nothing along the way to suggest some felony had taken place. 'Twas not until we had returned partway that I saw the threads.

A bramble bush bordered the road, and beside it a narrow opening which might once have been a path into the forest but was now mostly overgrown. Upon a thorn, at about waist height, I saw dark tendrils dangling. They were so few that I at first thought 'twas the filaments of a spider's web I saw. But spiders do not weave webs of dark blue wool.

I called out to Sir Aymer and as he approached I asked Brom what color cotehardie his mistress had worn the day before.

"Blue... dark blue," he said, then glanced to the threads.

Sir Aymer pushed the groom aside the better to see what I held. He grasped the woolen threads and held them against the palm of his hand.

"Where was this found?" he demanded.

I pointed to the bramble bush. "Just there."

Lord Gilbert had followed Sir Aymer across the road. He peered over the knight's shoulder, then followed my pointing finger to the bush.

"Are these threads the color Lady Philippa wore yesterday?" I asked.

"They are so few 'tis difficult to say," Sir Aymer said. "She did wear blue."

Lord Gilbert, observing that the place where I found the wisps seemed to be the overgrown entrance to a woodland trail, looked carefully at the thorny opening.

"Some time past, men, or perhaps foxes, have crossed the road here and entered the wood... or departed from it. 'Tis hardly a path, but let us follow and see where it might lead. Watch the thorns and nettles!"

Lord Gilbert plunged into the clinging briars. My employer is a man who, when he determines to do a thing, proceeds to do it, regardless of nettles or thorns. Sir Aymer, Giles, and I followed in the path he trod down for us, Arthur, Uctred, and Sir Aymer's servants behind.

Ten or so paces from the road the trees grew thicker, their shadows reducing the sunlight available to low-growing foliage, so that our passage was less entangled. But the path, if that was what we followed, also became less evident. If feet had trod this way only hours before, there seemed no evidence of it. Last year's oak leaves lay dry and undisturbed upon the forest floor.

Nearly undisturbed.

Clanfield's residents had picked the forest clean of fallen limbs last autumn for firewood, as was their right. The only branches littering the ground were those which had dropped in spring storms a few months past and had not yet been claimed. One of these boughs, nearly as thick through as my leg and three or so paces long, lay just to the right of Lord Gilbert's chosen path. I glanced to the limb as we passed and saw a thing foreign to a forest floor.

A golden brooch lay beside a mound of leaves. No sunlight penetrated the wood to gleam from the object and catch my eye. 'Twas mere happenstance that I saw the brooch as I passed. Or was it? If the Lord Christ sometimes involves Himself in the affairs of men, as the Scriptures attest, then perhaps it was He who sent my gaze to the brooch.

"Wait," I cautioned, and kneeled in the leaves to examine the brooch. A locking pin at the back of the ornament was yet closed upon a small patch of the blue wool which had evidently torn free with the brooch. An arm's length away a small pile of leaves indicated where someone had perhaps tripped over the fallen branch and stumbled to their knees. Could such a tumble cause the brooch to pull free of its wearer?

Sir Aymer and Lord Gilbert turned to the place where I

kneeled, and approached. "What is there?" Lord Gilbert said. "What have you found?"

I held the brooch before Sir Aymer. "Did Lady Philippa wear this?" I asked. I knew no maid would wear such a bauble.

"I gave it to her when we wed," the knight said.

"She tripped over this fallen limb," I said, "and the brooch ripped away. So I believe. Perhaps she or her captors were in haste and did not notice that the brooch had torn loose."

"But I do not understand why she did not cry out when men pulled her from the wagon," Lord Gilbert said. "Someone would have heard, even though the carter hears nothing."

"If a man holds a dagger to your throat and commands silence," I said, "most folk will obey."

Sir Aymer placed the brooch in his purse, then studied the disturbed leaves at our feet. They were so little upset that had I not seen the brooch I would not have noticed the slight upheaval.

I turned my eyes to the direction I assumed the lady had been taken. The trees thinned, and through dappled sunlight I saw a field planted to oats some fifty paces distant.

Our party set off for the oat field. We walked the near edge of the field in both directions but saw no footprints in the earth. Wherever Lady Philippa was taken it did not require that she walk through an oat field.

The field ended less than a hundred paces to the north. I followed the edge of the plot to where, at a square corner, it turned to the west. Two hundred paces beyond the corner the field ended at a road. The road north to Black Bourton and Alvescot.

Had Lady Philippa come this way? If so, was she brought here against her will, or of her own volition? Against her will, I felt certain. Would a lady stumble through shrubbery and thorns and a wood of her own choice? If so, why? To escape a husband? Surely there would be less arduous ways to flee a spouse. But perhaps not.

Alert to the chase now, our party hastened along the edge of the oat field until we came to the road. From the crest of the hill where we had left our beasts we had traveled perhaps half a mile through forest and undergrowth. Lady Philippa's captors would not lead her to a road except they intended to travel it. And likely not afoot.

The road was dry, dusty, and well used. The marks of horses' hooves, men's feet, both bare and shod, and cart tracks were faint in the dust. There was no way to discern which of the impressions in the road had been made by Lady Philippa and her captors.

"We must travel the road north to Black Bourton," I said. "Perhaps some folk there have seen men traveling with a lady." To Arthur and Uctred I said, "Wait here and keep your eyes open. We will retrace our steps to the horses, then return by the Clanfield road. If any man passes whilst we are away, ask him of his business and whether he has seen two women, a lady and her maidservant, in the company of men."

We were not seeking to follow an obscure track, so our return to the Clanfield road and our beasts required less than half the time it had taken us to first traverse the forest and scrubland. Sir Aymer mounted and spurred his palfrey to a trot, we others did likewise to keep up, and shortly Arthur and Uctred came into view.

No man, Arthur said, had passed while he and Uctred awaited our return. The two grooms mounted their beasts and again Sir Aymer set off at a trot , this time for Black Bourton. 'Twas but a mile to the village.

As in Bampton, men and their wives and children were at work mowing meadows and spreading the cut hay evenly. No man, or woman, was likely to journey through the village unseen. When strangers pass, inhabitants of such places are likely to lean upon their scythes and rakes and watch until the travelers are out of sight.

I called our party to a halt before a band of women employed upon turning the new-cut hay. The meadow was quite large, a yardland at least. Large enough that I thought it likely the women had been at the same work the day before. I dismounted and approached the meadow. Sir Aymer and Lord Gilbert followed. The women had stopped their work when they saw us approach on the road. Now they recognized Lord Gilbert and curtsied.

"Aye," the women agreed. Two strange men upon a cart had passed through Black Bourton the previous day, shortly after the noon Angelus sounded. No women were seen, but the contents of the cart were covered. A heavy cloth of coarse woven hemp was fastened over the cart bed. A load of wool being taken to market, one woman guessed. To this the others agreed.

I looked from Sir Aymer to Lord Gilbert. "Easy enough to hide Lady Philippa and her maid in the bed of a cart," Lord Gilbert said. Then, to the haymakers, "Which road did this cart take from here? To Bampton or to Alvescot or Shilton?"

"To Shilton," a woman replied.

"Of course," Lord Gilbert muttered. "The rogues would not take their captive past Bampton Castle and pass right under my nose. We shall return to the castle for our dinner, then visit Shilton and follow that cart. Are you yet determined to return to Coleshill this day?" he said to Sir Aymer. "Or will you come with me and Sir Hugh to Shilton?"

Sir Aymer did not immediately reply. "I still think the scoundrels will demand a ransom of me," he eventually pronounced. "I must be in Coleshill, where they will surely send their demand. I trust you and your bailiff to see to matters here. I will hold to my original intent and return to Coleshill after dinner."

He did so, leaving Giles, Maurice, and Brom. Lord Gilbert, I, Arthur, and Uctred, the squire, and the two grooms rode with Sir Aymer as far as Cowleys Corner. John again rode postilion ahead of the empty wagon. The heavy conveyance would slow their journey. Sir Aymer would be fortunate to reach Coleshill before dark.

The haymakers had returned to their work from their dinner when we again passed Black Bourton. There and at Shilton, men were busy raising a pile of sticks and logs for the Midsummer's Eve fire the next day.

The fellows at work in Shilton tugged forelocks when they recognized Lord Gilbert. Two had seen a cart pass the village the day before, but had been some distance from it and could not remember if it was covered or not, or if two men rode upon it, or one.

Lord Gilbert thanked these tenants and bade them return to their work. He stood in the road, gazing north toward Burford.

"Shall we ride on?" I said.

"To what purpose?" Lord Gilbert replied. "Carts passing through Burford will be as thick as boats passing under London Bridge."

He was right. Burford is a town of perhaps near one thousand souls. Carts by the dozen, loaded with Cotswold wool, some of the finest in the realm, will pass through the town this time of year. And most will be covered to protect their valuable cargoes.

"Perhaps the cart we seek turned aside at Alvescot, or passed through Brize Norton," I said.

"Mayhap. But then 'twould likely enter Witney, and there are as many carts and carters upon Witney streets as throng those of Burford. To seek one cart there of many would be a fool's errand."

The afternoon sun warmed me as we made our way back to Bampton. I drew my palfrey beside Giles and asked of Sir Aymer and Lady Philippa. Lord Gilbert heard and also drew alongside the squire. The youth looked to Lord Gilbert and answered my questions in monosyllables. I felt sure that Giles might say more if out of Lord Gilbert's hearing, although why this might be so, and whether or not his words might illuminate the circumstances around Lady Philippa's disappearance, I could not guess.

Kate prepared a supper of stewed herrings with barley loaves. Adela was capable of preparing a meal of stewed herrings but Kate has told me that she is accustomed to being mistress of her own house and finds it now difficult to change. So she will prepare my supper, with only such aid from Adela as is needful. The lass may do the laundry, that Kate is quite willing to forgo, and sweep the flags, change the rushes, and care for the hens.

Bessie needed no encouragement to consume a wedge of barley loaf, and the herrings seemed to please her. John is beginning to take notice of his parents' meals and seems enthusiastic about the discovery. I am always pleased to see my children eat heartily. Bessie is now nearly past the age when infants die of fevers and such, but John, only a year old, is yet to pass through the fearful age.

As we ate I told Kate and her father of what had been learned this day concerning the missing lady. And of what had not been learned. My father-in-law, Robert Caxton, had been a stationer in Oxford until declining custom due to the deaths of so many scholars because of plague, and the theft of some of his books and gatherings of parchment, drove him out of business. His poverty had reduced the man to naught but skin and bones when I persuaded him to remove to Bampton and live with us in Galen House.

"Is Sir Aymer wealthy?" Caxton asked.

"As wealthy as any other knight, I suppose."

"So the men who took his wife might expect more than a few pounds for her return?"

"Probably. And I heard no mention of children. Sir Aymer and his lady were traveling from Coleshill to his manor of Epwell. They would not likely leave their children behind, but none accompanied them."

"A knight will surely wish for an heir," Caxton said. "Without a wife such an acquisition is most difficult." He chuckled at his wit and nearly choked upon a fragment of barley loaf.

Chapter 3

In the past, when required to investigate dark matters, I have learned I am likely to discover the most from those who least wish to speak to me. Giles Stonor seemed reluctant to speak when we rode together from Alvescot, especially when Lord Gilbert rode with us. I resolved to seek the youth.

I broke my fast with the stale remnant of a barley loaf, consumed a cup of ale, kissed my Kate, and set off for Bampton Castle.

Giles was at the marshalsea, seeing to his palfrey which, he said, had seemed to favor its foremost right hoof as we neared Bampton the previous day. He and Lord Gilbert's farrier were examining the suspect hoof when I entered the stable.

"Sure an' there's a stone caught between the shoe and the beast's hoof," the farrier said, and went to work at the offending pebble with a trimming knife. Giles stood, stretched, and spoke.

"I've been expecting you."

"Oh? Why so?"

"You asked yesterday of matters of which I did not wish to speak. I still don't, but I think you are not a man to be put off."

"Why will you speak now but not yesterday?"

"I'd rather Lord Gilbert did not know some things about his friend, Sir Aymer."

"What things?"

"You ask and I'll reply. If you do not ask I'll assume you do not consider the unspoken issue of importance."

"Very well. Sir Aymer placed John in charge of his wife's wagon. He knew the man to be frail and nearly deaf and blind. Why would he do so?"

"Did you not ask Sir Aymer?"

"He said the man had served his father and grandfather before him and he did not wish to put him away. The old man desired to

34

be of service for his keep, and Sir Aymer's usual ostler is ill. Do you question this?"

"Nay. I've heard Sir Aymer speak of John in such words. But 'twas Lady Philippa who chose John to guide her wagon. He was devoted to her."

"Sir Aymer has no children?"

"None. He was wed to Lady Alyce nine years, before plague took her. She was barren, and Lady Philippa also."

"Does this trouble Sir Aymer?"

"Trouble? Hah! A stronger word might be fair. He is bitter about his marriages. I heard him tell Lady Philippa that had he known she could not bear he'd not have wed her. Should have bedded her before the marriage, he said. Then, if she was found with child he would have known she was fertile."

"Lady Philippa is not a happy wife?"

"Nay, I think not. But she bears her humiliation well, I think."

"Does she bear more than humiliation?" I asked.

"What is your meaning?"

"Did Sir Aymer mistreat her in his wrath?"

"When Sir Aymer has too much wine his words might become deeds."

"Have you ever witnessed such deeds?"

"Aye, once. 'Twas in the hall, after dinner. Sir Aymer had too much hypocras, I believe. I saw him speaking privily to Lady Philippa, and when she replied he seized her and threw her from her chair."

"Does he commonly consume too much wine?"

"No more than most, I suppose."

"Does he ill-use Lady Philippa at other times as well?"

"Not that I've seen."

"What of things you've heard of, but have not seen?"

"Shortly after Twelfth Night Lady Philippa kept to her chamber for a fortnight. We thought 'twas perhaps because she was with child and felt ill."

"Not so?" I asked.

"Nay. Milicent told me Sir Aymer had blackened her eye."

"Who is Milicent?"

"Her maid."

"Does Lady Philippa take pleasure in the company of other men?"

"Pleasure? She has not been unfaithful to Sir Aymer if that's your meaning. Not that I know or have ever heard of."

"Would you have known? Does the lady confide in any of Coleshill's residents?"

"Milicent."

"Would Milicent relate what Lady Philippa said or did, to you?"

The squire blushed faintly. I had struck a nerve.

"Does Milicent speak of these private matters to others of Sir Aymer's household, or only you?"

The blush deepened. "Only me, so far as I know."

"You have a particular friendship with the maid?"

The blush continued. The squire did not reply.

"Was... is Milicent a pert lass?"

"Aye, she... she is," Giles stammered.

Very well. I needed to ask no further questions on that subject, then.

"Has Milicent ever suggested that Lady Philippa is so unhappy that she would flee?"

"Nay. Where would she go? Her father was pleased with the match. He arranged it, and it cost him a few shillings, also."

"Lady Philippa came to Sir Aymer with a large dowry?"

"She did."

"Hmmm. If Sir Aymer demanded an annulment because Lady Philippa is barren he would have to return the dowry to her father."

"Aye," the squire replied. "That's likely why those who've served Sir Aymer longer than I say he was not much sorrowful when Lady Alyce was taken with plague four years past."

"He was then free to wed another who might provide an heir?"

"Aye, but so far, not so."

"As to where Lady Philippa would go if she fled Coleshill, has she ever confided in Milicent about other suitors, before she wed Sir Aymer?"

"Aye. You've never met Lady Philippa?"

"Never."

"A beauty she was… is. Often speaks to Milicent of lads who've sought her hand."

"Any names you remember?"

"One. She'd have wed Martyn de Wenlock."

"Why did she not? Her father?"

"Aye. Her father would not permit it. Not after Sir Aymer showed interest."

"Who is Martyn de Wenlock?"

"A scholar. He studies at some college in Oxford. I don't know which."

"What father would wish to see a daughter wed to a penniless scholar, eh?" I was once a penniless scholar, and understand the disagreeable condition. "Has Milicent spoken of Lady Philippa recently recalling the student?"

"Aye. Not a fortnight past. As Sir Ayner became more unhappy with her she spoke of de Wenlock more often. So Milicent said."

"Thank you. To another matter: as you traveled from Coleshill with Sir Aymer and his lady, did you see any suspicious men about? We have gone over this ground already, but think upon it again. Were there others on the road? Perhaps men who appeared, then were gone, and then were seen again?"

"I don't recall any such. There were folk upon the road, but most were afoot. I saw but one cart, as I remember."

"Where? Was it covered?"

"Just before we came to Clanfield. It wasn't covered. 'Twas empty, as I could see from horseback, but there was a hempen cloth folded in the bed. The carters had stopped at the side of the road where a stream flows near the road. One was holding a leather bucket to their beast to have water. The other was garbed as a friar, or clerk."

"Was this near to Radcot Bridge?"

"Halfway from there to Clanfield, I'd say."

"Did these carters then follow Sir Aymer's party to Clanfield?"

"I paid no attention. I suppose so. They were traveling the same direction."

"It seems odd," I said, "that they would not catch you and pass by, having an unladen cart, whereas you had to travel slowly because of Lady Philippa's heavy wagon."

Giles pursed his lips and considered this suggestion. "We did make slow going, that's true. Three runcies were just enough to surmount the hills we came to. Perhaps the fellows rested their beast before they traveled on."

"Aye, perhaps."

I released the squire and considered what I had learned from him. Sir Aymer was unhappy with his wife. She had produced no heir. Lady Philippa was unhappy for the humiliation of her barren state. And when drunk Sir Aymer mistreated his wife. Perhaps at other times, as well. The lady often recalled fondly a former suitor. Would she have plotted to abscond with him? Would the scholar have seized her against her will? Would Sir Aymer have sought his wife's death so to be free to seek a third wife and the heirs his first two wives had not provided?

What of the unladen cart Giles saw beside the road south of Clanfield? Was it coincidence that the women hay-rakers of Black Bourton saw a cart pass their village about the time Lady Philippa vanished? The cart they saw was covered, whereas the cart Giles saw was not. But a hempen cloth was folded in the bed.

I returned to Galen House for my dinner. Kate and Adela had prepared meselade. As I approached my door I noticed some men raising a pile of branches and limbs in the Bishop of Exeter's meadow, beyond St. Beornwald's Church, for the Midsummer's Eve fire. I lingered to watch them, and waved my hand in greeting when one glanced my way.

If, as I suspected, Lady Philippa had been the target of felons – mayhap the two carters along the road – the bailiff of Clanfield Manor might know of disreputable characters within his bailiwick.

I resolved to seek him. His reputation had traveled the few miles from his manor to mine, so I was unsure of how much aid the fellow might provide. Indeed, he was known for corruption and odious dealings with his tenants and villeins. He could get away with such behavior because the lord of Clanfield lived most months upon another of his estates, and Clanfield's bailiff was resolute in collecting fees, rents, and fines for his master. That he kept a portion for himself did not, apparently, trouble the lord of Clanfield so long as the manor was profitable to him.

Clanfield is but two miles from Bampton. What evil could befall me in two miles? If the men who seized Lady Philippa knew that I sought them and her, much wickedness might occur in two miles. At Bampton Castle I found Arthur and bade him prepare two palfreys, then sought Giles Stonor and the grooms Maurice and Brom. They would accompany me to Clanfield, I told them, and I bade them make their beasts ready.

Arthur has served as a groom to Lord Gilbert for many years, since before I came to serve as bailiff at Bampton. He is no longer young, but his sturdy appearance is often enough to cause men otherwise prone to violence to reconsider their intentions. And if they should not, he is able to subdue most men who will not be persuaded to live peaceably and obey the laws of the realm.

"You believe the lady disappeared while traveling through my bailiwick?" the Clanfield bailiff asked when I had found him and explained my purpose. The man's name was Thomas Skirlaw. A round-faced fellow with eyes set close together and a small nose half the size of my own. Not plump, but soft, as if toil was unknown to him. It likely was.

"I'm sure of it," I replied. "The woolen threads and the brooch indicate that she passed through the wood just north of the village. I believe it unlikely she would do such a thing unless coerced. Are there men of Clanfield who might see a painted wagon upon the road, realize that the wife of a wealthy knight likely traveled within, and plot to take her for ransom? Men who have access to a cart?"

I did not add that the bailiff's reputation might include him among such potential felons. 'Twould be impolitic to do so, regardless of the truth of the matter. And even if he was not one of those who had captured Lady Philippa, he might search for the culprits not to bring them to justice but to demand a share of their loot should Sir Aymer be required to ransom his wife.

But there was also a chance that he might deal justly, being perhaps chagrined that a lady traveling through his manor could be taken. The felony would not show his governance in a good light. So I stood before him and asked of disreputable men of his bailiwick.

Clanfield's bailiff pulled at his beard and produced the impression of a man in deep thought. "Henry Burton is not to be trusted, nor Bogo Bennyng."

"Any others?" I asked.

"Janyn Hoard has been accused of stealing another man's furrow so often 'tis a common matter of contention at hallmote."

"You believe any of these three have the pluck to venture stealing a lady from her wagon?"

"You believe one man did the felony?" Skirlaw said.

"Nay. Two women were within the wagon. Though I suppose one man might subdue two women were they surprised to the point of confusion and paralysis, and if he held a dagger to the throat of one of them."

"But you think not?" the bailiff said. "And the codger who drove the team being so blind and deaf that even if the lady managed to call out he'd not have heard?"

'Twas a question, not a declaration. I had already described John the wagoner to him.

"Aye. A man with the ears he was born with would likely have heard the lady or her servant gasp, even if they did not, or could not, call for aid," I said. "But the others of Sir Aymer's party were far enough from the wagon because of the hill that a soft cry of surprise would not, I suppose, have carried to them."

"Teach that knight to keep better watch over his lady, eh?"

"Aye, perhaps. The men you named, I wish to speak to them.

Will you collect them for me? This day. I would investigate this matter with each man privily, before they take the chance to put their heads together and create some tale to absolve themselves... if they are the felons I seek."

We spoke in the street, before the bailiff's house. He motioned to a bench made of a beech log split in half, drawn up before the village well, across the street. "Wait there. Bogo is with the reeve and several others, ditching. Janyn and Henry are haying upon Sir William's meadow. Or they're supposed to be."

The bailiff's concluding remark indicated that he thought it conceivable Janyn and Henry might abscond from their week-work without his oversight.

The bailiff strode away to the south, leaving Arthur and me with Giles and the grooms at the well. A few moments later a little lass appeared carrying a bucket. The child did not at first notice us. We stood in the shade of the roof and a nearby tree. When she did catch a glimpse of five strange men at her village well she skidded to a stop, peered suspiciously at us, then turned on her heels and hurried back in the direction she had come.

The lass was likely upon an errand for her mother. Perhaps the mother would come for water instead, and might be able to answer a question or two. I had in mind that the woman might have seen Lady Philippa's wagon pass through the village. She had.

The lass had disappeared behind a house which blocked my view down a side lane. Moments later a village matron marched into view, carrying the bucket. The woman eyed us with distrust, but held firmly to her course.

I stepped back to allow the woman unfettered access to the crank, and greeted her.

"I give you good day, madam."

Whether or not she was worthy of the appellation I cannot say, but I thought a bit of flattery might help my cause.

The woman did not reply, but her tight-lipped features did soften. She busied herself with the bucket, rope, and crank, ignoring me.

"I am Sir Hugh de Singleton, surgeon, and bailiff to Lord Gilbert Talbot at Bampton," I said.

Depending upon her opinion of Clanfield's bailiff, which was likely not high, it may have been a mistake to identify myself in such a way. But the woman needed to know that I was of a neighboring village, and that I had authority there. Perchance she had heard my name.

The woman filled her bucket, then spoke. "What does Lord Gilbert's bailiff want w'me?"

"Two days past travelers entered Clanfield on the road from Faringdon, bound for Bampton. A dozen or so men, mounted, and a painted wagon drawn by three runcies. Did you see them pass?"

The woman hesitated, as if considering how her reply might affect her future. Evidently she decided that responding could have no ill effects. "Aye. I did."

"After they had departed the village did another cart appear?"

"Carts is common," the woman said.

"Aye, but I'm interested in but one."

"There was a cart passed by soon after them gentlefolk with the wagon come through the village."

"Was there one man upon this cart, or two? Or more?"

"Two, as I recall."

"Did you know the fellows? Were they men of Clanfield?"

"Nay. Never seen 'em before."

"Did they take the Bampton road, or the way to Black Bourton?"

"I don't know. I 'ave too much to do to stand gawpin' at strangers passin' by."

From the corner of my eye I saw Clanfield's bailiff and another man approach. The woman also saw and immediately turned to leave the well. She apparently did not want to be seen in discussion with Bampton's bailiff. I thanked the matron to her back, then awaited the bailiff's approach.

"Sir Hugh, here is Bogo Bennyng."

The tenant tugged a forelock, but his expression did not reflect either deference or submission.

"I give you good day," I said. Then, to the bailiff, "Perhaps you could seek Janyn and Henry whilst I have discourse with Bogo."

'Twas not a question, and the bailiff understood this. I wished to speak to Bogo alone.

The man was clearly unwilling to speak to me. Had he something he wished to hide, or was he averse to conversation with any man who had authority over him – especially a bailiff?

In past conversations with men who do not speak willingly I have discovered that I may loosen a man's tongue if I require him to sit whilst I stand over him. And Arthur has come to understand his role in such interrogations. I pointed to the split log bench and invited Bogo to be seated. Arthur folded his brawny arms and stepped near to the fellow as he sat sullenly. Giles saw Arthur's intimidating posture and imitated it, but without the same effect. I also find it useful in such interrogations to press my face close to the man I question. But not this time. Bogo's odor would have driven a flock of sheep over a cliff. I kept my distance.

"You are at work ditching this day, I am told. Is this along the Faringdon road?" I said, and looked to the south, whence the man and his bailiff had come.

"Aye."

Bogo folded his arms and attempted to appear as imposing as Arthur. This was a failure.

"For how many days have you been at this work?"

"Since Monday."

"Two days past do you remember seeing a gentleman pass, with his grooms and valets, and his lady wife riding in a painted wagon?"

"Aye. I seen 'em. I don't know who was in the wagon. Covered, wasn't it?"

"After the travelers passed, who followed them?"

"Followed? No man. Not that I seen. Busy with ditchin'."

"A cart with two men riding did not pass?"

"Oh, aye. I forgot. None of us what was ditchin' followed. I thought that's what you meant."

"The knight and his party passed through Clanfield near to noon. Did you go to your dinner before or after the knight's party passed?"

"After."

"And then returned to your work along the Faringdon road?"

"Aye."

"How many labor at this work?"

"There's me an' Will an' Hubert... an' Walter, the reeve."

"These all returned to the work immediately after taking their dinner?"

"Aye."

"As did you? The others will say that you did not linger over your dinner?"

"Aye."

'Twould be a simple matter to walk south to where the ditch was being cleared and discover if Bogo spoke true. I was inclined to believe him. Being seated while Arthur, I, and Giles stood over him had modified the fellow's sulky demeanor. Yet I was suspicious enough that I considered seeking Clanfield's reeve to verify Bogo's claim.

That would have to wait. I saw Thomas the bailiff coming from behind the church accompanied by two men, dust-caked and sweating from their labor with scythes. Would the fellows be resentful of my questions, or pleased to be briefly released from their labor?

Janyn and Henry doffed caps and tugged forelocks as they drew near. Their demeanor was not so spleenish as Bogo's had been. Did this mean they were guilty of something and feared being caught out? Or did it mean they were innocent of wrongdoing and so had no anxiety concerning this interview?

I dismissed Bogo, and thought as I did so of a way to prove the truth of his assertion that he had returned to ditching after a brief dinner on the day that Lady Philippa went missing – and at the same time be free of Thomas Skirlaw's inquisitive ears as I questioned Janyn and Henry.

44

I motioned to the bailiff, drew him aside, and glanced toward Bogo as he walked away from the well. "Bogo said that two days past he saw Sir Aymer's party pass while he was at work clearing ditches. 'Twas just before dinner. He claims to have taken his dinner and then returned immediately to ditching. Kindly seek the reeve and ask if this is so. Or was Bogo tardy at returning from his meal?" Skirlaw rolled his eyes but did as I requested.

What Skirlaw had told Janyn and Henry of my reason for demanding discourse with them I did not know. "Did your bailiff tell you who I am and why I seek information of you?"

"Aye," one replied. "He said you was bailiff in Bampton. We've heard of you hereabouts, fixin' what hurts folks have done to themselves or others. And he said there's a lady gone missin' on her way to Bampton."

"Indeed."

"I know nowt of any missin' lady," the other man said before I could say more.

I motioned to the bench and bade the fellows sit. They did, caps in hand, and waited for me to continue. What questions might I ask? Should I inquire if, two days past, they had left off haying and seized a lady and her maid as she traveled the road from Clanfield to Bampton?

A foolish question. Of course they would deny such a charge. Did they see Sir Aymer and his party pass? Not likely. The hayfield was not near the road Sir Aymer would have traveled. Nor would they have seen a cart following the same road. What might I learn from Janyn and Henry?

"The crops were poor last year," I began. The men nodded agreement. "Some men may take desperate measures to feed themselves and their offspring."

Again the fellows nodded, no spoken reply being necessary.

"How many children do you have?" I asked.

"Four," one said. "Two... three soon," said the younger of the two.

"How are you providing for them?"

45

"Me wife waters the pottage," the older said. "An' we don't take corn to the miller no more. 'E keeps too much, so no loaves for us. The wife boils oats an' barley to make pottage."

"I suppose some men are driven to poaching," I said.

Neither man spoke for a moment, which was answer enough, then the younger said, "Some as know how to set snares may take a coney."

"What else may men do to have coin to feed their children?" I said.

The men exchanged glances but were silent.

"What? All men of Clanfield are upright, and will hear their babes crying in the night for their empty bellies but do nothing malfeasant?"

"I don't know what others may do," the younger man said. "Sir William has right of infangenthef an' Skirlaw is a man to use it. I'd be no use to me wife an' children under sod of t'churchyard."

"We of Clanfield," the older man said, "be not so foolish as to take a lady and hold 'er for ransom, either. That's what you're after, is it not?"

The man had divined my purpose. There was no reason to equivocate further.

"Aye. Lady Philippa Molyns is missing. There is evidence that she was taken from her wagon, along with her maid, not more than four hundred paces from where you now sit."

Janyn and Henry turned as one to gaze at the Bampton road. Did this mean they knew something of the lady's disappearance? Likely not. They knew of her travel to Bampton.

There was little more to learn from these two. If they had taken the lady, or knew who had, I had not the wit to pry the knowledge from them. I sent the fellows back to their scythes, and as they passed beyond the village church Thomas Skirlaw strode into view. I was about to admit to my companions the failure of this visit to Clanfield as the bailiff reappeared. He made straight for us and seemed hurried.

The man was unaccustomed to such exertion. He stopped

before me, caught his breath, then announced between gasps that Bogo had shirked his work two days past. According to the reeve Bogo had not returned from his dinner in a timely fashion. Rather, the man had been an hour or more late in returning to the ditching. The reeve, Skirlaw said, had assigned Bennyng an extra day at ditching for his tardy return.

Was an hour enough time to seize Lady Philippa and the maid? Not likely, especially if Bogo had acted alone. It would require more than an hour, I thought, to take the women, truss them up, and hide them in some secure location. Which would necessarily be close to the village. Likewise 'twould take more than an hour to drag an unwilling lady and her maid through a wood and bushes from the Bampton road to the Black Bourton road, there to meet some other man, or men, with a cart.

What of Janyn and Henry? Did they also return tardily from their dinners on the day Sir Aymer's party passed through Clanfield? Who would tell me if 'twas so? The haymakers had worked without supervision, so far as I knew. Would a tenant complain of another villager, or would such folk stick together?

Chapter 4

I thanked Skirlaw for the information and asked that he keep his eyes open. In particular I requested that he watch for any of his bailiwick who might in the future seem to have come by wealth they had not previously possessed. I felt sure that Sir Aymer would soon receive a ransom demand. Indeed, he had already.

We were halfway to Bampton when I heard a horse closing upon us. The rider was eager to reach his destination. I turned in my saddle to see if perchance Thomas Skirlaw had thought of or found new evidence regarding Lady Philippa's disappearance. 'Twas not the Clanfield bailiff who approached at a canter.

The fellow touched his cap and was about to pass us by when he recognized Giles and the grooms and slowed his beast. "You are Bampton's bailiff, are you not?" he said to me.

"Aye, I am."

"Then I have a message for you and your master. Sir Aymer this morning received a demand for ransom for Lady Philippa. Two pounds is required for her return."

Two pounds is a considerable sum, but should be within the means of a knight whose lands in two shires are of a respectable size. The lady's captors knew their man, I thought.

"I am to seek you," the rider said, "and tell you that you are asked to deliver the ransom."

"Why me? I have nothing to do with Sir Aymer's business. Who has named me to this duty?"

"The ransom note, in a way," the fellow said. "I will explain all when we reach Bampton."

I found Lord Gilbert in his solar, about to take his supper. Several guests attended him, gentlemen and ladies, but I did not wish for Sir Aymer's groom to divulge to all that his lord had received a ransom demand.

John Chamberlain announced us at the solar door and Lord Gilbert bade us enter.

"Ah, Hugh, have you news? Who is your companion?"

I glanced around the solar before I spoke. Lord Gilbert is quick-witted and divined my purpose. He turned to his guests. "Perhaps you will wish to attend your chambers to make ready for supper. I need to have conversation with my bailiff."

When the solar was emptied of Lord Gilbert's guests I turned to the messenger who accompanied me, whose name I had not yet asked. "This fellow caught up to Arthur and me, Giles, and the others, upon the road returning to Bampton, a mile or so back. He comes with news from Sir Aymer."

"Ah… good news, I trust?"

"Nay, m'lord. Well, perhaps. I am Roger atte Wood, in Sir Aymer's service. He bids me tell you that this morning a message was received demanding two pounds for Lady Philippa's safe return to him."

"Hmmm. Two pounds. A large sum but surely within Sir Aymer's competence. Will he pay?"

"Aye, m'lord. So he intends. But I am sent here to tell you that the villains require the ransom be delivered by some man not of Coleshill. Sir Aymer asks if Sir Hugh will be that man."

"What terms are required?" I asked.

"A man is to travel alone to Badbury Hill with the coins in four sacks. No coin greater than a quarter-noble, and no more than ten pence in farthings."

"Am I to be met upon this hill and exchange the coins for the lady?"

"I don't know the particulars. Sir Aymer will tell you more if you agree to the task. The message demands that a man appear with the money on Sunday, no more than an hour before sunset. I don't know more than that."

"Where is this Badbury Hill?" I asked.

"Near halfway between Coleshill and Faringdon. Folk dislike being near the place after dark. There are ruins of an old fort atop the hill, and men do say the ghosts of them that once lived there roam the hill to drive away any who would claim the place from the spirits."

I saw Roger shudder as he spoke.

"You must go, of course," Lord Gilbert said. Then, to Roger, "Has Sir Aymer enough coins on hand that he can meet the required amount?"

"He has requested of his tenants that they pay their rents early. He will remit a farthing per acre to those who will do this."

"His tenants agree to this bargain?" I asked.

"Some have not the coin on hand to do so, more's the pity. But enough have come to him that, with the means he has at hand, he has told me to assure you that your efforts in this business will not be in vain. The commons of Coleshill thinks highly of Lady Philippa."

"Sir Aymer is a man who wants his wife returned," Lord Gilbert said.

"Aye. He dearly wishes for an heir. He will enter his forty-third year shortly after Lammastide."

"Few men become new fathers at such an age," Lord Gilbert said. "More likely grandfathers.

"Go to the marshalsea and tell Andrew to have two palfreys ready for you on Saturday at dawn. Take Arthur. He, according to the ransom demand, cannot accompany you to the hill, but you'll not want to return from Coleshill alone. If there are felons about who would steal a lady from under the nose of her husband, they would not scruple to seize a solitary man traveling. And Sir Aymer's squire and grooms may as well return to Coleshill with you. This sorry business seems near to conclusion and there is nothing they can do here."

I notified Andrew, Lord Gilbert's page of the stables, and Arthur, then hastened home to Galen House. Kate had dressed the door and ground-floor windows with green birch branches, in honor of the season to come, which has already come, according to Bacon and other men who study such matters. The calendar, they claim, is much out of joint since the Romans devised it.

Kate guessed that on my return from Clanfield I would be ravenous. She and Adela had prepared hanoney for our supper. 'Tis a dish I favor, but so famished was I that I would have gladly attended to a simple bowl of oat pottage.

Our Bessie had been told a few days past of the great bonfire with which Bampton – as all villages within the realm – would welcome the arrival of summer. Her grandfather had explained to her the event and its significance. Now, as we departed Galen House my father-in-law took the hand of his excited granddaughter and led us north, past the Church of St. Beornwald, to the meadow and the pile of oak and beech limbs which would soon be set ablaze.

John Prudhomme was in charge of touching a flame to the mound of brush and limbs, but as befits his name did not do so 'til he saw Lord Gilbert and his guests pass the churchyard. The previous fortnight had been dry, so the tinder and then the heap of wood kindled rapidly. Sparks lifted to the dark sky and small boys darted about extinguishing those which were yet glowing when they fell to earth and threatened to set ablaze the bishop's meadow.

Kate held John, and I watched the red glow illuminate his face and glisten in his eyes. How many more Midsummer's Eve fires would those eyes see before he joined me, Kate, Bessie, and Sybil in St. Beornwald's churchyard? Midsummer's Eve is to be a joyous affair, but this wayward thought brought gloom. I did not share it with Kate. My spouse was intent on describing to our son the brilliant event before him. He was not old enough to understand. Next year he might be, if I could keep him safe from the many pestilences which beset children.

The fire burned low. John tired of the scene and his head dropped to Kate's shoulder. My father-in-law had seen many Midsummer's Eve blazes and so was ready to seek Galen House and his bed. Only Bessie was yet entertained by the dying embers, so it was with some difficulty that I persuaded her 'twas time to leave the celebration. I foresee the child, in a decade or so, developing a disposition which will hold my opinions in small regard. If so, she will be much like me at a similar age.

No men roused me from my bed Friday morning to announce that bones were found in the cooling pile of ashes which remained of the fire. Such a thing had happened two years past, and identifying the dead man and his slayer had left me with scars to remind me of the business. I have also scars which remind me of dealings with other felons.

My Kate had cheese and a maslin loaf ready with which I broke my fast Saturday morning. After a cup of ale I kissed Kate and Bessie, charged my father-in-law with their care, and set off for Bampton Castle.

Arthur, Giles, and Sir Aymer's grooms awaited me at the stables. 'Twas a dark, gloomy morning, so 'twas well to be off before rain might muddy the roads and dampen our garments.

Our mounts were fresh, so we arrived at Coleshill before noon. We passed Badbury Hill as we neared our destination and Giles pointed out the spot where, on the morrow, I was to deliver Lady Philippa's ransom. It looked a foreboding place. Perhaps the low clouds and mist encouraged such an appraisal.

Sir Aymer and his grooms and valets were ready to take their dinner when we arrived. Although I desired to know more of the ransom demands and see the document, I also desired to fill my belly.

Sir Aymer's cook presented him and his gentlemen guests with a pottage of whelks and rice moyle. Arthur, with the knight's grooms, was served a porre of peas, but he seemed content with the fare. As we dined, Sir Aymer told me of the discovery of the ransom demand.

Thursday morning the village priest had gone to the church to ring the dawn Angelus and found upon the door a scrap of parchment. The message was written in English and addressed to Sir Aymer. As Roger had said, he was to pay two pounds for Lady Philippa's return, and some man not of Coleshill was to deliver the coins to Badbury Hill one hour before sunset on Sunday.

"As you have had to do with this matter," Sir Aymer said,

"and are not of this place, I have asked for you to deliver the ransom."

"Does the writer say when and how your wife will be released from her captivity?"

"Nay. And the lack of such a promise concerns me. I am simply told that Lady Philippa is held and her freedom will not be restored until I pay two pounds."

"You have the sum? Your man said that the felons demand no coin greater than a quarter-noble and no more than forty farthings included."

"Perhaps Roger told you that I have remitted a farthing per acre of rents for tenants who will pay fees now that are due at Michaelmas. I have seven quarter-nobles. I have also a handful of groats, and the forty farthings. Near two hundred pennies make the total."

"Roger said the ransom must be delivered in four sacks. 'Twill take four stout leather sacks to do so," I said. "And I am to deliver the coins alone? I have but two arms. I should like to see the ransom note."

"You shall. 'Tis in my chamber. I could learn nothing from it, but perhaps you might."

I did.

After the void Sir Aymer bade me follow him to his chamber. From a small casket upon a desk he produced a fragment of parchment about as long and wide as a large man's hand. The writing was in a small script, the lines even, and the ink clear and not smudged. I have rendered the message as I remember it:

"Sir Aymer; A wife is a valuable possession. Yours should be worth to you two pounds. The coins must be delivered in four leather sacks, deposited between the highest and second rings of Badbury Hill Fort, upon the east side, no more than one hour before sunset upon Sunday next. It is our requirement that no coin be greater than a quarter-noble, nor shall there be more than forty farthings. Furthermore we require that the four sacks be carried to Badbury Hill by a man not of Coleshill. Do not fail to heed these instructions."

"What think you?" Sir Aymer said when I lifted my eyes from the document.

"The script is fine. Whoso wrote this is likely a scholar, skilled with a pen. See how delicate the letters are. This may be a woman's hand."

"A woman? How many women can write?" Sir Aymer scoffed. "Especially a woman who would consort with felons."

"Could Lady Philippa read and write?"

"Not well. She'd not put words together like this, if that's your meaning. The rogues who have her could not have forced her to write this," he said, and waved the parchment about.

"Miscreants who would steal a lady would not likely themselves be able to write," I said. "So perchance required some woman of their acquaintance to write for them. If, indeed, this demand is in a woman's hand. Mayhap 'tis not."

I took the message from Sir Aymer again and examined it more carefully, not attending to the words, but to the ink and parchment. 'Twas then I saw, faintly, that the parchment had been scraped clean before the ransom demand was written upon it. Likely the discarded parchment had been used for some other purpose before being fixed to the door of All Saints' Church in Coleshill.

Sir Aymer's chamber has glass windows. I took the parchment to one of these and pressed it against the pane. I sought some remnant of the writing which might have resisted the knife. Faint shadows of what had been written were visible. Between the lines of the ransom message, so that they were not much obscured, I saw the words *"Johannes autem cum audisset in vinculis"* – "When John had heard in prison."

I knew this phrase. I have read it several times in my Bible. 'Tis from the eleventh chapter of St. Matthew's Gospel. A scholar had indeed written upon this sheet of parchment at some time past. Who else would know Latin?

Neither Bogo nor Henry nor Janyn would be able to write, I was sure. And if they could, where would they find a scrap of parchment which had been previously used by some scholar?

Could Thomas Skirlaw read and write? Surely. Could he procure a fragment of disused parchment? Possibly. I must not be too quick to discard men of Clanfield from a list of possible evildoers.

Would such men require Lady Philippa's ransom be paid many miles from Clanfield? To secure four bags of coins, hide them, and transport them from Badbury Hill to Clanfield would require much effort. It would be more convenient for the knaves to demand the ransom be paid closer to Clanfield. Perhaps they considered that, and decided such a requirement might cast suspicion upon them. Whereas prescribing the coins be left at Badbury Hill might cast suspicion upon men who resided close to Coleshill.

Sir Aymer, it seemed to me, was only mildly troubled that his wife was taken and the scoundrels who had her demanded two pounds for her return. If some malefactors seized my Kate I would not sleep 'til I had found them out. Could it be that one or two of his trusted servants would collect the four bags of coins after darkness had come to Badbury Hill? The coins would be returned to him, the ransom message a fraud? Why would Sir Aymer do such a thing? If he knew more than he was willing to tell of his wife's disappearance, the demand for ransom would deflect any suspicion which might in the future be directed at him. By me, for example. Is this why I was asked to deliver the coins? To make me unlikely to suspect Sir Aymer complicit in Lady Philippa's disappearance?

Was the lady yet living? Sir Aymer was displeased with her – this I knew. Did he wish her dead so that he might wed a third wife and with her seek the heirs he had thus far failed to sire?

Would the bishops grant him permission to wed if there was no proof that Lady Philippa was dead? Perhaps. But perhaps not. To be sure of the bishops' acquiescence a corpse would be necessary. Or more sacks of coins delivered to a bishop's palace.

All of these thoughts passed through my mind as I peered at the ransom demand whilst it was yet pressed against the window.

"What do you seek?" Sir Aymer said as he peered over my shoulder.

I pointed to the faint Latin script and explained that the parchment of the ransom demand had been used previously for another purpose. While I spoke I observed Sir Aymer for any sign that he feared he had been caught in subterfuge. I saw no such token.

Sir Aymer had consumed his dinner with no sign of sorrow for his missing wife ruining his appetite. Likewise, at supper he consumed a dish of stewed herrings and showed no evidence that his loss might cause him to waste away.

Chapter 5

Next morning, after mass in All Saints' Church, Arthur approached me as we departed the churchyard.

"I've been keepin' me mouth shut an' me ears open," he said, and glanced about to be sure no man was near. I assumed the glance and the announcement meant he was about to tell me of something he had learned which I might find compelling. He was.

"That squire what rode with us yesterday from Bampton – Giles. 'E's downcast. 'Ave you noticed?"

"Aye. He seems troubled. Lady Philippa's disappearance has distressed him, I think."

"Mayhap, but I've 'eard one of Sir Aymer's grooms say 'e's more troubled 'cause Lady Philippa's maid is gone, too."

"Aye. I've spoken to Giles. His words indicated a fondness for the lass."

"More than fondness, I'm thinkin'."

"How so?"

"I 'eard Brom say Giles wears a silver chain about 'is neck with Milicent's ring upon it."

"Nothing unusual about a lass giving a lad a token," I said.

"It ain't the ring nor chain what's interestin'; 'tis what she said when she gave 'em to 'im."

"What was that? And how does Brom know her words?"

"The maid told Giles to keep the ring, but hid, to remember 'er. How could 'e forget a lass 'e was likely to see every day?"

"How, indeed? Did Brom overhear this?"

"Nay. The scullery maid did."

"And the lass told Brom?"

"Aye, so 'e said."

"Brom has not told anyone else of this? He has not told Sir Aymer? And Giles? What of him? Did Brom say if the squire has told Sir Aymer?"

"Nay. Brom said Sir Aymer 'as eyes for the lass 'imself. Most in Coleshill know it. Mayhap Lady Philippa knows also. He wouldn't be pleased to know Milicent an' Giles was sweethearts. If an' when Lady Philippa an' Milicent come home Giles might find 'imself sent away was Sir Aymer to know of this."

I suspected that Brom and the scullery maid may share kisses as well as overheard conversations. Likely Brom would prefer Sir Aymer not know of that, either.

After dinner I met with Sir Aymer to plan for my evening task. We decided Giles and Arthur would accompany me to near the foot of Badbury Hill. If some men knew what I was about and what I carried, I did not wish for them to discover me alone upon the road. Brom and Maurice would also attend, with Lady Philippa's wagon. If she was released she would need carriage home to Coleshill. About two or three hundred paces from the hill I would dismount, leaving my palfrey with the others. The wagon would wait there also. This would be far enough from the summit of Badbury Hill that the felons awaiting Sir Aymer's coin should not fear our presence and take flight, but close enough that, if I bawled out for help at the top of my lungs, I might be heard in the still evening air. And Lady Philippa and Milicent, if released to me, would have but a short way to walk to the wagon. At the back of my mind was the thought that the ransom demand had made no promise of their immediate freedom.

"There is one other thing I would like to do to prepare for delivering the ransom," I said.

"What is that?" Sir Aymer replied.

"If you seek your farrier and bring a hammer and a shoeing nail, I will show you."

The knight studied me with a puzzled expression, but did as I asked. In a few moments he returned with the hammer and the nail.

"Now, bring the sacks of coins and I will mark the coins so that forever they may be identified."

"They are in my chamber. I will return with them anon."

He did so, and 'twas but a matter of an hour, perhaps less, to take each coin, place it upon a table, and with the hammer and iron nail rap each coin smartly so as to leave a pronounced dent. I made the mark at the same location on each coin, at the base of the king's head.

"Coins are made to be spent," I said. "If one or more of these coins appear we may discover whence they came, and discover the felons who took your wife."

From two poles I made yokes with which to carry the bags, one sack tied at each end. Sir Aymer counted out the coins – he had done so several times, he said – to be sure of the amount, and we filled the leather sacks to be of equal weight and balance on the poles I would carry upon my shoulders.

I had little appetite for supper. Would the felons who seized Lady Philippa hesitate to strike me down if they suspected a trap? Would they strike me down simply because of my presence, trap or not? Such thoughts do not lend themselves to enjoyment of a hearty meal.

'Tis little more than a mile from Coleshill to Badbury Hill. There was no need to set out on my mission before the day was near done, even if the wagon would slow our pace.

The weather had remained cloudy and misty since my travel to Coleshill. Sunset this day would not be observable, and darkness would come earlier than on a cloudless evening. Our beasts were made ready, three runcies joined to the cumbersome wagon, and I was prepared to begin the business.

The priest of All Saints' Church attended our departure. I bade him say a prayer for my good success, and we set off toward the darkening eastern horizon.

The four sacks of coins and the poles to which they were fixed were deposited in the wagon. I saw no reason to be burdened with them until necessary.

Badbury Hill is visible from far off. I kept my eyes upon the summit as our party came near, but I saw no sign of any soul occupying the eminence. A small copse crowned the hill, in which men might hide and observe our arrival.

I called a halt to our progress. I dismounted and the others did likewise. I tied my palfrey to the wagon, placed the two poles with their sacks of coins over my shoulders, bade my companions listen and look sharp if I had to call for aid, then set out for the summit of Badbury Hill.

Rings of earthworks had been raised in four concentric circles about the hill. Broad paths were cut through these hummocks at two places so I was not required to climb over. When I had passed the second ridge from the top I left the path and walked the ditch. The raised earthworks on either side were two or three times my height. If men lurked the other side of the ridges they could be upon me in an instant.

The day was near done. So, even though the cloudy sky was yet light, the furrow of the ditch where I walked was in shadow. As I approached the eastern side of the summit I looked carefully for some sign that men might have made indicating where I was to leave the bags. I saw nothing.

A dying breeze sighed through the wood crowning Badbury Hill. I could well imagine why superstitious folk shunned the place. I was eager to complete my task and depart myself.

I walked thirty or forty paces – who would count at such a time? – to the northeast, but saw no sign of a receptacle or any other man-made object designed to receive the coins. I retraced my steps and in the fading light dropped the bags from my shoulders at what I thought to be the easternmost side of the hill.

Silence followed the clink of the falling coins. Surely if men were near they would hear and understand. I waited for several minutes, then spoke.

"I have placed the four sacks of coins as you have demanded. Will you now return Lady Philippa to her home?"

There was no reply. The eastern sky was now dark and the western horizon becoming so. Clouds would darken the moon, which would not rise for several hours anyway. If I wished to see my way back to the road and my companions I must not linger longer upon the hill.

I stumbled to the path cut through the ridges and made my way down the hill to the road. By the time I reached the others the road before me was but a pale path cutting through the darkness.

Giles heard my footsteps and called out: "Sir Hugh! Do you approach?"

Perhaps he worried that he and his companions were about to be set upon by men who had collected Lady Philippa's ransom and dispatched me. I answered and eased his mind.

"Where is Lady Philippa?" he said when I was near enough that he could see I was alone.

"I don't know," I replied. "I left the coins where I was told, and spoke to whomever might be near that I had done so. There was no reply."

"The scoundrels have dealt falsely with Sir Aymer," Giles said, and cursed them for their perfidy.

"It may be that they will not release her until they have collected Sir Aymer's ransom," I said, "and they will not do that until they are sure they will not be seized when collecting the money. Perhaps there was no man near to hear when I spoke. You said folk hereabouts believe Badbury Hill the habitation of vengeful spirits, and so avoid the place at night. Perhaps the felons know this, and so plan to retrieve their loot in the dark, when no others are likely to be about. Then, after they are assured of the ransom, they will set Lady Philippa and Milicent free."

"You believe it so?"

"I hope it will be so," I replied. "Meanwhile there is nothing to do but return to Coleshill. At dawn we will come back here. Perhaps Lady Philippa and Milicent will be atop the hill, waiting for us."

It is difficult enough to turn a wagon such as Lady Philippa's in daylight, upon a broad way. In the night, on a narrow, muddy road, with skittish runcies, 'twas doubly onerous. In the process one rear wheel dropped into the ditch, which due to the misty rain of the past day was deep in mud. We were all of us required to put a shoulder to the wheel, with Maurice swatting the horses' rumps to make them exert themselves.

Sir Aymer awaited our return before the manor house, and seemed genuinely dismayed to learn that his wife was not with us. I explained my theory that the ransom might be collected in the night, and Lady Philippa found in the morning where I had deposited the coins. If he had to do with his wife's disappearance, and even now was sending a groom to collect his money, he was a skilled player. Nevertheless, I did not discount the possibility that he had something to do with Lady Philippa's disappearance. I fear I have become mistrustful of all men. 'Tis due to my post, I believe, for as bailiff of Bampton Manor my dealings are most often with miscreants in whom the truth does not dwell. Honest men seldom have cause to attract my notice.

Does the Lord Christ serve in the same way, as bailiff of heaven and earth, anxious for His wayward subjects? I must seek Master Wycliffe's opinion when next I meet him.

I slept fitfully that night, eager for dawn. Before I sought my bed Sunday evening I had agreed with Sir Aymer that at daybreak we would ride to Badbury Hill. Would Lady Philippa and Milicent await us there? Would the sacks of coins be removed?

The first grey light of dawn roused me from what slumber I had found. I dressed myself and hurried to Sir Aymer's hall. The knight was there before me, eager to be away and anxious for what we would find at Badbury Hill.

We hurriedly swallowed maslin loaves, gulped cups of ale, and assembled Giles, Arthur, Brom, and Maurice. Giles and Arthur would accompany me and Sir Aymer. Brom and Maurice would follow with two extra palfreys. No wagon this time. If we found her, Lady Philippa was not going to walk a muddy road back to Coleshill.

Yesterday's drizzle had become showers broken by occasional shafts of sunlight as the sun rose above the eastern horizon. Sir Aymer spurred his beast to a canter and we others did likewise to keep up. We were mud-spattered by the time we came to Badbury Hill. Sir Aymer did not dismount at the foot of the hill, but rode his palfrey up the path cut between the earthen rings 'til he reached the ditch between the topmost and second rings. There he leaped to the sod. I did likewise.

"Which way?" he said.

I pointed to the dexter side and said, "Follow me. I will show you where I left the sacks – if they are now gone."

I set off for the east side of the hill, with Sir Aymer, Giles, and Arthur close behind. We found no sacks of coins. But where I had left the coins the wet grass was beaten down. More than one man, I thought, had been here in the night to collect Sir Aymer's two pounds. Even the poles I had used to carry the bags over my shoulders were gone. I had made the felons' work easier.

"This is the place?" Sir Aymer said when he saw that I had stopped to study the ground.

"Aye. See yon flowers. I placed the sacks here, at the base of the ditch, and just below those daisies. See how the wet grass is trodden down. More than one man came in the night, I think, to remove the sacks."

"Then where is Lady Philippa? The scoundrels have their ransom. Why do they keep her? Will they demand more of me?"

"Mayhap. Or perhaps they intend to be far away when she is freed."

"How could they be far away if my wife is released here?"

"She may be released near to Coleshill," I replied. "The ransom demand does not specify."

Indeed, the message said nothing at all about the lady's release, but I thought it impolitic to mention this at the moment.

"I believe," I said, "that the men who collected the ransom may have been close by, watching, when I dropped the sacks here last evening. Perhaps if we walk the hill we will find some evidence of their presence."

I sent Giles and Arthur back to the path which cut through the rings, where we had left our beasts, with instructions to walk the upper side of the topmost earthwork and the lower side of the second ring. Giles volunteered to search the higher ring and Arthur the second.

Sir Aymer waited until we heard their voices beyond the ridges, then we four began to walk slowly to the north, seeking signs of the nocturnal visitors who had absconded with Sir Aymer's coins.

We passed the northmost part of the rings and came to another path which cut through the ridges, much like the track to the south which we had ascended. Because this path did not lead to a well-traveled road it was more overgrown and thus 'twas easy to see where beasts had pushed aside the grass. Arthur found dung.

The sod of the track was too thick and firm to allow horses' hooves to leave a print, even though the soil was soft after days of mist and gentle rain. But the bruised verdure was easy to follow, so we did, to the base of the hill. Here was a meadow where sheep grazed behind a stone wall. A few of the newly shorn creatures lifted their heads to see if we might be a threat, decided not, and returned to cropping the wet grass.

There was no sign that horses had leaped over this wall, no soil gouged out by beasts taking flight or returning to earth. Oddly enough, verdure along the wall seemed to indicate that beasts may have approached this place from both directions.

Not so. I chose to follow the meadow wall to the west, and within twenty paces the crushed foliage ended. Grass, weeds, and bracken beyond this place showed no sign of disturbance.

We retraced our steps and this time followed the crushed vegetation to the east side of Badbury Hill and beyond, to the road from Coleshill to Faringdon. I saw in the mud of the road what seemed to be the hoof prints of two horses entering the road from the northern verge. These hoof prints soon merged with others recently made, so that following further was impossible. We stopped in the middle of the road.

"What now?" Sir Aymer said. "We have followed the spoor and learned nothing, but that my money is gone and my wife is not freed."

"We have learned two things," I said.

"What? That the rogues have escaped with two pounds is one. What is the other?"

"Three things, then. Aye, they have escaped. For now. But where the miscreants followed the stone wall upon their arrival at the hill, they went past the north track which leads to the summit, passing through cut-out places in the rings, as does the path to the south. It may have been dark, but even so men familiar with Badbury Hill would not likely lose their way and need to backtrack, as I believe they did. 'Tis my belief the men who now have your money are not much familiar with this place."

"Not of Coleshill, nor Faringdon either, you think."

"Aye."

"What else did we learn which escaped me?" Sir Aymer said.

"There are the ruts made by cartwheels here, in the mud of the road, but not newly made, I think."

Sir Aymer, Giles, and Arthur peered at the mud beneath their feet. Sir Aymer looked up, puzzled. "What does this tell you?"

"The men who took away your ransom had no intention of setting Lady Philippa and Milicent free here. If so they would surely have brought them to this place in a cart or wagon, but even if they were upon palfreys the beasts would have left behind their prints. Look there, to the verge, where the trace we followed enters the road. The hoof prints of two horses are there, no more."

"Perhaps," Giles offered, "Lady Philippa and Milicent were upon one beast and their captor another?"

"Mayhap. But did one man carry off four heavy sacks? And if Lady Philippa and Milicent were brought here, why were they then carried away again and not released? Nay, they are yet hid somewhere. Perhaps their captors will yet release them, but the rogues had no intention of doing so last night on Badbury Hill."

We set off to the west upon the road, toward Coleshill, and soon came upon Maurice and Brom, waiting with the spare horses. We ascended Badbury Hill to retrieve our beasts, then returned, defeated, to Coleshill.

Chapter 6

Arthur and I took our dinner with Sir Aymer, and a solemn meal it was. Sir Aymer had mistreated his wife, I had been told, and had an eye for Lady Philippa's maid. Nevertheless the knight seemed genuinely woeful that paying the ransom had not brought his wife back under his roof. I was nearly prepared to discount any thought that the man might have some part in his wife's disappearance. Nearly. And was his doleful visage due to the continued absence of Lady Philippa, or the loss of two pounds?

I bade Sir Aymer "Good day" after dinner, requested that he inform me if he heard again from Lady Philippa's abductors, then with Arthur set off for Bampton and home, defeated.

"You told Sir Aymer them scoundrels what've got the lady likely didn't know much about that hill," Arthur said as we passed Badbury Hill. "Suppose them knaves in Clanfield wouldn't know much about the place either, 'cept it bein' close to where the lady lived."

"True enough," I replied. "But which of them could write a ransom note, and in a skilled hand?"

"That bailiff... Skirlaw?"

"True again. But the demand was written upon parchment which was scraped clean of ink from a passage of the Gospel of St. Matthew. Where would Clanfield's bailiff come by such a fragment?"

"Why would some man scrape away what was wrote there?"

"Mayhap an error was made in copying, or the copyist made a smudge," I said. "Some error rendered the parchment worthless for its intended purpose."

"A monk, then, wrote Sir Aymer demanding ransom for 'is wife?"

"I doubt that. But 'tis likely that scrap was first put to use in a monastery, or perhaps a stationer's shop, before it was later fixed to the door of All Saints' Church."

We passed through Faringdon and were halfway to Clanfield, near to Radcot Bridge, when we met a train of carts and packhorses. Two men led the train, mounted upon matching grey palfreys and attired in linen chauces, fine woolen cotehardies, and silken doublets. Their beards were trimmed short, in a "V", and as we passed I heard a fragment of their conversation. The men were Italian wool buyers, the carts and runcies behind laden with sacks of Cotswold wool bound for Portsmouth or Southampton or some such port.

I did not count the carts or packhorses. There must have been a half-dozen carts and ten or twelve beasts. The animals seemed fatigued under their loads. Doubtless the group would seek an inn in Faringdon.

The packhorses were tied together in groups of three, two beasts following a third, upon which the driver rode, with a smaller sack of wool fixed to his saddle behind him. I paid the travelers little attention as they journeyed south and we to the north. But the last rider caught my attention. His companions ahead of him had worn short cotehardies of grey or brown or black, but this fellow wore blue. An uncommon color for a man of low rank.

The shade of blue seemed much like the wisp I had found tangled in the bramble and the fragment of blue torn from Lady Philippa's garment with her brooch. I drew my palfrey to a halt and peered over my shoulder at the departing beasts, carts, and riders.

Arthur looked to me, puzzled. "What are we stoppin' 'ere for?"

"The last rider... did you note his cotehardie?"

Arthur then also turned to follow my gaze. "What am I supposed to see?" he said.

"How many drovers and suchlike folk wear blue?"

"Not many. Ah, I see your point. That fellow's wearin' a cotehardie much the same color as that we found seekin' for Lady Philippa."

"Indeed."

"What you going to do?"

"Learn where he came by the garment, if I can."

I turned my palfrey and with Arthur close behind I spurred the beast to a trot. We soon overtook the pack animals and carts, and received astonished glances from riders as we passed. We had but moments earlier been seen traveling in the opposite direction.

When we drew alongside the men who led the procession I slowed my palfrey to a walk and bade the fellows "Good day." They nodded, puzzled, but did not halt.

"Whence do you come this day?" I asked.

"Burford," one replied. The man was surely Italian, here for Cotswold wool. His accent proclaimed it so.

"I am Sir Hugh de Singleton, bailiff to Lord Gilbert Talbot at his manor of Bampton."

The wool buyers looked to each other as if each thought my announcement might be of significance to the other. Eventually both men shrugged, then the nearer spoke.

"I am Antonio Benedici. How may we serve the bailiff of Bampton?"

"Halt your band for a moment. There is a matter I wish to discuss with you."

The man turned in his saddle and with a raised hand indicated to those who followed that they would stop. He then turned again to face me.

"The last man of your company," I said, "wears a blue cotehardie. It does not seem defiled with mud and dust of the road. How long has he possessed the garment?"

Benedici looked to his companion as if silently asking whether or not he should answer. He received another shrug in reply.

"Why must you know?"

"A felony has been done near this place. A blue garment of much the same hue as your drover wears plays a part in the crime. Lord Gilbert has charged me to seek those responsible."

"What crime has been done?" the other man said.

"A woman has been carried off. When she was last seen she wore a cotehardie of the same dark blue that distant fellow wears.

How and when did he come by it? Your other carters and drovers wear brown and grey, as do most of the commons."

"We have seized no woman," Benedici replied indignantly.

"If you will not answer perhaps I must compel you to come with me to Bampton, where your carts and wool sacks may be examined." How Arthur and I might compel six men to reverse their journey I did not at that moment consider. There are limits even to Arthur's strength. But Lord Gilbert's name is stronger yet.

I hoped the threat would loosen tongues. It did.

"The man you speak of, he found the cotehardie this morning. His own was tattered."

"Come. I must speak to the fellow, and you must require of him that he provide truthful answers to my questions."

Once again I passed the line of carts and runcies, this time with the wool buyer following. I reined my palfrey to a stop before the blue-clad drover and studied his garment. I saw what I had not noticed the first time I passed by the fellow. Near to the cotehardie's left shoulder, high upon the breast, the garment was torn. A patch of wool nearly the size of a mussel shell was ripped away.

"This man," Benedici said in his accented English and nodding to me, "wishes to know how you came by your new cotehardie."

The drover glanced resentfully at me, as if he thought I intended to take it from him, which at that moment I did.

"Found it, didn't I," the man muttered.

"Where?"

"Aside the road, in a thicket where beech trees was coppiced."

"What were you doing there?"

"We stopped so we could relieve ourselves."

"And you entered the thicket?"

"Aye... for privacy, like."

"And this cotehardie was there?" I said.

"Aye. But for the tear there's no reason 'twould be cast away."

"Was it well hidden, in the coppiced grove?"

"Aye."

I looked to the hem of the garment. It had been crudely hacked short so as to be more comfortable for a mounted man.

"I am Sir Hugh de Singleton, bailiff to Lord Gilbert Talbot at his manor of Bampton. I seek the woman whose cotehardie you now wear. She was seized upon the road north of Clanfield, on the way to Bampton."

"I didn't find it near that road," the drover said. "'Twas by the road to Black Bourton."

"Where an oat field lies east of the road?" I said.

"Aye. So 'twas."

"Did you cut away part of the cotehardie there?"

"Aye."

"And discarded it?"

"Aye. Tossed it aside the wall. No good to me."

I was uncertain if possession of the cotehardie would help me find Lady Philippa. What use the garment would be to my search was small compared to the value of the garment to the poor drover. I decided to allow the man to keep it. I would return by way of the Black Bourton road and seek the fragment the drover had slashed away.

I briefly considered requiring the Italians to allow me to peer into the carts, under the wool packs, to see if Lady Philippa and Milicent might be hidden there. But I had already demanded much of the fellows, and feared that even if they had no women hidden in a cart they might rebel against any further imposition. And women concealed in a cart would hear my words and make themselves known. If they were concealed against their will.

I bade the wool buyer "Fare well," and with Arthur at my side set off for Radcot Bridge, which was visible in the distance.

Rather than taking the Bampton Road at Clanfield we traveled north to the oat field I had first examined days earlier. As the drover said, I found the scrap he had severed from the cotehardie close against a corner of the field.

I raised my eyes to the nearby wood and some twenty paces away saw a copse which resembled a coppiced grove. The shoots had grown thick and tall and would provide dense cover for a man who wished to do nature's work privily. Indeed, I soon found evidence that the drover's tale was true.

But although I stumbled about between stumps and shoots I could find nothing to indicate that Lady Philippa had disrobed here. The place was so difficult to enter that I would not have investigated it but for the drover's testimony. Perhaps, I thought, the lady donned some other garment at a place not so thickly overgrown, and the blue cotehardie was then tossed into the copse because the trees grew so densely that those who placed it there believed it would never be found.

For what reason would Lady Philippa change her apparel? To escape detection. But was this substitution her doing, or the plan of some other? Some other, likely, else why a ransom demand? And when the lady departed this place, what then was her garb?

Hiding anything in a coppiced grove is not a sure way to conceal it. The shoots which emerge from the stumps, when new and tender, are useful as arrow shafts. Grown larger they may become fence posts and rails in places where stone is lacking. When larger still the growths may be used for rafters for sheds and small barns, even for modest houses. Perhaps the man, or woman, who discarded Lady Philippa's cotehardie was unfamiliar with the ways of villagers and verderers. A lady might be so ignorant, and also her captors if she had been taken by city folk. Any of these might not understand that coppicing is done for a purpose. A coppiced grove is likely to occasionally be visited, and what may be hidden there discovered.

Folk in Black Bourton and Alvescot told me they had seen a cart pass to the north the day Lady Philippa disappeared. Was she hidden in the cart, under a canvas, wearing only her chemise? Or was it planned before she was removed from her wagon that she would change from her blue cotehardie to some other garment? If so, who made these plans? Such a provision would not be made upon short notice. Would men of Clanfield have time after seeing the wagon pass through their village to acquire some other clothing for their victim?

I had inspected the place several days earlier, but now that

Lady Philippa's clothing had been found Arthur and I performed another search. We found nothing else to indicate that folk had passed the copse and field a few days before.

The sun was low in the northwest. I told Arthur we would give up the search, and with the fragment of Lady Philippa's cotehardie across the pommel of my saddle we returned to Clanfield and the Bampton road.

At the entrance to Bampton Castle forecourt I dismounted and bade Arthur see the palfreys to the marshalsea.

"And let Lord Gilbert know I will call in the morning to tell him all."

Chapter 7

'T was nearly dark when I reached Galen House. My Kate had not yet barred the door for the night, so I did not need to bruise my knuckles to gain entrance.

"I have looked for your return all day," Kate said. "What has delayed you? You were to deliver the lady's ransom last evening, were you not?"

"Aye, I was. And did. But I am too weary and hungry to relate all at this moment. If you feed me I will regain enough strength to tell the tale."

"Come," Kate smiled, and led me to the kitchen. There, upon our table, I saw thick slices of cyueles and a wheaten loaf with honeyed butter. 'Twas good to be home.

My father-in-law had retired to his bedchamber, but left his bed when he heard my voice and looked on approvingly as I consumed his daughter's culinary creation. Kate sat across the table waiting for me to eat my fill before speaking of my journey to Coleshill and return.

Adela had already put Bessie and John to bed, and gone to her home in the Weald. I drew a bench from the kitchen to the back garden and Kate, her father, and I sat upon it, backs against the warm kitchen wall, and watched the dark sky over Lord Gilbert's forest to the west.

"A feminine hand, you say?" my Kate commented when I had related the tale of my unsuccessful journey to Coleshill.

"Mayhap. The characters were writ small, as the parchment was not large. Of necessity the letters were precise. It may be that is why I took the message to be inscribed in a feminine hand."

"A careful scholar might be responsible for such a script," Caxton said. "Poor students often write small to save parchment. Even copyists. I have seen it so. There is a monk at Osney Abbey who can place two chapters of the Gospel of St. John upon half a leaf, and the entire Gospel upon less than a gathering. Of course, only the young can read such work."

"Sir Aymer's squire learned that Lady Philippa was courted by a scholar before she wed Sir Aymer," I mused.

"You suppose the man would seize her?" Kate said.

"Men have done stranger things for love," I replied. "Consider Paris and Helen."

"But why demand ransom, then?" Caxton asked. "If some disappointed swain took her he'd not likely return the lady for any amount."

"Aye," Kate said. "But two pounds would pay for lodging and food for two for many months."

"You think the disappointed suitor has her, and that Lady Philippa is complicit in the business?" I said.

"Neither she nor the maid cried out when they were taken. Why so?"

"If a dagger was to their throats and silence commanded they might obey," I replied.

"Mayhap," Kate replied skeptically.

"Who is this unsuccessful suitor?" Caxton asked. "Have you a name?"

"Martyn de Wenlock."

"Of which college?" Kate asked.

"That I do not know. But 'twould be of interest if he remains in Oxford, or has departed his college in the past few days."

"You think," Caxton said, "that if he took the lady he would flee the town?"

"Aye. Too many folk might recognize Lady Philippa if she was kept in Oxford."

"Unless she was made a prisoner," Kate said. "Which I doubt. If this scholar had to do with her disappearance, likely she was a willing accomplice to her abduction."

"And the maid's gift to the squire puzzles me," I said.

"The ring?"

"Aye. Why say to Giles that the ring would cause him to

remember her except that without it he might forget her?"

"Which he would not do was she serving her lady daily at Coleshill," Kate said. "Perhaps she wished to escape Sir Aymer's attentions – you said many of the knight's servants knew of this – and had resolved to flee her employment. Mayhap the ring had naught to do with her disappearance with the lady she served… that was merely happenstance." I pursed my lips and Kate continued. "Nay, I don't really think it so, either. 'Twas but a thought."

"Will you seek this de Wenlock fellow?" my father-in-law said.

"I am charged to find the lady, but I have few threads to pull which might unravel the riddle. The scholar is one, so I will seek him in Oxford and give him a yank, to see if he can be tattered."

"When will you be away?" Kate asked.

"Tomorrow," I sighed. "A trail is like a pease pottage, best when hot."

The next day I awoke early, as does every man whose wife possesses a rooster. Kate has named hers Roland, for he sings well and believes that the sun rises to hear him crow.

Arthur is not reluctant to travel. The man seems to enjoy adventure even though he nears the age when men would rather sit by a fire and entertain grandchildren than set off upon the back of a horse. So when I found him at Bampton Castle he readily accepted my requirement that he make ready two palfreys so as to accompany me to Oxford. While he did so I sought Lord Gilbert and told him of the sorry business at Coleshill.

"So Sir Aymer has lost two pounds and a wife," my employer said after I related the tale.

"So it seems, although I suppose the lady may yet be released."

"Not likely, though, eh?"

"Aye."

"What now? Do you wish to wash your hands of the matter and allow Sir Aymer to seek Lady Philippa on his own?"

I did not immediately answer. The thought of abandoning the

search had not before occurred to me. Now, when I considered it, the idea had some appeal.

But I dismissed the notion. If I forsook the quest it would be ever with me, like a splinter in a thumb, reminding me of its presence until I had it out. Until Lady Philippa was found.

"You do not reply," Lord Gilbert said.

"Words often do not improve upon silence. I am considering what I must do."

"Must do, or wish to do?"

"Occasionally they are the same," I replied.

"And occasionally not."

"In this matter I believe they are. I wish to see the business concluded, and for my own tranquility I must find the solution."

I could not then know, seated in Bampton Castle's solar, how little tranquility the resolution of Lady Philippa's disappearance would bring to me and others.

"I will not require of you that you pursue the matter," Lord Gilbert said. "The lady was not taken upon my lands, so you are free of the obligation to find her."

"But I have your consent if I wish to proceed?"

"Certainly. Sir Aymer is a friend. I would see his wife returned to him. What will you now do to continue the search?"

"I have told Arthur to prepare palfreys. We are off to Oxford to seek the scholar who courted Lady Philippa before she wed Sir Aymer."

"Scholars can be a testy lot," Lord Gilbert mused. "I well remember the St. Scholastica Riots."

"Aye. Some prefer tumult to scholarship."

"If Lady Philippa scorned the fellow he may resent her rejection."

"Possibly. But Sir Aymer's squire told me the match with Sir Aymer was Lady Philippa's father's doing."

"Ha. I can believe that. Felbridge was always seeking preferment."

"Felbridge?"

"Sir Warin Felbridge. Lady Philippa's father. A minor knight of Sussex. Never misses a chance to appear above his station. Would surely be furious if his daughter chose to wed a poor scholar. No matter that the fellow might rise some day. Some scholars do."

"And some," I said, "remain paupers. Unless some great lord employs them."

Lord Gilbert grinned. "Aye, but some become bishops and who will live better?"

"But if they become bishops they will not marry."

"Has that ever stopped a bishop from taking to himself a woman?"

The question needed no reply.

"If," Lord Gilbert continued, more seriously, "Sir Warin demanded his daughter wed Sir Aymer, and 'twas against her will, mayhap she plotted to go off with the scholar."

"Mayhap," I agreed. "This must be considered."

"Sir Aymer would be furious to know his wife preferred another man."

"Any man would," I agreed.

"He has always seemed a pleasant enough fellow. I would think Lady Philippa would be content with such a man."

I did not reply for a moment.

"Ah... silence again. You know something of the match which you will not speak of."

"I do. And you speak true. I'd rather not speak of what I have learned."

Lord Gilbert frowned, but did not demand that I tell him of Sir Aymer's mistreatment of his wife because she had produced no heir. Perhaps he deduced this. Lord Gilbert is no dolt. He employed me, did he not?

Lord Gilbert bade me a safe journey and I departed the solar for the marshalsea. Arthur awaited me, impatient to be off. He enjoys the chase and capture of felons as a baron enjoys following his hounds in pursuit of a stag.

'Tis sixteen miles or thereabouts from Bampton to Oxford. We arrived before the noon Angelus Bell rang from the tower of St. Aldate's Church, and took a dinner of roasted capon and barley loaves at The Fox and Hounds before we set off for Queen's College, where my master at Balliol College, John Wycliffe, now resided, taught, and studied for the degree of Bachelor of Theology. Master Wycliffe is well known amongst Oxford's scholars, if not always admired, and likewise knows many who bend over books in Oxford's halls and colleges. I thought he might know of Martyn de Wenlock.

I found the scholar at his work, confounding a flock of lads who had been sent to Queen's College because they were thought precocious. Most were foolish enough to believe this, until they sat at Master Wycliffe's feet and were disabused of the notion. When I was a lad it took but a few days of Master John's instruction before I understood how much I had yet to learn.

Wycliffe has a room at Queen's College, and 'twas there I found him. Arthur and I waited outside his door until his lecture was done and the students departed.

Too much study, crouched over books, or writing his own, in the dim light of candle or cresset has, I fear, weakened Master Wycliffe's eyes. He held a glass between his face and a book he had just opened. I had seen spectacles before, but this was the first time I had seen a glass used. When I entered his room he looked up, blinked, and waited for me to speak. Perhaps he thought I was a scholar who had returned to have some point clarified.

"'Tis Hugh de Singleton," I said.

"Ah... Master Hugh. Nay, Sir Hugh. I have heard of your elevation. 'Tis of much benefit to have the ear of a great prince."

Master John knows the truth of this. Prince John of Gaunt, Prince Edward's younger brother, is well disposed to Master John and his views.

"You have come from... Bampton, is it? On some business, no doubt. Is it a matter with which I might help you?"

"Aye, on both counts. A lady has disappeared while traveling to Bampton."

"And you seek her? How may a bachelor scholar assist in the search?"

"The lady is wed to Sir Aymer Molyns, of Coleshill, beyond Faringdon. But before she became Sir Aymer's wife an Oxford scholar paid court to her."

"You think the lady may have abandoned her husband to run off with this scholar? What is the fellow's name?"

"Martyn de Wenlock. Mayhap she did abscond with him, or perhaps he seized her against her will."

"While traveling? Upon the road to Bampton? Surely she did not journey alone. How could such a thing be?"

Like most scholars, I think, Master Wycliffe enjoys puzzling out a riddle. I told him of the events of the past week and he listened intently, chin resting upon a fist.

"What if the lady is found with the scholar, and has plotted to leave her husband to be with the lad? Will the knight have her back?"

"Hah! You must ask him that. He desperately desires an heir, as I told you, and without a wife he'll have none."

"True. Men who have wealth and lands want to pass these on to children and grandchildren. I have neither, nor will have, so I escape the worry.

"Speaking of descendants, how is your Kate – begging your pardon, Lady Katherine – and your children?"

I assured the scholar that I had left them this morning hale, then returned to the matter which brought me to his door.

"Do you know this Martyn de Wenlock?" I asked.

"Nay. He is not of Queen's, I think. But surely some men of my circle will know him. Come." He stood. "We will visit the other halls until he is found."

Arthur followed me and I followed Master John as we departed the college and entered the High Street. We found de Wenlock at the third place we sought him.

Nay, that is not strictly true. We found those who knew him, and we learned of the man, but we did not find him. Not then.

We sought de Wenlock first at University College, then at Merton College, with no success. But William de Daventre, the provost of Oriel College, knew the man we sought. De Wenlock had studied there.

"Where will we find him?" I asked when the provost replied that he knew Martyn.

"Not here. After Trinity Term he left the college. But a few days past."

"Where did he go?" I asked.

"He never said. Not to me. Mayhap he'll return for the Michaelmas Term. Scholars come and go, as their interest waxes and wanes, and as their funds bloom and wither."

"Who are de Wenlock's friends? Did he share a room with another scholar of Oriel?"

"Aye. Robert Lewys."

"Where did the two reside? Is Lewys yet in Oxford?"

"The two had a chamber here, at the college. Whether or not Lewys remains I cannot say, but I suppose so. I've not heard that he is away, either for the summer or permanently."

"Will you lead us to the lad's chamber?" Master John asked.

"Follow me," the provost said. We did.

Robert Lewys was not at home, which was a disappointment. I had hoped to learn what I could from him of Martyn de Wenlock, and then set out for Bampton. Assuming that what I might learn would exculpate de Wenlock from collusion in Lady Philippa's disappearance.

We might have prowled the inns of the High Street for hours and not found Lewys. It was best to await his return to Oriel College.

The wait was not so long as I had feared it might be. The scholar tottered back to his lodgings less than an hour later. He had surely been at an inn, and likely not drinking mere ale. He reeled from one side of Grope Lane to the other, and I despaired of learning anything of importance from a man who had consumed too much wine.

The provost greeted Lewys when he came near, and the fellow

was so startled to hear his name and see four men awaiting him that he stumbled and fell to the mud of the street.

Rising was an ordeal, and finally Arthur took the man's arm to set him upon his feet. The scholar swayed so that I thought he might collapse again. Evidently he had enough wit about him that he realized the probability, for he took two staggering steps and leaned against the doorpost.

"Robert," the provost said, "here is a man who wants words with you about Martyn de Wenlock." As he spoke, the provost looked to me. Lewys then did also, and I saw him try to focus on my visage which was, no doubt, spinning before his eyes.

Robert clumsily doffed his cap, then ceremoniously replaced it askew upon his pate, the liripipe falling to his waist.

"I am Sir Hugh de Singleton, seeking Martyn de Wenlock. I am told that he has departed Oxford. Is this so?"

Lewys swayed against the doorpost and glanced to the provost, as if considering whether or not he should, or must, answer. Or could.

"Aye. Gone, is Martyn," the fellow finally said, his tongue thick between his teeth.

"Where, and when will he return?"

"He won't return. So he said."

"Where has he gone?"

The scholar again seemed to consider his words, or perhaps the wine had dulled his memory.

"Cambridge," he finally said.

"Does he intend to study there?"

"Aye. Peterhouse College."

"Why did he choose to desert Oxford for Cambridge?" I asked.

Lewys was again silent for a time, as if a reply was too much for his addled brain to consider.

"A lass," he finally said.

"A lass? In Cambridge?"

The scholar shook his head and the action caused him to stagger. Arthur reached out a hand to steady him. Between Arthur and the doorpost Lewys regained some stability, then spoke.

"Nay, here, in Oxford."

"So 'tis not a lass in Cambridge who draws him, but a lass in Oxford who repels him?"

This concept seemed too deep for Lewys. His brow furrowed and his eyes rolled from me to Master John to the provost.

"He saw her at Whitsuntide. Said 'twas too much to bear." The scholar hesitated. I prompted him.

"Saw whom? And where?"

"Philippa. He saw her here, with her husband."

"Lady Philippa was here, in Oxford? Did she see Martyn? Did they speak?"

The scholar's reply was to retch violently. He grasped his stomach, then his neck, and we who questioned him had to step away hastily to avoid our shoes being fouled.

Lewys emptied his belly, stood, regained the security of the doorpost, then wiped his mouth upon a sleeve. Do drunken men understand how witless they appear?

Lewys had lost the thread of our conversation along with the contents of his stomach. He looked to me with a vacant expression and I repeated the question.

"That's right. She's a lady now. She wed some knight, Martyn did say. She was here upon Oxford's streets with her husband. Martyn didn't say if he'd had words with her."

Spewing out his belly full of wine seemed to have returned Lewys to a more lucid state.

"Seeing the lady caused de Wenlock much woe?" I said.

"Martyn said she lived but a long day's journey from Oxford, so she'd likely seek the town often – for new gowns and such – and 'twas more'n he could bear to see her again. He said he'd go where she'd not be."

"Cambridge?"

"Aye."

"And he departed Oxford as soon as Trinity Term was done?"

"Aye."

"Did you see him away? How did he travel?"

"Walked, didn't he? He had but three books. He carried them along with all his worldly goods in a sack over his shoulder. The last I saw of him he was bound for Southgate."

A lad who had departed Oxfordshire two weeks earlier, possessing so little he could carry his belongings in a sack, seemed an unlikely candidate to carry off a lady from under her husband's nose, although surely he could benefit from the addition of two pounds to his purse.

I wondered if Lady Philippa now resided in or near Cambridge. And if so, was she taken there against her will? The thought of traveling there to seek Martyn de Wenlock and ask him of Lady Philippa did not appeal. But I could see no other way to learn of what – if anything – the young scholar might have had to do with Lady Philippa's disappearance. As it happened, I was able to answer that question, or so I thought, without the journey.

Chapter 8

"'T is past the ninth hour," Master Wycliffe said as we left Oriel College, its provost, and Robert Lewys. "Darkness will overtake you, I think, before you can return to Bampton. Will you sup with me? There are empty chambers at Queen's College where you may stay the night, and a stables just round the corner on Catte Street where your beasts may be cared for."

The thought of an evening in discourse with my mentor appealed. I had thought to return so far as Eynsham and spend the night there at the abbey before journeying on to Bampton, as I have done in the past when matters called me to Oxford. But Master John needed to exercise little persuasion to change my plans. Arthur, so long as he could consume a good meal, was amenable.

We dined at an inn on the High Street, upon a roasted capon and maslin loaves. Whilst we consumed the fowl Master John saw a friend enter the establishment, hailed him, and invited the fellow to join us, saying the capon was fat enough to feed four. Arthur seemed dejected to hear this conclusion.

The man wore a scholar's gown and accepted the offer with alacrity. His visage was hollow-cheeked and his neck scrawny. His appearance indicated that he rarely found a plump capon before him.

"Hugh, here is Eustace le Scrope," Master John said, and introduced me then to his scholarly friend. "Eustace is of Balliol College and a fine scholar."

Such an accolade from Master Wycliffe is praise indeed, for Master John is known for his corrosive wit in disputation with scholars who display faulty knowledge or reasoning. This penchant has earned him both virulent enemies and loyal friends. Few of Oxford's scholars have no opinion regarding Master Wycliffe and his views.

Conversation over the capon bones was mundane. Perhaps

I expected the exchange of brilliant thoughts and phrases. But even scholars are not immune to the pleasures of gossip. So my mind drifted to thoughts of Lady Philippa's disappearance. Then something Arthur said brought me alert.

"The maid's father paid for her return?" Arthur said.

"Aye," le Scrope replied. "Three pounds. He could well afford it, as the rogues surely knew."

"Of whom do you speak?" I asked.

"My cousin, Sir Thomas le Scrope, of Didcot."

"I apologize. I was wool-gathering and did not follow the conversation."

"Eustace was telling us of the taking of his cousin's daughter," Wycliffe said. "I had told him of your search for the missing lady and her two-pound ransom and he spoke of a similar abduction."

"When?"

"'Twas at Candlemas," Eustace replied, mildly annoyed at my inattention, but willing to be patient.

"And it was a lass abducted? A young lass, you say?"

"Aye. Joan was but thirteen years."

"How did it happen?" I asked. Eustace looked a little askance at this, but had the courtesy to go over it again.

"Joan was marching to the church with other matrons and ladies. 'Twas her first time to be of age to do so. When of a sudden four mounted men galloped into the town, scattering the procession, and one was heard to call out, 'Here is the lass.'"

"These fellows knew whom they sought?" I said.

"Aye. 'Twas not a random taking. The scoundrel seized her and threw her across his saddle whilst his companions wielded swords and challenged any to interfere. Men who saw this happen bore only daggers and were no match for the miscreants."

"Were the men masked?" I asked.

"Aye."

"Even so, were they recognized? Could they be identified?"

Eustace shrugged. "Most folk of Didcot know who seized the lass, but none have the courage to say so."

"The rogue is known about Didcot?" I said.

"Aye."

"They have a powerful protector, then? Powerful enough that your cousin paid three pounds rather than see the evil-doers arrested."

"Aye. You have it so. If he sought their capture his barns would burn within a fortnight, and mayhap his house as well."

"Who protects this outlaw band?"

Eustace was silent.

"You fear to say? For dread of what the brigands might do if they learned you named their protector?"

"Even Oxford scholars are not immune from the retribution of sinful men," Eustace said softly.

Le Scrope leaned toward me as if to share some secret and in a whisper spoke a name.

"'Tis bandied about that Gaston Howes took the lass."

"This man is leader of a band of felons?" I asked. "Who is his dark champion?"

Eustace fell silent again, raised a morsel of maslin loaf to his mouth, and glanced about the noisy inn as he chewed. The man was determined to ensure that no other was paying attention to us or our conversation before he would continue. His covert survey of the room evidently satisfied the scholar.

"Sir John Willoughby," le Scrope said, raising his cup as if the ale would wash his mouth clean of the name.

"Willoughby? There is a judge of the King's Eyre of that name, I believe," I said.

"Aye, so there is."

"And Sir John is kin to the judge?"

"He is. Distant cousin or some such, I've heard tell."

Here was interesting information. A band of felons had recently seized a maid and demanded three pounds' ransom of her father for her release. The ransom was paid even though 'twas likely he knew who had carried his daughter off. The felons had a powerful protector, who himself had an even more powerful defender. I felt sure that of the three pounds Sir Thomas paid in ransom more than a few shillings went to Sir John Willoughby and his cousin the judge.

Would such rogues go so far from Didcot that they would seize Lady Philippa Molyns? Likely the supply of ladies near to Didcot whose ransoms would make them worth carrying off is small. And perhaps husbands and fathers of the area, who fear for their wives and daughters, pay to ensure the ladies will be let alone. Who could know? Men so threatened would not likely tell others of their inability to safeguard their spouse or daughter.

"Your search for the missing lady of Coleshill has brought you to Oxford, then?" le Scrope said. "Have you information that those who took her may be of this place?"

"I have not. But there is – was – a scholar of Oriel College who courted the lady before she wed Sir Aymer Molyns. I thought to seek out that scholar and discover what, if anything, he might know of Lady Philippa."

"You failed to find the man?" Eustace said.

"Aye. We are told he has removed to Cambridge, to avoid the ache of seeing the lady upon Oxford's streets – which painful encounter did befall him some weeks past."

"You think that he might have carried her off, or she might have willingly fled her husband to be with this scholar?"

"Aye. I do. Mayhap she now resides in Cambridge, willingly or not," I replied.

"So – will you travel to Cambridge in search of this scholar?"

"If I must. He has been there but a few weeks, so few folk of Cambridge will know the name Martyn de Wenlock."

Le Scrope had been leaning upon the stained, scarred table. He abruptly sat straight up, his eyes wide and his mouth open.

"Martyn? Cambridge?" he said.

"Aye. You know the man?"

"Know him? I saw him yesterday. When was he to have gone to Cambridge?"

"A scholar who shared a room with him said he departed Oxford the day after Trinity Term ended."

"Hmmm. He may have done," le Scrope said. "I'd not seen him for several weeks. But I did see him yesterday."

"You are sure it was he?"

"I have no doubt. I've known Martyn going on three years."

"Did he say where he now resides?"

"Nay – I knew no reason to ask the question. 'Twas but a greeting as we passed one another on Cornmarket Street, near to St. Michael's at Northgate."

I looked to Master Wycliffe. "Master John has invited me and my man to stay the night in a vacant chamber at Queen's College. My home is in Bampton, and I meant to return there on the morrow. But now I think not. Are you engaged tomorrow, or could you prowl the streets with us? We do not know de Wenlock and would not recognize him. Perhaps if we walk the length of Cornmarket Street he might reappear there."

Le Scrope had enjoyed a free meal, so perhaps he felt obliged to assist me in my search. He agreed to meet me, Arthur, and Master Wycliffe at the gate to Queen's College at the third hour next day. Master Wycliffe's sight has declined, to be sure, but not so that he can no longer recognize a face he knows – and he professed himself keen to be included in our hunt for the man we sought.

I slept little that night, and the fault was not (only) Arthur and his snores. My thoughts were upon Lady Philippa, Martyn de Wenlock, and the solution to the lady's disappearance, which I considered might be near. Would the scholar leave Oxford to avoid seeing a lady whose occasional appearance brought sorrow for what was lost – then suddenly return? Did de Wenlock reappear in Oxford because he knew Lady Philippa was near? Why do so if her presence brought mourning? Perhaps it no longer did. But why not?

Or did he return because he knew he would no longer be grieved by the lady's appearance on Oxford's streets?

Whatever the answer, I hoped I might discover it the next day.

'Twas not the first time my hopes were dashed, and likely will not be the last.

Master Wycliffe, as most scholars, breaks his fast with only a cup of ale. He had a ewer full, and shared the brew with Arthur and me. There remained yet two hours 'til Eustace le Scrope should appear before Queen's College, so Arthur and I left Master John to his studies and sought a stationer. It is my custom to write a careful record of felonies I have been charged to resolve, and I needed to renew my supply of parchment. I thought the events in which I was now embroiled would be worthy of the writing. Back in the day when my father-in-law owned a shop in Oxford he supplied this need, thankful for my service to him in removing a splinter from his back which had gone deep and festered. I had no need to purchase ink, for my Kate had produced the stuff for her father, and made all I could require from oak galls and copperas.

But those days are gone, and on this morning I had to part with an eye-watering sum to purchase four gatherings – vellum is not cheap. Then Arthur and I wandered the familiar streets, passing the inn where once upon a time, on the first floor, I had hung with pride my sign indicating that a surgeon resided there. Arthur knew the place well, for he had accompanied Lord Gilbert on the day, many years past, when another groom's beast, startled at a cat dashing across the street before it, wheeled and bucked and with an iron-shod hoof struck and lacerated Lord Gilbert's leg.

'Twas Arthur who ran up the stairs to seek me that day, having noticed my sign, and met me hurrying down, having glanced through the window at the commotion and seen the wound made.

So it was that I met Lord Gilbert Talbot, stitched up his lacerated thigh, and was shortly after invited to serve him as bailiff to his manor of Bampton. How the course of my life waschanged by a frightened cat! We never know what interventions may make all the difference.

Would I have met Lord Gilbert and entered his service? Most unlikely. Would I have sought parchment and ink to write of the felonies I had solved in Lord Gilbert's employ? Would I have met

Kate at her father's stationer's shop? Would I have two babes and a beauteous wife? Even if I did, it would not be Kate, not my Bessie, not little John. Then did the Lord Christ send that cat before the groom's skittish horse so to set me upon His chosen path? Does He work such things? Or was it my decision to take lodgings above that particular inn that set in train all that has since come to me? Ah, these questions must be crammed with so many others into my bulging mystery bag, to be opened and explained when I meet the Lord Christ face to face.

Arthur and I reminisced as we made our way through the streets back to Queen's College. I found Master Wycliffe awaiting us, then, whilst he was away kindly depositing my bundle of parchment in his chamber, le Scrope appeared. Minutes later we walked together to Cornmarket Street where two days past Martyn de Wenlock had been seen.

We sauntered up and down the street 'til noon, seeing no sign of de Wenlock but plenty of other young scholars – free of their studies until the Michaelmas Term – frolicking in the way, chasing each other about and poking fun, as lads will do. As I once did. All serious, sober men were once lads who gamboled about in the joy of youth. Do lads ever consider the approach of age and responsibilities? Why should they? I seldom did. Do old men remember when they were lads intent upon a lark? Not often, I suspect, and sometimes when they do, with remorse.

At the same inn on High Street where we had enjoyed our roasted capon just a few hours before, we sought dinner. 'Twas a fast day, so no capons or pease pottage thick with pork were offered. The inn provided eels in bruit, which cost me sixpence and two farthings. I paid the innkeeper with seven pence, and received in return two farthings. I felt an oddity as I slipped the farthings into my purse. My fingertips detected an indentation on one of the coins. When I drew it out for a second look, I knew well the mark. I had put it there. Here was one of the farthings I had punched at Sir Aymer's house in Coleshill but a few days before. Whoso had gathered the ransom had perhaps purchased a meal or lodging at this inn. Or purchased some goods from a man who then spent the coins here. Whatever the circumstance – he had likely been this way.

I sought the innkeeper and asked if he remembered a man who had paid for his services with a damaged coin. The fellow stared at me as if I was daft. I showed him the farthing and the flaw inflicted upon it. "Nay. As long as folk pay the coin 'tis of no concern to me. Lots of coins change hands here in a day. If you don't want that one, I'll exchange it for a better."

"Nay. 'Tis well enough," I replied.

Chasing after the man who had spent the dented farthing would be a fool's errand. But Sir Aymer's ransom had come to Oxford, that was sure.

"Don't forget your gatherings," Wycliffe reminded me.

I would have, had he not spoken, for my mind was consumed with thoughts of a missing lady, an elusive scholar, and blemished coins.

As we approached Queen's College le Scrope suddenly said, "There he is!" Then he shouted to a distant scholar, "Martyn... Martyn de Wenlock!"

A black-gowned figure fifty or so paces distant turned to see who had called his name. The youth had a pleasant face, light hair, and an intelligent expression as yet unlined with the cares of maturity. He sought among those upon the street for the man who had called his name, saw Eustace, and smiled in recognition. All in all I did not deem his countenance that of a bereaved lover. Perhaps, I thought, de Wenlock had found another lass. But in case not I warned le Scrope, as Martyn approached, that he should not identify my mission.

Eustace, as many scholars, is quick-witted, and understood that he must devise some reason for calling out de Wenlock upon the street. When Martyn came near he said, "I heard you had abandoned us for those pretenders in Cambridge! I am pleased to see 'tis not so."

"I had thought to do so," de Wenlock said, "but changed my mind."

"I am right glad to hear it. Will you continue at Oriel College, or enroll elsewhere? Oh – do you know Master Wycliffe?" De Wenlock bowed to Master John. "He is now at Queen's College," le Scrope continued.

"I had heard," de Wenlock said, "that you departed Canterbury Hall for Queen's."

"We at Queen's always welcome bright lads," Wycliffe said with a smile.

De Wenlock began to glance about, as if impatient to be away. Le Scrope saw this and apologized for delaying him.

"Think nothing of it," de Wenlock smiled. "We will meet again over a cup of ale when I am less hurried."

"Indeed. Fare you well."

De Wenlock again bowed to Master John, then with a wave turned on his heels and hastened north on Northgate Street before le Scrope had a chance to introduce me and Arthur. We had met the scholar upon High Street. He was walking then beyond the city wall, and left us to continue along that way. What could be beyond the city wall, I wondered, that he hastened to see? Or who, that he hastened to meet? Could it be that Lady Philippa was somewhere near?

"Come," I said to Arthur. "I intend to follow de Wenlock. He seems too joyful for a thwarted lover."

"Unless 'e's found a new maid to take the place of the one 'e lost," Arthur grinned.

"Aye, perhaps."

I said a hurried "Good day" to Master John and Eustace, promised Wycliffe I would call for my parchments shortly, and set out in haste to follow de Wenlock. Arthur and I stayed close enough that he remained in sight, but far enough behind that I thought us safe from recognition if he turned to observe the street behind him.

He did so, but his gaze did not linger upon us, so I believed we were not noticed. Although Arthur is a hard man not to notice. At a muddy lane de Wenlock turned to the east, then at Broad Street turned south again, walking briskly, 'til a few moments later heading west he approached the Northgate where he had departed the city but moments before.

"What's all this about, then?" Arthur muttered. "'E set off like the 'ounds of 'ell was after 'im and now 'e's come back to where 'e started."

"He saw us," I said. "And although he does not likely know me or my mission, he has some secret to hide."

"The lady?"

"Possibly."

"What you plan to do? Keep followin' 'im?"

"We will not need to. He is stopped just inside the Northgate and seems to be awaiting someone. Perhaps us."

This was so. As we approached, de Wenlock left the wall of St. Michael's Tower where he had leaned whilst we came near, and stepped out to stand squarely in our way.

"You accompanied Eustace le Scrope," he said with an accusing tone. "Now you are following me. Why so?"

Clearly I am not adept at deception. I decided to speak plainly.

"Because I wish to learn what you may know, or see what you may see."

"Who are you, and what is it you think you may learn or see by pursuing me?"

"I am Sir Hugh de Singleton, bailiff to Lord Gilbert Talbot at his manor of Bampton. Now, as to what I wish to learn or see, I believe you may know."

This declaration brought a blank stare in reply. "I've heard of Lord Gilbert Talbot. And where's Bampton?"

"You've heard of Robert Lewys," I said. De Wenlock nodded. "He told me yesterday you departed Oxford for Cambridge when Trinity Term ended. And he told me why. You sought to escape seeing Lady Philippa Molyns, whose love you once sought, but lost."

"I never lost her love," the scholar replied softly.

"Hmmm. But you lost the lady. And Robert said you told him you could not bear the sorrow of seeing her again – which in Oxford you might do, as Lady Philippa resides but a long day's journey from here. If this is so, why have you returned?"

De Wenlock shrugged, then perhaps realizing this was no good answer, spoke. "I missed Oxford and my friends here. I didn't like Cambridge."

"Friends like Robert Lewys? Have you resumed lodging with him? He did not say so."

"Nay," Martyn scoffed. "Robert is a drunkard. I've lost track of how many times he spewed up his guts in a stupor, then collapsed upon his pallet leaving me to remove the filth."

"If not with Robert at Oriel College, where do you now lodge?"

"I have a chamber above the Red Dragon."

"On Little Bailey Street?"

"Aye."

I knew the place, and the proprietor. Above his tavern were six rooms, no larger than cells, where impecunious scholars might lodge.

"How long since you returned to Oxford?"

"Why these questions? Why does a bailiff of some place I've not heard of wish to know of my coming and going?"

I hesitated. He sounded genuinely puzzled. If de Wenlock knew why I wanted to know of his movements for the past days, telling him could not likely harm my investigation. If he did not know of Lady Philippa's disappearance – which seemed to be the case – then he had nothing to do with it, and informing him would likewise do no injury to my search for the lady. He might even help us find her. So I thought. I told him.

The lad's eyes widened as he heard from me that Lady Philippa had not been seen for eight days. He seemed genuinely surprised at the news, but I take little stock in such expressions. Some men, and women also, are skilled at deception.

I returned to the previous question. "How long since your return to Oxford?"

"You believe I had to do with Philippa's disappearance?" he cried indignantly. "Why would I do so? The lady has wed another. I am bereft, with no hope of gaining what is lost."

"Mayhap. When did you return?"

94

"Near a fortnight past."

"What day?"

"Exactly?"

"Aye, exactly."

De Wenlock counted back the days in his mind, then replied, "'Twas the nineteenth day of June... a Sunday."

"And you have not departed Oxford since returning that day?"

"Nay. When did Philippa vanish?"

"Two days after. Can any man corroborate your claim that since Sunday ten days past you have not forsaken Oxford, even for a day?"

Martyn shrugged again, glanced about blankly for a moment, then brightened. "He who owns the Red Dragon. He has seen me every day, and will attest what I say is so."

From where we stood on Northgate Street to Little Bailey Street and the Red Dragon was but a walk of ten minutes, not more. I told de Wenlock we would visit the proprietor and learn if what he said was so. We did, and it was.

"Aye," the wizened old fellow agreed. "Martyn 'as 'is dinner 'ere every day. Not known 'im to miss a meal since 'e took lodgin' up the stairs."

As he spoke he glanced up to the board ceiling above him.

"He took lodging upon a Sunday?"

A moment's hesitation while the old codger thought. "Aye," he agreed. "Two weeks Sunday."

Martyn de Wenlock might know of Lady Philippa's abduction even if he had naught to do with it. I could not be sure, one way or the other, but he had not participated in the event. I had but one more question for him but did not want to ask it before the man's landlord. I motioned to the door and said, "Come with me for a moment."

"When you set off on Northgate Street and my man and I followed, where did you intend to go? You made haste, that was plain. When you discovered yourself followed, you returned to the Northgate. What was your purpose?"

De Wenlock was adept at shrugging his shoulders when he would rather not answer a question. I have discovered that when a man wishes to escape a question it is often best to say no more. This may allow a mendacious man time to invent a falsehood, but the silence often results in such discomfort for the interrogated that they will spill out the truth.

"There's more'n one lass in Oxford," de Wenlock finally said.

"Quick work," I replied, "to meet a maid having returned to the town but ten days past. Or did you know of her before you departed for Cambridge? Nay," I answered my own question. "You'd not have fled the sight of Lady Philippa had another lass taken your fancy."

De Wenlock shrugged again.

"Why so secretive? Most lads don't care if others know they are courting a lass. Especially when the others are men they've just met and don't know."

Another shrug.

"Lady Philippa's father was not pleased with your suit, I understand. Who wishes for a penniless scholar for a son-in-law, eh? Is this true also of some new maid?"

Another shrug.

I began to understand that a twitch of de Wenlock's shoulders was all I was likely to get from him. If he was in Oxford eight days past he could not have taken Lady Philippa with or without her connivance. Although others could have done so with his knowledge and scheming. I must consider this possibility even if I thought it improbable. And I wished to leave Oxford to its residents and be off home. But before I dismissed de Wenlock I asked to see his purse. This caused more than a shrug. The scholar raised his eyebrows but I assured him I had no intention of taking coins from him. The inn was filled with patrons and the street busy, so perhaps he thought it safe to hand the pouch to me. If he raised the hue and cry a dozen men would be after me in an instant.

In the purse I found a groat, six pennies, and five farthings. None of them had a blemish where I had marked the ransom coins. I handed the purse back to de Wenlock without explaining my purpose, then dismissed him. He touched a forelock in respect. I considered that Arthur and I were about to set off on a long, dry ride to Bampton, so I spent four farthings on two cups of watered ale to fortify us for the journey.

Chapter 9

'T was near to the ninth hour when I retrieved my gatherings from Master John and we mounted our palfreys to set off across Bookbinders' Bridge, so darkness was close upon us when we reached Bampton. As we traveled I had opportunity to consider what I had learned in Oxford and what I had not. Most provoking was the knowledge that not far from Bampton a maid was taken and three pounds demanded for her return. Would those rogues travel such a distance to seize Lady Philippa as her wagon departed Clanfield? If there was no more likely victim closer to them, surely. Men who become accustomed to ill-gotten gain generally will not give up the source of their income for honest labor, unless compelled.

Kate expected my return. She had kept a pottage of peas and beans near the fire. As I consumed a bowl I told her and my father-in-law of Oxford.

"Mayhap," Kate offered, "the rogues who seized the lass near Didcot did the same to Lady Philippa – or perhaps they did but supply the notion to others. Didcot is not near, is it?"

"Nay. But near enough that events there may be heard of here, or even beyond, to Coleshill."

"And near enough," Caxton added, "that a man might travel from Didcot to Clanfield and return in a day. A long day."

I fell to sleep that night considering why felons would demand three pounds' ransom for a lass of but thirteen years, but only two pounds for a married woman. It must be, I decided, that the felons considered the wealth of father and husband. Which might mean that whoso seized Lady Philippa and the lass knew the husband and the father well. If the rogues were the same.

It had been to dark on Wednesday evening when I had dismounted at Church View Street, walked to Galen House, and sent Arthur on to Bampton Castle. I did not follow him after my supper as I know that, since Lady Petronilla's death four years past, Lord Gilbert seeks his bed early.

So on Thursday morning, after a barley loaf and ale, I went to the castle to keep my employer informed. There was little to tell him: only the Didcot abduction, and Martyn de Wenlock's departure from Oxford and hasty return.

When I told Lord Gilbert of de Wenlock's reason for leaving the town and then returning, he raised an eyebrow. He does this when skeptical or questioning. When I first entered Lord Gilbert's service I tried to emulate this trait. This was unsuccessful. My brows rise or fall together and I have given over the struggle.

"What of the maid in Didcot?" Lord Gilbert said.

"She was taken whilst marching to the church for Candlemas," I explained.

"With others to see?" Lord Gilbert asked in disbelief.

"Aye. The abductor was a rogue named Gaston Howes, so all men believe. He and his companions were masked. Three pounds' ransom was demanded for her release."

"Her father paid?"

"Aye, he did."

"The Howes fellow... if he is known in that place, why is he not arrested?"

"He has a protector."

"Who? Likely I will know the fellow."

"'Tis said Sir John Willoughby shields the rogue."

"Hmm," Lord Gilbert nodded, "I'm not surprised. Sir John will be secure behind Sir William Willoughby."

"The judge? Sir John's cousin, I believe."

Lord Gilbert nodded again. "Aye, the same."

"Money flows from hand to hand and the rogues escape punishment for their villainy."

"So it seems," Lord Gilbert agreed. "Have you carried this business as far as you wish, or will you continue to seek Lady Philippa? I tell you again, you have no obligation to do so. Sir Aymer can seek for his own wife. Perhaps she has already been returned to him."

"If so it would be helpful if Sir Aymer would report it."

"Aye. But perhaps he believes you must have abandoned the search by this time, so he feels no need to inform us."

"Perhaps."

"But you do not believe it so, do you?"

"Nay. And this is why I doubt it was those felons from Didcot who took Lady Philippa."

"Because when the ransom for the maid was delivered she was released?"

"Just so. As far as we know, Lady Philippa is not free, even though Sir Aymer met the demand for two pounds."

"So you will not travel to Didcot?"

"Nay. Not yet. But I do not intend to forget Lady Philippa."

"You will continue to seek her, even though you are not required?"

"Aye."

"Where? What will you do next? Who may have knowledge of the lady, think you?"

It was my turn to shrug. In truth I did not know what direction my next steps must take. I knew only that I could not find ease 'til the matter was resolved.

My interview with my employer was nearly completed when there came a rapping upon the solar door.

"Enter," Lord Gilbert said.

'Twas John Chamberlain who was at the door. "A rider has come from Coleshill," he said.

Lord Gilbert looked to me. "Lady Philippa is set free," he said.

"Nay, m'lord," John replied. "Sir Aymer wishes Sir Hugh to attend one of his servants. The man was injured two days past. His arm is out of joint."

"The rider said nothing of Lady Philippa?" I said.

"I asked it of him. She is not released."

"Where is the messenger?"

"I sent him to the kitchen for a loaf and ale."

"Good. Come," Lord Gilbert said to me. "We will learn what we can from the fellow."

'Twas Maurice we found at a table in the kitchen. He stood when he saw Lord Gilbert enter and tugged a forelock.

"What news?" Lord Gilbert said.

"I am sent to ask your surgeon to attend Sir Aymer. John Cely's arm is out of joint at his shoulder. Sir Aymer asks if you can put it right."

"Is John Cely the man who guided Lady Philippa's wagon?"

"Aye, the same. He was pitching hay from the loft. He lost his footing, bein' old an' wobbly on 'is feet, an' fell to the ground."

Lord Gilbert looked to me. "Can you mend such an injury?"

"Aye, probably."

"Your mistress has not been returned to Sir Aymer, my man said. Is this so?" Lord Gilbert said.

"Aye. She is not returned."

"Has there been a further ransom demand? Do her captors require more coin?"

"Nay. Nothing is known of them."

"Is there no physician or surgeon near to Coleshill who can deal with the man's injury?" Lord Gilbert asked.

"There is a physician resides in Faringdon. Sir Aymer sent for him yesterday. He could do nothing but torment John, yanking his arm about. His howls were pitiful." Maurice shook his head, compassion clear in his face, as he remembered.

"Sir Aymer sent me to fetch you as soon as dawn came this morning. He begs you to come quick. The man is in much pain."

"I will, surely. A shoulder out of joint, which is likely what afflicts John, can be put right. But this must be done soon after the injury. After a few weeks the remedy becomes more difficult. I will have the marshalsea make ready a palfrey, visit my home to tell Kate I am away, and return within the hour."

"What?" Kate said when I told her my plans. "You intend to ride to Coleshill without first having your dinner?"

"Apparently not," I replied. "Is there something ready now?"

"I will seek Adela and hurry the meal."

'Twas worth the wait. I enjoyed stewed herrings with maslin loaves for my dinner, and was not too much beyond the hour when I returned to Bampton Castle. I found three palfreys, Arthur, and Uctred awaiting me.

"I 'eard you was called to Coleshill," Arthur explained, "and thought you'd best not travel alone. Uctred wants to come along for the journey. There's little enough to keep a man busy these days."

This was indeed true. The work of ploughing and planting was done, the labor of harvest yet to come. Other than hoeing weeds and repairing houses, barns, roofs, and fences there is small demand on a man's time and labor come midsummer.

Four strangers passing through a village – Maurice returned to Coleshill with us – always attract attention. So it was in Clanfield. Folk tending their onions leaned upon hoes to watch us pass, and in a field planted to dredge I saw Janyn Hoard and another man unknown to me raking weeds from the furrows. The other spared but a glance but Janyn watched until we passed from view. He was not near the road, but close enough that I saw distrust in his eyes. Perhaps it was my imagination. Due to the nature of our duty we bailiffs are accustomed to receiving malevolent glares. So much so that we expect them.

Badbury Hill was green and gold in the slanting sunlight as we passed the place. How many days had passed since I ventured to the top – well, near the top – to leave several hundred coins where directed?

We halted before Coleshill's manor house in time for a late supper. Sir Aymer's grooms took our palfreys in hand, and Arthur and Uctred and I were invited to a meal of beans yfryed. I did not see the injured wagoner and asked Sir Aymer of him.

"He ate his dinner, but complains of the hurt and will take no supper. How will you deal with his shoulder?"

"I require a length of stout hempen rope, perhaps three yards long, and an old kirtle or some such garment which may be folded to a pad."

"That's all?"

"Aye. Maurice says you have still received no messages from those who took Lady Philippa."

"True."

Sir Aymer's shoulders seemed to fall. "I have no wife. I have no word from those who have her. What is worse, I know not what I may do now to find her."

While we ate I told Sir Aymer of the lass of Didcot seized at Candlemas.

"Sir John Willoughby safeguards this Howes fellow?" he said.

"Aye. Do you know Sir John?"

"I do," he said with contempt. His tone of voice intrigued me, but I did not press him for an explanation. I thought it likely Sir Aymer would account for his opinion without prompting. He did.

"Our fathers fought at Crécy. Or, I should say, *my* father fought at Crécy. Sir John's father was present, but no one saw him while the battle raged. 'Twas not 'til the French withdrew that he was seen."

"Men may lose track of one another in the heat of battle," I said.

"Aye, they may. But Crécy was fought upon muddy ground, after days of rain. Those who fought were bespattered with mud and filth. Not so Thomas Willoughby. No man saw him 'til after, when our archers were stopped from slaying the wounded French knights."

"I have heard that the archers slew many wounded after the battle," I said.

"They did. Knights whose ransoms could have amounted to hundreds, nay, thousands of pounds. But of course the commons care nothing about that. No French knight would ransom himself from an archer. My father and others stopped the slaughter, and the kindness proved profitable. He held two French knights and gained twelve pounds for their release."

"And Thomas Willoughby?"

"He and his squire collected three knights, I heard."

"And his armor was unstained?"

"It was."

"Did the men who were present speak of this in the days after the battle?"

"Not when Sir Thomas was within earshot."

"But at other times?"

"Aye. And Sir Thomas knew they did so."

"Was your father one of these?"

"He was. Sir Thomas would speak of Crécy as if he alone saved King Edward, when all know 'twas the bowmen, not the gentlemen in their armor, who vanquished the French that day."

"Sir Thomas harbored a dislike for your father because of this? Does the son also resent what was said of his father?"

"Surely. And has little regard for me or others because of it."

"I wonder if he would set Gaston Howes to seize your lady as revenge for your father's opinion of his own?"

"Hmmm. I had not considered such a thing. He might, I suppose. But he would need to abduct half the ladies of the realm if he wanted to avenge all the words spoken by knights behind his father's back. But when will you deal with John's shoulder? The light is failing. Must you wait 'til morning?"

"Much light is not necessary. A few candles or cressets will serve. Putting a dislocated shoulder aright – and I must see the man before I know if this is truly his injury – is more a matter of touch than sight."

John Cely was brought to the hall when supper was done and a moment of testing the joint told me that dislocation was his complaint. The arm was not broken, nor was his collarbone. I saw the raised lump of his right shoulder before his cotehardie and kirtle were removed. The old fellow gasped with pain when his arm was raised to remove the garments.

I asked for a cup of ale, and in it placed a thimbleful of crushed hemp seeds and another of the dried flakes of lettuce sap. I have had good success with these herbs when I wished to reduce a man's pain while I treated his hurt.

The dosage requires an hour or so to take effect, and I shouted into the codger's ear so as to make known to him the reason for delay in putting his shoulder right. He nodded understanding, and I pointed to a bench and bade him sit. 'Twould be a sorrow if the herbs so dazed him that while standing he toppled to the flags. I might then have two injuries to deal with.

I repeated to Sir Aymer that to complete the repair to John's shoulder I would need rope and some worn discarded garment. He sent Brom to fetch these items. And while we awaited his return and the effect of the hemp and lettuce Sir Aymer and I renewed our dinner conversation regarding Sir John Willoughby and Gaston Howes.

"I cannot charge Sir John with this villainy on nothing more than a suspicion," Sir Aymer said. "And if I did, his cousin would not permit his arrest."

I agreed that we lacked evidence. We mulled over our possibilities – threats, an armed band appearing before Sir John's door, or plotting to seize Sir John's oldest son for exchange? All these we abandoned, for the good reason that we could not be sure if the felon he protected was guilty of taking Lady Philippa.

So an hour later, when John Cely swayed upon the bench as if he was about to entertain Morpheus, we were no nearer to a plan to seek Lady Philippa than when the conversation began.

Brom laid the rope and kirtle before me. I tied two loops at either end of the rope, about as far apart as from my chin to my waist. I shouted into John's ear that he should rise, and Maurice took hold of his good arm to assist the feeble old groom to his feet.

I draped the folded kirtle over the crook of John's right arm, as a pad for the rope, then drew a loop from one end of the rope over his right hand and rested it upon the kirtle. This left the other loop dangling a foot or so above the flags.

I took firm hold of John's useless arm with one hand where it had been drawn from his shoulder, then placed my left foot in the dangling loop. I told Maurice to hold firm, then took hold of John's right wrist and raised it 'til the loop was tight about the folded kirtle and his elbow. The old groom seemed untroubled by this, but his equanimity would soon change, I knew.

Of a sudden I put my weight upon the dangling loop whilst I continued to raise John's wrist. The tightening rope pulled down upon his upper arm, as it could not move the lower arm due to my hold upon the wrist.

The codger winced and cried out, but I pressed down with my foot the harder. I felt, and heard, a popping sound. The dislocation was no more. The tightening rope had drawn the bone back into its proper place in the shoulder socket.

I felt the joint to be sure the remedy was complete and successful. As I did I saw a tear trickle down the old man's cheek. He looked to his right shoulder and smiled through his tears when he saw the disfiguring knob was no more.

Next I took the old kirtle, ripped it in half, and made a sling. I shouted into John's ear that for a fortnight he must rest his arm in the sling and do no labor. A shoulder which has become dislocated, and restored, is likely to be dislocated again if much force is too soon applied to the joint. John nodded, and Sir Aymer, who had until then watched the procedure in silence, said, "There is no need for John's labor 'til Lammastide, and perhaps even then he will not be needed."

The long day was past when I finished with John Cely. Sir Aymer paid my fee, sixpence, and with Arthur and Uctred I went to the chamber Sir Aymer had assigned me, and sought my bed.

Arthur spoke, and his words were not conducive to sleep. "Did you watch the old fellow whilst you an' Sir Aymer was talkin' about Lady Philippa?"

"Nay. What would I have seen had I done so?"

"He suffers the disease of the ears, 'tis said. You needed to shout in 'is ear to make yourself understood."

"Aye, I did."

"Mayhap 'e hears more'n folks think."

"Why do you say so?"

"He was sittin' on the bench whilst you an' Sir Aymer was speakin' of the lady. His head was goin' back an' forth, to you, then to Sir Aymer, dependin' on who was talkin'."

"What of it?" I said. "He could see who was speaking. Perhaps he has learned to follow a man's speech by watching the movement of his lips. I've heard it said that there are men who can do so."

"Mayhap. But I thought 'is eyes was cloudy-like. So how could 'e see a man's lips movin' so clear? An' 'is face said 'e understood what you an' Sir Aymer was sayin'. Some of it, anyhow."

Arthur's words planted a seed of doubt which sprouted overnight. Were John's ears as defective as men thought? Surely his eyes were. The white of his cataracts was plain to see. Before I fell to sleep I devised a plan to learn if John Cely could hear more than others thought. After I broke my fast I would try the scheme.

Chapter 10

Sir Aymer provided maslin loaves and ale to fortify us for the return to Bampton. I told him I wished to examine John Cely before we set out, to reassure myself that all was well with the groom's shoulder, and he sent Brom to rouse the man from his bed and bring him to us.

"Watch the old fellow while I speak to Sir Aymer," I said to Arthur and Uctred. "I will have my back to him so he will not see my lips, even through his clouded eyes. I wish to learn if my words cause him distress."

Arthur nodded understanding. I had spoken these instructions in a whisper, so Sir Aymer, who was speaking to Brom, would not hear.

John appeared, rubbing rheum from his eyes, a few moments later. He had the sling about his neck, supporting his mended shoulder. I shouted into his ear that I wished to inspect my work once again before I departed Coleshill. The old codger looked to his shoulder while I removed the sling and pressed my fingers against the joint. This examination caused him to wince, but I was satisfied all was well.

Then I turned from him and in a normal voice addressed Sir Aymer. "I am pleased. It is sometimes the situation that if the dislocation of a man's shoulder is profound, the tissue holding the bones together will die."

This is not so, but neither Sir Aymer nor John Cely would likely know it. I lied. For a good cause. May the Lord Christ forgive me.

"If so be it this happens, the only recourse is to amputate the dying limb. Such surgery may also be fatal, but if 'tis not done a man will perish."

Sir Aymer stared at me open-mouthed. The information shocked him, as it surely would John, if the man heard it. I did not then turn to see the fellow's reaction, if such there was. I would rely upon Arthur and Uctred, who had also heard my falsehood, to tell if there was any sign that Cely heard and was anxious for his life.

I did not need to hear their opinion. When I finally turned back to the old fellow to replace the sling I saw his mouth agape. He said nothing, but it was clear to me that while John Cely might have a disease of the ears he heard more than most folk thought.

The stairs from the upper floor of Sir Aymer's manor house opened into a corner of the passage between kitchen and hall, beside the screens passage. I heard footsteps and from the corner of my eye saw movement. 'Twas a woman of perhaps twenty years. Her complexion was dark, as those who work in the fields, under the sun, but she wore a spotless linen chemise and a bright green woolen cotehardie. Her hair was braided with yellow silk ribbons.

Sir Aymer followed my gaze. "My guest," he said. "Isobel Davies."

I bowed a greeting and wondered if she was his only guest, or if a man would follow her down the stairs. None did. Isobel bowed in return and silently passed into the kitchen.

"What am I to do if John's arm seems to fail him?" Sir Aymer said.

"Send for me straightaway," I replied. I knew this would not happen, but I must continue the subterfuge as I was now certain Cely could hear more than he would admit. Why this might be puzzled me, but I considered that when Lady Philippa was taken he likely heard more of the event than he would say, even if he saw nothing of it. A man may feign deafness, but the white film over his eyes can be no sham.

Arthur and Uctred confirmed my opinion of John's reaction to the suggestion that I might need to lop his arm off. "Watched 'is Adam's apple bounce like the tail of a suckling lamb," Uctred chuckled.

"Will you truly saw 'is arm off if need be?" Arthur said. I thought his features seemed pale, as if he feared I might require his aid in such a surgery.

I assured him that such a surgery would not be required as we walked to Sir Aymer's stables to ready our beasts for the return to Bampton. We found Giles Stonor there, attending to his steed.

"Were you able to deal with John's displaced shoulder?" he asked.

"Aye. It was corrected last night."

"He will be as good as new?"

"None of us will ever be good as new," I replied.

"Aye, 'tis so," Stonor agreed. "But will the fellow be able to use the arm as well as he could three days past?"

"Ancient folk do not heal of wounds and injuries so quickly as a lad like you, but in a fortnight he may discard the sling which now supports the arm. By Martinmas the dislocation will likely be as restored as ever it can be." But there was something else I wanted to ask Giles Stonor. "Who is Isobel Davies?"

"You met her?" The squire grinned.

"Aye. Sir Aymer said she is a guest."

Giles softly snorted in derision. I waited for an explanation.

"She's not Sir Aymer's first guest at Coleshill," he said.

"The second, then? Or have there been more? All women?"

"The second, so far as I know. When I came to Coleshill as a page to Sir Aymer, his guest was Maud Corbet."

"How long did that visitor remain?"

"Till Sir Aymer made his suit for Philippa Felbridge."

"After plague took Sir Aymer's first wife he took up with Maud? But he did not wed her?"

"Nay. She was of the commons. Her father is but a smith of Highworth."

"No dowry there, eh?" Arthur observed.

"And Isobel?" I asked. "What of her?"

"Her father had a yardland and more of Sir Reginald Peor of Faringdon."

"Had?"

"He's been dead these three years, she said. Her mother has the tenancy now."

"But the woman does not prosper?" I guessed.

"That's right. She does not. So when Sir Aymer offered, Isobel accepted."

"When was this?"

"She's been here four days."

"It didn't take him long to seek feminine companionship," I observed. "Of his two wives and first mistress," I continued, "he has no offspring?"

"None. His wives were as barren as granite, and Maud also."

"Sir Aymer seems honestly distressed that Lady Philippa has not been returned to him."

"Aye. He's fond of her. He'll warm his bed with Isobel 'til his lady is released, and then he'll send Isobel away."

"Does she know of Lady Philippa?"

"Aye – and she knows that when the lady reappears she'll be sent packing. Perhaps with a few shillings for her trouble."

"And she is content with this?"

"Who can say? Last year's harvest was poor, her mother has three younger children to feed, and there's a month and more 'til this year's harvest. I suspect Sir Aymer left a groat or two with Isobel's mother to fill the vacancy of her departed daughter."

Then if Lady Philippa never returned to Coleshill, what would become of Isobel, I wondered? Sir Aymer would surely not wed the lass, even if it became known that Lady Philippa had been slain – and for the same reasons he did not take Maud to wife; she is of the commons, and would come to him with no dowry.

"Isobel has an advantage that Lady Philippa had not," Giles continued. "She will not be beaten if she does not conceive. Probably not."

"Was Sir Aymer so furious that he abused Lady Philippa often?"

"Not often, but as I told you, when he'd consumed too much wine he'd consider his childless state and berate her."

"And words would betimes lead to blows?"

"Aye."

Two pounds Sir Aymer had laid down for his wife's return.

I wondered again if she did not wish to be free of her captors, whoever they might be.

Holy Writ asks, "Who has sorrow? Him that looks upon wine when it is red in the cup." Solomon might have added that the drunken man's wife would sorrow as well – or the drunken woman's husband.

Giles fell silent and glanced over my shoulder. I turned and saw Sir Aymer enter the stable. Arthur and Uctred stepped back respectfully.

"I have given much thought to your search for my wife," he began. "I see that I have been inconsiderate. Lord Gilbert was not answerable for her seizure, and my loss is not of your bailiwick. You should feel yourself free of any responsibility to me or Lady Philippa."

I nodded understanding and wondered why he would not wish to see all possible be done to recover his wife. Perhaps he was satisfied with her temporary replacement.

"You and your men will continue to seek her?" I asked.

"Surely, but 'tis my judgment that the rogues who have her will soon demand more coin of me. They saw I was willing to part with two pounds, so will likely demand more. Meanwhile I might search the country from here to London and not find my wife. She will be hidden away where no man will find her."

This was true, or nearly so, but I could not at the time know it. My thoughts rather centered on Sir Aymer's lack of concern for his wife's whereabouts and well-being. I did not understand the man. One day he was determined to seek his wife; another he seemed careless as to her fate.

The grooms had saddled our palfreys while I spoke to Giles and Sir Aymer. I bade the knight and his squire "Good day," Arthur and Uctred tugged their forelocks, Sir Aymer wished us fair travel, and we rode from Coleshill.

I could not help but gaze at Badbury Hill as we passed. Arthur and Uctred did likewise. What secrets did this place hold, I wondered? Well, I knew of one, and was about to discover another.

Arthur and I looked away but Uctred continued to observe the hill. "Look there!" he yelled, and pointed to the copse of trees which adorned the crown of the hill. I did, and saw a figure disappearing into the grove, about two hundred paces from the road.

~ "A fellow come out of the wood, right there, an' when 'e saw I was lookin' at 'im 'e scurried back into the trees!"

If, I thought, some man did not want to be seen prowling about Badbury Hill it may be that he had done so before and suffered consequences for it. If he frequented the place, perhaps he would know of men who came in the night some days past and made off with four sacks of coins. Perhaps he was the man who did so. Was he then also involved in seizing Lady Philippa? If not, and those who took her did not gather the coins, mayhap that was why the lady was not released. But why, then, had Sir Aymer not received an angry message threatening Lady Philippa and demanding the uncollected ransom?

I motioned for Arthur and Uctred to halt, and hurriedly devised a scheme to speak to this man who clearly did not want conversation with travelers upon the Faringdon road. I sent Arthur ahead, to the path we had followed from the back of Badbury Hill to the road. I told him to climb the hill from the rear. Uctred and I would wait here 'til we were sure he was in place, then we would leave our palfreys at the fringe of the hilltop wood and enter from opposite sides. Perhaps we might snare the reticent fellow and learn something from him.

The grove at the top of Badbury Hill is no more than a hundred paces from one side to the other, but thick with fallen branches, even whole trees down, and so contains many places where a man might hide – especially one familiar with the place. The clutter of fallen, uncollected branches, must, I thought, be due to the reputation the spot had for uncongenial spirits.

Was the fellow armed? Likely. Would he use his dagger if discovered? There was but one way to answer that question. Discover him.

"The fellow ducked into the wood just there," Uctred said,

and pointed to what may have been a game trail where deer, who concealed themselves in the grove in the day, ventured out to the grassy rings to graze in the night.

I entered the shadowy copse, following the track, and but a few paces into the wood saw our quarry. 'Twas but a youth. Had the lad lain silent against a log we might have passed him by. But out of fright he took to his heels. He soon vanished amongst the foliage, but we heard him crashing through the undergrowth and followed the sound.

Moments later I heard Arthur bellow, "Hold, you rascal! I have you!" The sound of feet running through leaves and twigs became the thrashing of someone captured and attempting escape.

Uctred and I broke into a tiny clearing and saw Arthur sitting upon a struggling lad. The captive was screeching a demand for his freedom. Arthur saw us approach, grinned, and seized the fists that were ineffectually pummeling him.

"Daft lad," Arthur observed. "Ran right into my arms. Lookin' behind 'im as 'e came. Never saw me 'til I had 'im."

"Let him stand, but keep a tight hold of him," I said.

Arthur did so, and moments later a youth of likely no more than fifteen years stood quaking with fright before me.

"It was only coneys," he said with a quivering voice. "I never took no deer."

We had caught a poacher, likely while he was placing his snares. I did not know what gentleman held Badbury Hill – and nor, apparently, did the lad, for he perhaps thought I was the man and was likely to see him hanged or blinded. In such a pass I would have quivered myself.

"You set snares here atop the hill? For hares and coneys?"

The youth's eyes dropped. "Not many. Only three."

"Are you successful?"

My question surprised the boy. "Sometimes," he finally said.

"Once or twice each week? Or more? Or less?"

"About that."

"I am Sir Hugh de Singleton, bailiff" – at this announcement the youth started as if pricked with a goad – "of Bampton. Have you heard of the town?"

The lad shook his head.

"As I am not of this place, it means nothing to me if you snare a coney or two. But there is another matter I do care about. Answer my questions and I will have my man release you.

"You set snares in the day, when you can see what you are about. Is this so?"

"Aye."

"Do others do so also?"

"Not many."

"Because they fear the spirits said to abound in this place?"

"Aye."

"But you do not?"

"I fear 'em, but I fear the pangs in me belly more," the youth said.

"Just so. You lay your traps in the day. Do you then return next day to see if they've succeeded?"

"Sometimes."

"When else are you likely to return?"

"I come at night."

"When the spirits are said to be about?"

"Aye. But I've never seen any. I've heard 'em, though."

"If you've heard ghosts here, how do you dare visit at night?"

"There's other folks what's hungry."

"Ah... and they know you, or someone, sets snares here, atop the hill. Is that it?"

"Aye. There's folk who'll come an' take from me snares in the daylight. They can't see in the dark to know where my snares is set, but a man can 'ear a coney tryin' to free itself."

"Do you come in the middle of the night, or just before dawn?"

"I come up early. Coneys come out soon as sky grows dark, an' if I've caught one I need to have it before someone else might."

"Five or so days past did you inspect your snares in the night and see or hear other folk about the hill?"

"Aye. I thought they was spirits, at first."

"At first? But not so? Did you see men?"

"Aye, I did."

"Show me where you saw them."

With Arthur keeping a strong grip upon the lad's wrist there was little chance he would free himself. Although if he could he would likely show his heels to the three of us. Uctred's joints are stiff with age, Arthur's legs are stout and short, and my Kate's cookery has slowed me somewhat.

I followed Arthur and the lad from the copse and when free of the trees the youth turned to follow the path cut through the rings. Beyond the first ring he turned into the trough between the first and second rings and went straight to the place where I had deposited the four sacks of coins. There he halted.

"You saw men here? How many?"

"Two. I thought they was specters at first, but when I crept close I saw they couldn't be."

"Couldn't be? Why not?"

"No spirit goes about in a priest's robe, I think."

"It was dark. Are you sure one of the men was a priest?"

"A friar, mayhap, or a monk," the youth said. "When 'e bent over I seen 'is rosary danglin' from 'is belt. I knew then 'twas no spirit."

"Indeed. What specter would go about with a rosary fixed to his belt? Show me where you were when you saw these men. Arthur, go with him."

The lad scrambled up the first ring, which gave Arthur some trouble, as he maintained his grip on the boy's wrist. Just over the lip of the first ring the lad fell to hands and knees and peered into the trough. He was no more than six or seven paces from where I had left the four sacks of coins. Even in the dark a lad with sharp eyes could identify a priest.

I motioned for Arthur to return with the youth. When he did so I said, "You were near enough to hear men speak. What did they say?"

"I couldn't hear much. They was whisperin'."

"But what could you hear?"

"One said, 'Are there four? I see but three.' An' the other said, 'There's four – here's another.'"

"Nothing more?"

"They turned an' I feared they might see me, so I crawled back to the trees, as quiet as I could."

"You did not see them depart?"

"Nay."

"What was it they had four of?" I asked.

"I don't know. It was too dark to tell. Whatever it was, though, they could carry it off."

"How do you know this?"

"I stayed hid in the wood until dawn, then I came back here. I wanted to see. But whatever they had there was four of, they took away."

"Did you see any other men come here shortly after dawn?"

"Nay. I'd got nothin' in me snares, so I went back 'ome."

"Where you may now go," I said. Then, to Arthur, "Release him." He did so.

"As you came here to poach your lord's coneys, I think you will not speak of this encounter. Am I correct?"

"Aye."

"Good. Tell no man of who I am, nor of the questions I have asked."

The lad promised silence, scurried off to the path through the rings, and disappeared.

I had heard tell of villainous priests and abbots who protected felons in return for a share of the loot. Was Lady Philippa held by such men? If the scoundrels who seized the lass in Didcot were the same who now held Lady Philippa, they would not have returned to Didcot in the night after they collected the ransom. No man, even a felon, would want to be upon the roads in the night with four sacks of coins. Likely they sought an inn or some such lodging, perhaps in Faringdon.

Why had I not thought of this before? If two men, one a priest or friar, had sought accommodation at some inn in Faringdon, the proprietor would have been more likely to remember soon after the event than he would be now. Nevertheless, I decided to seek the owners of such establishments there.

Faringdon boasts but one inn. We dismounted before the place, and to improve the proprietor's mood purchased three cups of ale.

'Twas yet morning, so custom was slight. One man was before us, and he emptied his cup soon after we entered the inn and straightaway departed. Three strange men will do that to wary folk, especially if one of the three is constructed like Arthur.

I could think of no way to tactfully introduce the subject of Lady Philippa's disappearance, and I soon learned there was no need to do so. Everyone in Faringdon knew of it, the man said, when I spoke of the matter.

"About five days past, did two travelers seek lodging for the night – one a priest, or friar?" I asked. "They would have come after dark."

The fellow scratched his shaggy chin. "Nay," he said at length. "None like that 'ave sought shelter 'ere."

Would two men travel at night laden with bags of coins? Perhaps accomplices waited on the road for the two to collect the coins, then in a larger party the rogues might travel at night in safety. To Didcot? Or Clanfield? Or might two men find other shelter than an inn? Or might an innkeeper, for a few coins, obligingly forget men who stayed under his roof? How could I know?

We left Faringdon on the Radcot road, as I had done several times in the past few days. A half-mile or so to the north of town, at a settlement folk call Wyke, there is a grange. Would a priest or monk seek lodging in such a place? Monastic houses are pledged to offer hospitality to travelers, but must a subsidiary grange also do so?

This particular grange is large, containing houses for the lay brothers and a great barn for storage of grain 'til it may be sent to

Beaulieu Abbey. I told Arthur and Uctred we would visit the place, and turned my palfrey from the road to the lane leading between the stone walls to the main buildings. A lay brother emerged from the barn, saw us approach, and waited, hands upon hips.

"I bid you good day," I said.

"And to you," the fellow replied.

"Do travelers sometimes seek accommodation for the night here?" I asked.

The fellow glanced to the sun, climbing in the sky, and then cast a puzzled eye to me. Why would I seek lodging when the day was not half done? I explained.

"About five days past, did two men seek shelter here for the night? One was garbed as a priest, or perhaps a monk or friar. They would have come after dark."

"Nay. We've little call to provide lodging." He looked about, then said, "Them as travel on Radcot Road ain't much taken with what they see an' pass by... just barns an' such."

"But if men did desire hospitality, would you provide it?"

"Aye. Such as we 'ave we'd share."

I knew of no abbeys or priories nearby where the men I sought might have found shelter, but I wondered if there might be other granges near. I asked.

"Oh, aye. At Great Coxwell," the lay brother replied.

I remembered the name. "That is a hamlet just off the road from Faringdon to Coleshill, is it not?"

"Aye. They be Cistercians of Beaulieu Abbey, as we are, and" – here he glanced to the barn he had just left – "they 'ave a great stone barn, as we do." There was pride in his voice.

"So would they provide for travelers upon the road?"

"I can't say for sure." The man shrugged. "They likely would. Though they wouldn't 'ave a hosteller or almoner, of course."

"Of course."

I thanked the man for his conversation and bade him "Good day."

Arthur and Uctred followed me down the lane to the Radcot

road and when we came to the thoroughfare I surprised them.

"We will return to Faringdon and seek the Great Coxwell Grange. 'Tis close by, I think, to Badbury Hill." And indeed it was.

Chapter 11

'T was but two miles to return through Faringdon to Great Coxwell. The lay brother at Wyke spoke true. An immense stone barn dominates the hamlet. The structure is, I guessed, fifty paces long by fifteen or so paces wide, and the peak of the roof is as high as the barn is wide. A prosperous grange, indeed. And as we approached I glanced over my right shoulder. Less than a mile distant I saw the grove of trees atop Badbury Hill.

"I thought them Cistercians was supposed to be poor folk," Uctred said, gazing at the massive barn.

A large house, not nearly so large as the barn but having the appearance of prosperity, stood beyond the barn. A dormitory, I thought. The house had a wattle-and-daub chimney from which a wisp of smoke rose. I drew my palfrey to a halt before the building and rapped upon the door. A lay brother opened to me.

"I am Sir Hugh de Singleton, bailiff to Lord Gilbert Talbot at Bampton. Are there monks in residence here at Great Coxwell?"

"Nay. How may I serve Lord Gilbert?"

"He has assigned me to assist Sir Aymer Molyns."

"Him whose wife has disappeared?"

"Aye, the same. You know of the felony?"

"'Tis the talk of the neighborhood."

"What do folk say?"

"If the lady does not return Sir Aymer will soon find a replacement."

I did not tell him that such was already the case.

"Do you seek the lady? Is that your assignment?"

At that moment I heard a pounding, as if a man with a mallet was striking a board. A man was. The lay brother glanced over his shoulder in the direction from which the drumming came, then spoke.

"'Tis time for our dinner. We have no guest table, but you are welcome to share our humble meal."

Humble it was. Barley loaves and an oat pottage flavored with leeks. The ale, as with most monastic houses and their subsidiaries, was fresh-brewed. Arthur, Uctred, and I shared the meal with nearly twenty lay brothers and a dozen or so servants.

"I am Edgar," the man who had greeted us at the door said as we ate. "If you seek Sir Aymer's wife, why do you visit Great Coxwell? There are no women at the grange... a few in the village."

"I do not seek her here, but you may know something of the men who seized her."

Edgar looked up from his bowl with a puzzled expression.

"About five days past, did two men seek lodging with you for the night? One garbed as a priest, or perhaps a friar or monk."

"Aye. Two men did so. They came to us late. We were already abed when they pounded upon the door and asked shelter for the night."

"Did these visitors state their business, or why they came late to your door?"

"Nay, they said only they'd traveled far that day."

"What names did they give?"

"Hmmm. That's odd, now you mention it. They never said their names and I did not ask. Perhaps they told some others of the grange."

When the meal was done Edgar asked the others but neither the servants nor the lay brothers remembered a name.

"They were particular about their beasts," a lay brother volunteered. "I offered to leave my bed to care for 'em, but one said, 'Nay, we'll not trouble you.' He asked the way to the stables an' saw to 'em 'imself."

This was hardly surprising. If the two palfreys carried four bags of clanking coins tied to their saddles, the visitors would not want others to know of it.

"Did they, perchance, mention a destination when they departed?"

"Nay. One said to the other that they should arrive before dark, but he never said where that might be."

"Did you see the fellows leave?"

"Nay. They were up and away before dawn."

Monks are accustomed to leaving their beds before sunrise, but in the long days of midsummer perhaps not much before. If one of the grange's guests was indeed a monk perhaps he both arrived and departed in darkness.

Both Didcot and Oxford, to say nothing of Clanfield, may be reached in a day's riding from Great Coxwell. Indeed, even a man afoot, if he sets a good pace, might be in Didcot or Oxford before sunset.

I thanked Edgar for his hospitality, and with Arthur and Uctred retrieved our beasts and set off once again through Faringdon, past the grange at Wyke, and to Clanfield. We saw few travelers upon the road, and one we did see, near to Radcot Bridge, on seeing us appear over the crown of the bridge immediately left the road, hastened across an oat field, and disappeared into a wood. Perhaps he carried something another man might find worth stealing and feared the losing of it.

Several hours of daylight remained when we entered Clanfield, so I halted before the bailiff's house. I left Arthur and Uctred with the palfreys and approached the dwelling. A lass answered my rapping upon the door, and when I asked for Skirlaw she said, "Who shall I tell my father wishes to see him?"

"Sir Hugh, bailiff of Bampton."

I had thought little of Prince Edward's offer to grant me knighthood when the honor was conferred, but since then I have discovered that folk often judge a man by his title rather than his character or reputation. And a title can be announced in a moment whereas character and reputation in other men's eyes develop more slowly. And as long as they take to grow, a man's character and reputation may be spoiled in a moment's conversation, whereas a title, deserved or not, remains.

The maiden bade me enter the hall and wait while she fetched her father. I heard her voice in the next room, then the sound of a bench scraping across the flags. A moment later Skirlaw appeared, wiping his mouth with the back of a hand. Perhaps the bailiff had been enjoying a cup of ale. He offered me none.

"Ah, Sir Hugh. Have you found the missing lady of Coleshill?"

"Nay. Have any of Sir Reginald's villeins or tenants given evidence of new-found prosperity?"

"Aye. A man of this place has put two glass windows in his house but a few days past. A glazier from Burford came to do the work."

"Who? Janyn or Henry or Bogo?"

"Nay. None of those. 'Tis Clanfield's reeve, Walter Ticknor."

Folk of a village like Clanfield elect their reeve from amongst themselves, and generally choose well. A man who attempts to cheat his neighbors or browbeat them to his will is not likely to be chosen. In this they are unlike bailiffs, who are selected by the lord of the manor and may be as wicked as a pardoner yet retain their post so long as they please their employer.

"Clanfield's reeve? Is he a man known for avarice?"

"Aye. Never misses a chance to enrich himself."

This is not unusual. What man will not seize an opportunity to add a few coins to his purse?

"Why, then, do folk of Clanfield prefer him for reeve?" I asked.

"This puzzles me," Skirlaw admitted.

"Has he been caught in misdeeds?"

"Nay. Too clever, is Walter."

Here was information which came near to an accusation. But I sniffed animosity on the part of the bailiff. Did he and the reeve disagree? Likely. If so, what might be the cause? Here were questions which I could not ask the bailiff. Well, I could, but his answers would be predictable.

What of the reeve? Would the man speak plainly to me of his wealth, or lack thereof? Would he tell me the reason for his bailiff's dislike? If he did so the cause would surely be the fault of the bailiff. Who in the village might speak plainly to me? Janyn? Henry? Bogo? Not likely. What of the matron at the well?

"Send word to me at Bampton if your reeve spends more than a reeve ought," I said, and turned to the door.

"You are not going to seek Walter?"

"If he took Lady Philippa Molyns he did so within your bailiwick. You must deal with the felony yourself. If you suspect him, why have you not already done so?"

"Folk of Clanfield are... uh, confused."

I understood. If Skirlaw arrested the reeve on such flimsy evidence, residents of the village would rebel against him, Walter being admired, Skirlaw probably disliked. A man whose duty entails collecting rents and fines will not be popular. Sir Reginald would learn of insurrection upon his manor and be displeased. Displeased with his bailiff, whose duty it is to prevent such occurrences. It would not be the reeve who would lose his post.

I left Skirlaw spluttering behind me and told Arthur and Uctred to follow. We led our palfreys past the well, to the lane where I had seen the matron vanish after I spoke to her at the well.

I found the woman in her toft, at the end of a wooden hoe, scratching weeds from a patch of cabbages and onions. She looked up from her work when, from the corner of her eye, she saw us approach, then with the back of her hand wiped sweat from her forehead.

"I bid you good day," I began. "Do you remember me?"

"Aye. You be the bailiff what's from Bampton," she said.

"If you overheard an argument between Clanfield's bailiff and reeve, which would you believe spoke truth?"

The woman's mouth fell open and her eyes flicked about as if seeking some village inhabitant interested in her reply. Her gaze finally settled on me.

"You seek to bring me trouble?" she said. "I've affliction enough without addin' Walter or Thomas to the list."

"Neither man will learn of your reply," I said.

"You still seekin' the lady what traveled through Clanfield then disappeared?" she said.

I did not remember speaking earlier to this woman of my assignment. Word of Lady Philippa's disappearance, I thought, was now no secret in Clanfield.

"Aye, the lady is yet missing."

"She was in the painted wagon you asked about?"

"She was."

"Why, then, do you ask of Walter an' Thomas? You think they, or one of 'em, knows somethin' of the lady?"

"She vanished, along with her maid, but a few hundred paces north of Clanfield. This is sure. Who better to know of strange business hereabouts than a bailiff or reeve?"

"Father Andrew," she said.

"The village priest?"

"Aye. Always an ear to the ground, an' willin' to tell what 'e knows."

"A gossip?"

"That 'e is. Most folks don't confess all to 'im. Sure as sun'll rise tomorrow he'll not keep quiet."

"You know of instances when he has broken the silence of the confessional?"

"Aye. Last year Simon confessed that..."

"I've no wish to learn of what Simon may have confessed."

The woman seemed disappointed that she was not to continue the tale. I decided to visit the priest before I left the village. One of the men who had sought lodging at Great Coxwell was perhaps a priest. But before I would seek the man I returned to my question.

"If I seek the truth of matters in Clanfield will I find it with your bailiff or your reeve?"

As before, the woman hesitated. "What folk do say in Clanfield is likely to be soon known to all," she said.

"No man will learn of your opinion from me," I replied.

"So you say."

I once again reassured the woman that whatever she might say of her reeve and bailiff would remain our secret, but could not convince her to speak. Her reticence was understandable. She must remain in Clanfield; I would leave. What remained of her life would become onerous should she name bailiff or reeve as untrustworthy and the man learn of her opinion. He would not learn of it from me.

But knowledge may not always be suppressed. Arthur and Uctred stood behind me and heard the exchange. Did the woman fear that after too much ale one of them might repeat her words? They might, I thought.

But I had learned one thing from the matron. Her village priest had a loose tongue. If I sought him could I persuade him to wag it?

Nay. The priest might speak of village matters to his parishioners but to outsiders he was as tight-lipped as a mussel.

Arthur, Uctred, and I led our palfreys from the matron's house to the priest's and when I pounded on the door the priest's housekeeper opened to me. Her employer, she said, was within and she would fetch him.

She did so. A moment later a ruddy-faced, plump, black-clad, jovial priest appeared in the doorway between living quarters and kitchen. From over his shoulder I saw the housekeeper peering from the kitchen, attempting to hide behind the jamb. If the priest did not relate our conversation to the village his housekeeper likely would.

"Ah," the priest began. "You're Lord Gilbert's bailiff."

"Indeed. Do you also know my assignment?"

"Aye. You seek a lady who went missing near here some days past."

"I do. Your duties bring much village news to your ears. Have you heard any folk of your parish mentioned as having to do with the disappearance?"

"People will talk, won't they?" he said.

And, according to one of his parishioners, so will priests, but I did not say so.

"What do they say... about the vanished lady?"

"Nothing of consequence," he replied.

"What is said which is of no consequence?"

"That the lady's husband paid a ransom for her return. Five pounds, 'tis said." The priest shook his head to indicate disbelief. "Five pounds," he said again.

"Two pounds," I said.

"What?"

"Sir Aymer paid two pounds' ransom, not five."

"Hmmm. Folk do exaggerate."

"They do. If a parishioner suddenly has more in his purse than his neighbors think meet, do they gossip about his unexplained wealth?"

"Of course," the priest said.

"Who is the subject of wagging tongues in the village?"

"Any man who has made an enemy."

"That might include most of the village, would it not?"

"Indeed," the priest agreed.

"So the disappearance of Lady Philippa has set villagers against each other?"

"Only those as had disagreements before. It's just given them another cause to be at one another's throats."

"You believe the accusations floating about are groundless?"

"Aye, mostly."

"I would hear of some which you believe justified."

The priest made no reply. I waited. Fruitlessly. If the fellow was garrulous at some times he was not now, not with me. Perhaps he also knew that behind him his housekeeper had an ear cocked in our direction.

I knew better than to ask if any man of Clanfield had confessed to him of the felony. Loquacious as he might be, he would not break the seal of the confessional to a man not of Clanfield.

"You will not name any who may be suspect as having to do with the felony?"

"Nay. Because I do not believe any man of my parish guilty. If I name some who are most spoken of you will seek them out. Then folk will talk the more, and you will have wasted time you might have more profitably spent elsewhere."

'Twas true, I thought. If I appeared before some Clanfield villager's door, and his neighbors saw, they would assume I had reason to suspect him of the felony. He would be thought guilty even if 'twas not so. On the other hand, it might be so. But the priest was not going to provide me with names, this was clear. No matter how much he might gossip to and about his parishioners, he would not share village rumors with an outsider.

I thanked the priest for his time and tactfully reminded him that I served a lord greater than his own. This was not precisely true; he served the Lord Christ, than whom no man, even King Edward, is greater. But the lord of Clanfield does not rank with Lord Gilbert, Third Baron Talbot. Lord Gilbert was determined, I told the priest, that Lady Philippa's whereabouts be discovered. Soon. And my employer would be angry, when the lady was finally found, if he learned that there were men who had obstructed my search. Actually I was not sure that Lord Gilbert now thought it either his duty or mine to return Lady Philippa to her husband. But it would be as well if the Clanfield priest did not know this. The priest nodded understanding. Most men are acquainted with the fury of angry nobles, by word of mouth if not first-hand. Word of mouth is best.

I turned to leave the priest's house but before my second step another question came to mind.

"Have you traveled from Clanfield in the past few days?" I asked the priest.

"Nay. Why would I do so? My duties keep me here."

Of course he would say so. Had he been the priest seen at Badbury Hill he'd not admit it. 'Twas a foolish question.

I returned to Arthur, Uctred, and our beasts. As I mounted my palfrey I saw Father Andrew's housekeeper, bucket in hand, appear from behind the vicarage and stride toward the village well. I raised a hand to my companions to indicate that I wished to leave the place slowly.

The housekeeper walked vigorously, purposefully, toward the well. We followed twenty or so paces behind. I drew near to the woman as she fastened an iron hook to the pail, the hook being knotted to the hempen rope wound about the crank.

I heard the bucket splash at the bottom of the well. The woman waited a few moments for it to fill, then turned the crank.

Meanwhile, from the corner of her eye, she watched me dismount and approach.

"You thirsty?" she said.

"Nay," I replied. And if I had been, I'd not take water from a well I did not know.

"Has Father Andrew's duty taken him from Clanfield recently?" I asked.

The woman was silent. The only sound was the squeak of the crank as her bucket rose into view.

"He went to Faringdon," she said as she drew the bucket from the hook.

"When? Why did he travel there?"

"When? Near a week past. He goes there two, maybe three, times each year, does Father Andrew. His mother resides there, an' his two sisters."

"When he travels there does he spend the night away?"

Faringdon is but three miles from Clanfield. A man may easily walk there and return in a day.

"Sometimes he does, sometimes not."

"Did he return the same day on his most recent visit, or remain overnight?"

"He come back next day."

Here was an interesting discovery. When I asked the priest if he had traveled from Clanfield in the past few days he had replied that he had not. Did he think that visiting Faringdon a fortnight past did not qualify as "the past few days"?

"Did he have a companion with him?" I asked the housekeeper. "Did he travel with another man?"

"Nay. I don't think so. Not that I saw."

"Does Father Andrew own a horse?"

"A priest of Faringdon parish own a horse?" the woman scoffed.

I thanked the woman for her time, mounted my palfrey, and as I nudged the beast to set off for Bampton glanced over my shoulder to the priest's house. The priest stood in the open door, watching us depart. He was too far distant to know for certain, but I thought his expression not so congenial as before.

The grange's barley loaves and oat pottage did not satisfy past the ninth hour, and 'twas well past that of the clock when we passed Cowleys Corner, and the wall of Bampton Castle came into view.

Duty and desire may often be in conflict. My desire was to leave Arthur and Uctred to deal with the beasts and set off afoot for Galen House. Kate would likely expect me home this day – perhaps wondering that I had not returned sooner – and a meal would await me.

Lord Gilbert had told me I need no longer concern myself with Lady Philippa's disappearance. But so long as I continued to seek the lady he would wish to be informed of any new knowledge which came my way.

So with Arthur and Uctred I dismounted at the castle drawbridge and sought my employer. I found him with Sir Henry Hering, Bampton Castle's new marshal, laying out the site for an enlargement of the castle larder. Lord Gilbert saw me approach, made a final comment to Sir Henry, and turned to meet me.

"What news?" he said in his bluff fashion. "Your face says Lady Philippa is yet missing, even though your lips are silent."

"I did not know I am so easily read," I replied. "But you speak true. I have no thought as to where she might be or who took her there. I have learned that two men were seen in the night upon Badbury Hill retrieving the ransom, and one of those wore a priest's robe. Later that same evening two men, one garbed as a priest, or mayhap a monk, sought lodging for the night at a grange at Great Coxwell."

"Great Coxwell?" Lord Gilbert mused. "The place is little more than a bowshot from Badbury Hill."

"Indeed."

"The scoundrel will have a protector. No monk or village priest would be so bold as to steal a lady on his own, I think."

"Would Sir John Willoughby protect a rascal priest?" I wondered aloud. "Perhaps the other man who collected Sir Aymer's ransom was Gaston Howes."

My stomach chose that moment to growl loudly. Lord Gilbert heard, lifted an eyebrow, and dismissed me.

"Your Kate will have a supper ready, I think. You'd best be off. Be cautious if you intend to seek felons who have a powerful protector."

I promised to do so, then hurried across the castle yard, under the castle gatehouse, thence to Church View Street and my supper.

Chapter 12

'T was a fast day, so my Kate, with Adela's assistance, had prepared a dish of haddock in balloc broth for our supper. My goings and comings have, of late, been unpredictable, but Kate's guess that I would return this day was accurate.

When we were first wed Kate and I fell into the habit of drawing a bench to the toft after supper, there to rest from the day's travail in the fading sunlight and speak of events. We continued the custom after Bessie, then Sybil and John were added to our household, tucking them first into their beds. When Kate's father came from Oxford to live with us he would often join us. The bench is large enough for three.

After supper Adela took Bessie and John to their beds – not without some protest from Bessie, who has begun to believe herself old enough to participate in adult matters. Why is it, I wonder, that children wish to be older and the aged wish to again be young? We prefer what we have not, and disdain what we have.

This thought occupied me as I placed the bench against the west wall of Galen House. When Kate and her father joined me I spoke of Bessie, whose protest had only moments before ceased.

"'Tis a happy child who is content with her lot," Caxton said.

"Then many children are unhappy," Kate said.

"Aye, and their parents also," her father replied.

"Perhaps this is no bad thing," I said. "If all men were content with their lot, who would go to Oxford to study and improve themselves? Who would undertake to build a great cathedral, or even improve a village church? Had I been content with my bachelor state I would not have pursued you," I said to Kate.

"Ah," she smiled. "And did the capture improve your condition?"

"I am well fed, with two healthy babes, and my bed is warmed on cold winter nights. I would be a dolt to think otherwise."

"There are dolts among men, then," Caxton said.

"Aye, and among women, also," Kate added.

As neither her father nor I took exception to this remark the subject seemed exhausted and we three fell silent, basking in what remained of the sunlight before the oaks of Lord Gilbert's forest obstructed the light.

Kate sat to my left, her father to my right. Because she was farther from Caxton, Kate likely did not hear his faint sigh. No, 'twas more a gasp, and I saw his hand reach for his belly. In the past weeks I had seen that his appetite was not so hearty, and his belly seemed swollen. I did not like these developments, but had not mentioned them to Kate. Holy Writ tells us the evils of each day are enough. We must not worry about the evils which may attend tomorrow. So I had not spoken to my wife of my concerns lest she fret about her father's health. But I resolved that some time when Kate was not present to become alarmed I would examine my father-in-law.

I had spoken of Badbury Hill and Great Coxwell and the discoveries there while we consumed our supper. Kate revisited the subject.

"In the dark I suppose a monk, a priest, and friar appear the same," she said.

"Unless they be Cistercians. Even in the night the pale robe of a Cistercian monk would surely be distinguished from that of a priest."

"If 'twas a monk, then, whoso made off with the ransom was likely a Benedictine, eh?" Caxton said.

"Aye, and likely not of the grange at Wyke or Great Coxwell, either monk or lay brother."

"Do you suppose the two fellows who retrieved the ransom did so for themselves or were they doing the work of some other?" Kate wondered. "It must be some other charged them with collecting the coins," she added. "Two men would not be strong enough to seize two women from a wagon, I think. Unless they were willing to be taken."

"If you were wed to a man who berated and beat you because you failed to conceive," I said, "would you connive at your own disappearance?"

Kate stared pensively at the golden westerly sky before she answered. "Had I someplace to go, aye. I would. But a bad place is better, I think, than no place."

"Why, then, a ransom demand?" her father asked.

"Mayhap the place she would go had little wealth," I said. "Such as the lodging of a poor scholar."

"And to demand a ransom would disguise the fact that the lady was complicit in her own disappearance," Caxton said.

"It could be so," I replied. "But how could the lady convince a priest or monk to aid her in the business?"

"A few shillings would be enough, I think," Kate said. "Or even less, had the lady some kin in holy orders, willing to help her."

Here was a new thought, and worth pursuing if no other paths took me to Lady Philippa. But first I had a mind to visit Didcot and there seek Gaston Howes and mayhap Sir John Willoughby. But not alone. If Howes led a band of knaves in service to Sir John, I would learn nothing from him unless I appeared at his door backed by more force than he could muster.

I serve a greater lord than Howes, for Lord Gilbert outranks Sir John Willoughby, who is but a knight, and not even a banneret, and this I determined to use. That evening, after we had replaced the bench in the kitchen and sought our beds, I decided to send a message to Sir John, over Lord Gilbert's signature, and closed with his seal, if Lord Gilbert would agree. He did.

I sought my employer early next morning, after a maslin loaf and ale. When I explained my mission he readily agreed to the part I wished him to play – which was simple enough. He had but to sign his name to a letter which I would dictate to his chaplain's clerk, whose duties include serving as Lord Gilbert's secretary.

The clerk was summoned to the solar, told of his task, and sent for ink, parchment, and pen. He returned shortly and wrote to Sir John Willoughby the letter I dictated. In brief, I told Sir John that I, Lord Gilbert, Third Baron Talbot, had taken an interest in the disappearance of Lady Philippa Molyns, née Felbridge, and had learned of a similar offense near Didcot. In a few days my bailiff,

Sir Hugh de Singleton, would visit him seeking to discover if the men who took for ransom a lass named Joan le Scrope might be the same who seized Lady Philippa and demanded two pounds' ransom for her return. I ended the missive with a remark that the recipient would surely offer Sir Hugh all assistance he required, considering the rank of him who signed his name.

Lord Gilbert returned to the solar as I concluded dictation. I offered him the document, which he read and approved, then he took the clerk's quill and with a flourish signed his name. The clerk folded the parchment while Lord Gilbert removed his signet ring. A candle was tilted so as to drip wax upon the letter, and the clerk pressed Lord Gilbert's seal into the wax.

"If Sir John will not help you find this Gaston Howes," Lord Gilbert said, "what then? Do you expect me to send household knights to Didcot if he will not yield to this request?"

"Your name upon this parchment will suffice, I believe. Can even his cousin, a judge of the King's Eyre, protect him if you go to the king, or Prince Edward, and request that influence be applied to produce the information I seek?"

"You are as acquainted with the prince as I. You might ask this of him yourself."

"Indeed, but I do not wish to presume upon Prince Edward's goodwill."

"The prince does not take umbrage at those who might presume on his goodwill if they have previously done him good service. As you have done."

"We may hope," I replied, "that the prince's intervention will not be required, and this letter with your seal upon it will suffice."

"Indeed. In the letter you tell Sir John that you will visit him in a few days. Who will deliver this message?"

"I thought to send Arthur and Uctred, garbed in your livery, your badge upon their tunics."

"'Tis sixteen miles, thereabouts, to Didcot. Do you expect them to travel there and return the same day?"

"Nay. Neither the beasts which bear them nor their own

rumps should be so abused. I would send them tomorrow, after mass and dinner. They may return Monday. There is a priory near Didcot where they may seek lodging Sunday evening."

"Very well. Then you will go to Didcot on Tuesday?"

"Aye, or perhaps Wednesday. If I give Sir John a few days to consider his position I may find him more amenable."

"You may. Or you may provide him with time to invent falsehoods and prepare an uncongenial welcome. Will you travel to Didcot alone?"

"Nay. Mysterious events can happen to a lone traveler. Arthur and Uctred will return there with me."

Neither Lord Gilbert nor I thought to ask Arthur and Uctred if they desired to travel to Didcot even once, much less twice. Grooms in service to a great lord are not asked where they wish to go nor when they wish to go there. They are told. And expect this to be so. And life within the walls of a castle can be boring at times.

By the time the letter to Sir John had been written, signed, and sealed 'twas near time for dinner. Thus I knew where to find Arthur and Uctred, and awaited the ringing of the bell which would bring them to Bampton Castle's hall.

"Have you ever been to Didcot?" I asked Arthur.

"Did what?"

Here was answer enough. "Didcot. A town a few miles beyond Abingdon."

"The place what that scholar spoke of, where the lass was took at Candlemas?"

"Aye. Lord Gilbert and I wish for you and Uctred to travel there tomorrow, after mass and your dinner. In Didcot you will seek Sir John Willoughby and deliver to him a letter from Lord Gilbert."

"This is about Lady Philippa?"

"It is. Perhaps. Men who succeed at a felony may think to try the same evil again."

"Willoughby? I recall the name," Arthur said. "That scholar spoke of a knight who protected them what stole the lass. That 'im?"

"Aye. But you need do nothing but place the letter into his

hands, then return on Monday. Steventon Priory is not far from Didcot. You may spend the night there. We intend to allow Sir John to consider Lord Gilbert's words for a day, then Wednesday you and Uctred and I and perhaps a few others will confront Sir John with what is known of his business, and try to learn if there are matters unknown which can be brought to light."

"A few others? You think Sir John will take amiss what Lord Gilbert 'as to say?"

"He may. Or he may seek to avoid causing a great lord anger, and cooperate."

"So when you visit Didcot on Wednesday you think it best to prepare for the worst, eh?"

"Aye. Safer to prepare for villainy which may not occur than expect good fortune and be confounded."

I left Arthur and Uctred to their meals and returned to Galen House and my own dinner. Kate and Adela had prepared whelks in bruit with maslin loaves. The day was warm and pleasant, my belly was full. Bessie and John played and giggled. Why, then, was I dissatisfied? Should a missing lady I had never met so upset my life? Probably not. Should I dismiss the matter, tell Arthur and Uctred to remain at the castle tomorrow, and require Sir Aymer to find his own wife? Lord Gilbert had granted me such permission. Would I be less fretful if I gave up the search, and never learned Lady Philippa's fate, or if I continued the quest, perhaps unsuccessfully?

And success seemed unlikely as I thought of what little I knew and what I must yet discover before the lady could be found and returned to Coleshill. Bogo Bennyng had been absent from ditching past the time he should have returned to his labor, and this at the time when Lady Philippa had vanished. Father Andrew had traveled to Faringdon near the time Sir Aymer's ransom was collected. Might he and Bogo be comrades in villainy? Here were loose ends which needed tying up. But how?

Sir Aymer mistreated his wife because she did not produce an heir. Would this cause the lady to seek escape, or even seek another husband? Or a lover? And what of John Cely, deaf and near blind, but perhaps not so deaf as folk believed?

What of Martyn de Wenlock? He fled Oxford to avoid the pain of seeing Lady Philippa, so he said – but then abruptly returned. A young man's heart may be fickle. Had he found a new love in Oxford which brought him back to the town? How could he, if he was in Cambridge? Was he, for a few days, in Cambridge? The innkeeper said he was in Oxford the day Lady Philippa was taken. Did he speak true? Might a few pence have affected his memory?

Who were the men who retrieved Sir Aymer's coins upon Badbury Hill, and whence did they come? Were they the same who sought shelter for the night at Great Coxwell? Surely. When they departed the grange where did they travel? To Didcot? Was one of the fellows Gaston Howes? Would a man who had brazenly seized a lass at Candlemas now travel by night, and with a priest, to collect a ransom? And what fine hand wrote the ransom note?

After mass and dinner the following day, I sent Arthur and Uctred on their way, Lord Gilbert's letter to Sir John Willoughby tucked safely into a leather pouch hung about Arthur's thick neck. Tied to his belt was a purse which contained ten pence for ale, meals, and lodging at an inn if they could not be accommodated at Steventon Priory.

What transpired over the next two days I learned from Arthur upon their return. Before he spoke I knew that matters had gone amiss and when I traveled to Didcot it must be with a sizeable contingent of Lord Gilbert's grooms and pages. And a few household knights.

Arthur and Uctred's faces were bruised and lacerated when they appeared at Bampton Castle's gatehouse late Monday afternoon. Their cotehardies and tunics were torn and muddied, and the shoulder of Uctred's garment was bloodied from a torn ear.

They had been attacked, that was clear. Whoso did this must have outnumbered them, or likely their appearance would be no better than Arthur and Uctred's. Neither man is incompetent at defending himself.

I had been awaiting their return in the castle yard, and when I saw them appear I hurried to greet them. As did others. One glance as they dismounted was enough to confirm they had been in combat. Excited voices asked the predictable questions. I shouted for silence so Arthur could explain the cause of his battered appearance.

"Traveled to Didcot yesterday in good time," he began. "Asked folk for Sir John, found 'is manor 'ouse in Coscote, an' give 'im the letter. Told 'im 'twas from Lord Gilbert, so 'e knew that before 'e broke the seal. Did that before 'e dismissed us."

"What did he say?" I asked.

"Nothin'. Frowned, thanked us, an' sent us on our way. Didn't even offer a cup of ale for our trouble."

"Were you then set upon when you departed Sir John's house?"

"Nay. We traveled to Steventon Priory to seek a bed, as you suggested. It's not much of a priory. More like a grange. Only two monks and a few lay brothers. We arose this morning, took a loaf an' ale, an' set out for 'ome, thinkin' the task was an easy one.

"We'd traveled no more than a mile when a dozen or so mounted men accosted us. Some come out of a copse before us, the others was behind so we couldn't retreat."

"We don't look so good," Uctred joined the conversation, "but there's more'n a few of them fellows sore an' cut up as well."

"They knew of the letter," Arthur said. "The leader – must've been, cause 'e stood aside an' let t'others 'ave sport with us – said, ''Ere's your lord's reply.'"

"They made no attempt to slay you there, upon the road?"

"Nay. Only one or two drew daggers, an' them only after I'd drawn me own. Just fists an' clubs."

"What of your ear?" I said to Uctred.

He raised a hand to the lacerated appendage and tenderly touched it as if to assure himself it was yet at least partially attached to his skull.

"Some knave with a club took aim at me 'ead," he said. "I seen the blow comin' but couldn't dodge fast enough – it just caught me ear. It would've laid me out on the road for sure, if I 'adn't ducked."

The clamor surrounding Arthur and Uctred was heard in the solar. Lord Gilbert opened the upper door, peered out, saw his pages and grooms clotted together just inside the gatehouse, then apparently saw Arthur and Uctred. Even from that distance he could see that all was not well.

Lord Gilbert plunged down the stone steps from solar to castle yard growing more red-faced with each step. By the time he reached the group clustered about Arthur and Uctred his visage glowed, and his brows had narrowed to a scowl. He guessed what had happened.

"Is this how Sir John replies to my letter?" he said to me.

"It seems so. They were set upon this morning, after spending the night at Steventon Priory."

Lord Gilbert required Arthur and Uctred to tell him what they had already told me. He listened, hands on hips, jaw set. Sir John Willoughby, I thought, had got himself some trouble. Even a cousin who was a judge of the King's Eyre could not save him from the wrath of the Third Baron Talbot.

When Arthur and Uctred had told this tale for the second time, Lord Gilbert turned to me, his eyes flashing.

"Tomorrow we will visit Sir John and teach him the error of his ways. A company of my household knights and grooms will change his behavior."

"You intend to lead this band?" I said.

"Aye. No man deals so with my retainers."

"It might be best if you did not."

"Oh?" Lord Gilbert lifted an eyebrow. "Why so?"

"When you lead men into battle do you throw your entire force into combat when it is first joined, or do you hold back men as a reserve in case some part of your line requires support?"

"Ah, I take your point. You wish for me to be the reserve, to be called upon only if needed."

"Just so. We may allow Sir John a day or two to believe himself safe from your wrath, then on Wednesday I will travel to Didcot with some of your household knights and grooms."

Arthur and Uctred, although sore and bruised, would not hear of remaining at Bampton on Wednesday morning. Uctred's ear was held firmly to the side of his head by four stitches and a length of linen wrapped tight. 'Twas the second time I had been required to fix a torn ear back to its proper place. One becomes more skilled with practice. Perhaps Uctred's ear will not project from his head like a banner in the breeze. The gristle of an ear is difficult to pierce, but Uctred bore the sting well.

Sir Ralph Alward, Sir Jaket Bek, and Sir Humphrey Mauduyt rode with me Wednesday morning as we led seven of Lord Gilbert's grooms across the castle drawbridge. The knights carried swords, we others but daggers. I was uncertain of the assistance that Arthur and Uctred could offer if we became involved in a brawl, and the realization came to me that Arthur was no longer a young man. As for Uctred, he had seemed aged as long as I had known him. As if he had never been a young man.

Chapter 13

The way to Didcot led past pleasant fields and forests. We crossed the Thames at Newbridge and approached Didcot before noon. Men at work in the fields watched guardedly as we passed, seemingly ready to abandon hoes and rakes and run toward the nearest wood if we showed interest in them. Such is the state of the realm that strangers are viewed with mistrust, and armed strangers with fear.

The inn at Didcot did not expect eleven hungry men at the tables for dinner. The innkeeper had only a kettle of boiled stockfish and maslin loaves, which, I assume, was enough to feed his customary patrons. He promised to put another kettle to the fire, and provided ale while we waited. By the time the meal was done most of our company had consumed not enough fish and too much ale. I worried about our performance if conflict lay before us.

It did, but not before enough time had passed that an excess of watered ale no longer dulled a man's faculties.

Arthur and Uctred knew the way to Sir John Willoughby's manor, Coscote, a mile south of Didcot. Perhaps a hundred souls live in Didcot, even fewer in Coscote. There are many empty dwellings in both villages. Plague has struck hard. A knight who has seen rents collapse as his tenants die or move to another manor might throw in his lot with a felon to replace his lost income.

Sir John's manor house was a substantial structure in need of repair. The oiled skin of a window on the upper storey was torn, and the daub was chipped away in several places. Two barns and a stable occupied the space behind the house, but the thatching of one of the barns was so rotted that anything stored therein would soon become damp and moldy. Between the barns was a dovecote, the roof of which was nearly as dilapidated as the barn.

Several men of the village saw us approach, and one took

to his heels and disappeared behind the manor house. Sir John would be expecting us.

Some who watched as we drew near were close enough to our path that they could be recognized had Arthur or Uctred seen them before. When accosted, perhaps. I leaned toward Arthur and told him to keep a sharp eye for any man who might have been among those who waylaid them upon the road. He nodded, as did Uctred, who overheard the conversation.

There was no rail before Sir John's house where we might tie our beasts. Apparently if men arrived mounted they knew to guide their horses to the stable. I was concerned that Arthur and Uctred were in no fit condition for a brawl, if such was in our near future, so I left them and one other groom with the beasts, then with the three knights and four grooms approached the manor house door.

I needed to smite the door but once and it opened. A groom swung it wide, saw four men before him garbed as gentlemen, and tugged a forelock.

"We seek Sir John Willoughby," I said in my sternest voice.

"Please enter," the fellow said, and swept a hand toward the hall as an invitation. "Who shall I say desires to see Sir John?"

"I am Sir Hugh de Singleton, bailiff to Lord Gilbert Talbot at Bampton, and these are three of his knights."

The groom's eyes darted from me to the knights, then dropped to the swords which hung from their belts.

"Please wait here. I will find Sir John." As if we would think he did not know his master's whereabouts.

Sir John seemed in no hurry to greet us. The groom disappeared and we stood awaiting Sir John, resting weight upon one foot, then another, for half an hour or more. I wondered what pressing business delayed the knight. I discovered soon enough.

An open door led from the hall to a screens passage and then a buttery and pantery. From the door I heard voices. At first I thought this must be the groom returning with his master. Not so. Many more than two voices came to my ears. A moment later the hall entrance door banged open. I turned with a start at the unexpected sound and saw a well-dressed man garbed in a fine blue cotehardie, grey tunic, and pale chauces standing arms akimbo in the opening. Another movement caught my eye. Two men stood shoulder to shoulder in the screens passage. Each held a dagger. Behind them I saw more faces. I did not take time to count. Either faces or daggers.

"What does Lord Gilbert mean," the gentleman in the entrance doorway said, "sending armed men to Coscote?"

I looked to the faces behind the speaker. None of these were Arthur or Uctred. Had they been assaulted again? Nay, they would have cried out a warning.

"You are Sir John Willoughby?" I asked.

"Aye. Lord of this manor and ready to defend it."

"Why should it need defense?"

The question seemed to take Sir John by surprise.

"Uh... there are evil men about. These are troubled times," he finally said.

"Indeed. Three days past two of Lord Gilbert's grooms delivered a letter to you. They were set upon next day as they returned to Bampton. They are outside your door at this moment, tending to our beasts. Likely you saw them there. Lord Gilbert requires of you two things: a reply to his letter, and punishment of the men who attacked his grooms."

"I cannot assist Lord Gilbert in either matter," Sir John said, and folded his arms.

At that moment I heard an incomprehensible shout through the open door. I and all others. This bellow was immediately followed by another, and then the constant roar of men in combat.

No man took heed of any other as we all pushed through the door, to the toft, to learn what the uproar was about.

Two men rolled about in the dust, kicking, shouting, attempting to do each other harm. One of these was Uctred. From the corner of my eye I saw Arthur. His arms were wrapped tight about a man I did not recognize. One of Sir John's grooms, I thought. The fellow struggled, seemingly intent upon joining the fray, but in Arthur's grip he could as well have been bound to a gatepost with hempen cords.

Sir John shouted that the combatants must cease the brawl. He might as well have commanded the wind to cease. Uctred and his foe regarded no man but the other.

The struggle did, however, end only moments later. Uctred found space to draw back his fist and deliver a blow to the other fellow's chin. A tooth popped free of the man's mouth, blood gushed from his lip, and he collapsed limp upon the dirt. Uctred stumbled to his feet and as he did Sir John turned to a retainer and shouted, "Seize him."

Arthur and I reacted to these words at the same instant. He shoved the man in his grasp to the ground and drew his dagger. My dagger was also in my hand, and together we jumped to Uctred's aid. Lord Gilbert's knights saw this and a heartbeat later three swords were unsheathed and forming a steel ring about Uctred.

"Your man has attacked one of mine," Sir John said. "I will see justice done!"

"'Tis already done," Uctred said, and pointed to his vanquished opponent. The fellow was just beginning to twitch himself back to wakefulness. "That's one of them what set upon me an' Arthur two days past."

"What? Edmund? Nay. He'd do no such thing." Then, to his grooms, Sir John again said, "Seize the fellow."

A few grooms placed hands upon the hilts of their daggers but none took a step toward Uctred. Five men encircled him armed with two daggers and three swords. Five quickly became ten as the rest of Lord Gilbert's grooms advanced toward the place of combat and joined us who had placed ourselves between Uctred and harm.

"Are you sure this fellow was one of those who attacked you and Arthur on Monday?" I asked Uctred.

"No mistake. Look at 'is finger."

I did, and saw that one digit was wrapped in a dirty, bloodied linen fragment.

"You recognize his wounded finger?" I said.

"Recognize? Hah! I give it to 'im."

"How so?"

"Him an' two others 'ad me down. He was tryin' to gouge me eye. I seen 'is fingers close to me face so I bit on one. He let out a yelp an' from then on I 'ad but two rogues to contend with."

"Look about you," I said. "Do you see any others who were among those who waylaid you? Arthur, do you recognize any man?"

Arthur and Uctred scanned the crowd of men who had gathered behind Sir John. I thought it seemed as they did so that several men retreated a few steps and placed themselves behind others. One of these had a fat, purple lip. Some unyielding object had recently made contact with it.

"I can't say as I do," Arthur said. "I wasn't givin' faces much attention at the time. I was more heedful of clubs an' fists."

The two groups of men facing each other over the fallen groom were of near equal size. But among the men behind Sir John I saw no swords. Only daggers, and these yet sheathed. None of Sir John's retainers seemed eager to use or face a blade.

The man Uctred had bested raised himself to his knees, swayed a bit, then struggled to his feet. I stepped toward the dazed fellow and, taking an arm, drew him to the circle of Lord Gilbert's men who encompassed Uctred.

The stupefied fellow tried to resist when he saw to which group he was taken, but wobbly as he was could do little to object. He found himself surrounded by armed men who gazed upon him with choleric expressions upon their faces.

Whether or not the fellow had wit enough to answer my questions I did not know. There was but one way to discover this. I asked him who had sent him to attack men upon the road Monday after they had departed Steventon Priory.

Sir John took exception to the question, as I thought he might. He stepped toward me and said, "Edmund is not fit to be interrogated." He was about to say more, I believe, but glanced over a shoulder and saw that none of his retainers had followed. They stood as if rooted. The only man who moved in response to Sir John's approach was Sir Jaket, who, sword in hand, stepped to intercept Sir John.

Edmund, meanwhile, glanced about as if seeking some way of escape. He found none, for even as bewildered as he was he could see that none of Sir John's grooms were eager to do combat to free him from my control.

Sir John scowled fiercely at Edmund, assuming, I suppose, that a truculent stare would close the fellow's mouth. But an angry glance is no match for drawn swords and daggers. Through thickening lips Edmund pointed to his master and said, "Sir John sent us."

"Nay," the knight said. "He is so dazed he knows not what he says."

"Us?" I said. "Who else? My men were attacked by half a dozen or so. Who accompanied you?"

"Osbert."

"And who else? More than two attacked my men."

As I spoke I saw a man detach himself from the group behind Sir John and disappear through the manor house doorway. Osbert, perhaps.

"Just Osbert. We was to help Gaston."

"Gaston Howes?"

"Aye."

"Why would the man need aid from two of Sir John's grooms?" I said.

The scowl on Sir John's face deepened and from the corner of my eye I saw him shake his head.

"You'll need to ask 'im," Edmund said.

There was peril in doing so, I thought, but likely the man spoke true. I had one more question for Edmund.

"Where is Gaston to be found?"

Again Sir John shook his head. Perhaps Edmund did not see. Or perhaps he thought Lord Gilbert Talbot a greater threat to his future than Sir John Willoughby.

"Just there," he said, and pointed to a house perhaps a hundred paces from the manor house, on the opposite side of the street.

The time had come, I decided, to use my rank. "I am Sir

Hugh de Singleton, bailiff to Lord Gilbert, Third Baron Talbot. I was knighted by Prince Edward, your next sovereign, for services I rendered him. Neither baron nor prince will be pleased if they learn that men of Coscote have hindered my investigation of the disappearance of Lady Philippa Molyns.

"You," I pointed to Sir John, "come with me. We will seek Gaston Howes. The others will remain here. Sir Jaket, accompany me and Sir John."

The knight nodded and sheathed his sword, although his hand did not stray far from the hilt. I told Sir Ralph and Sir Humphrey to remain before the manor house and see to it that none of Sir John's retainers followed him and me and Sir Jaket. None appeared zealous to do so. Sir John's grooms did not seem eager to risk blows or slashes to defend his conduct. Perhaps his behavior to his own people had been occasionally offensive.

As we turned to the dwelling Edmund had pointed out I saw a man run from behind an abandoned house and sprint across the road, disappearing behind the house Gaston Howes occupied. This house was remote from its neighbors. The nearest dwelling was fifty or so paces to the south. To the north of Gaston's house was a pile of rubble which had once been a house, now fallen to ruin, most likely since plague had taken its occupants.

I saw as we approached that Howes' residence seemed in better repair than Sir John's manor house. The thatching was nearly new, the daub of the walls freshly patched, and the skins of the windows whole and untorn. Whatever business Gaston Howes followed, it had prospered. Well, I knew what business he followed. With a formidable protector, theft can be lucrative.

The house was the only one in the village, other than the manor house, which had behind it a sizeable barn. As this structure came into view two men suddenly appeared between the house and the barn. They glanced in our direction, then turned and took to their heels across a new-mown hayfield beyond which lay a dense wood. Men who flee a bailiff likely do so because they are guilty of something. Of course, most men are guilty of something.

But they hope that only the Lord Christ knows all and will forgive.

One of those who fled toward the wood was the man who had left the group before the manor house and I had next seen running to Gaston's dwelling. He and a man I assumed was Howes were now halfway across the stubble to the wood.

Should I chase after them? If I did so I must leave Sir Jaket with Sir John, to be sure he did not abscond. What then? If I caught Osbert and Howes before they found the wood I would be one against two. If I could not apprehend them before they reached the wood, the copse was dense enough that they might melt into the grove. Or hide themselves so as to set upon me as I stumbled after them. I decided to refrain from a chase. Valor is commendable, but those who possess too much of the virtue seldom live long enough to bounce grandchildren upon a knee.

"That was Gaston Howes, was it not?" I said to Sir John.

"Aye," he smirked.

"The man who ran across the road as we left your manor house... 'twas Osbert?" I said.

"I don't know. I didn't see him."

"How much of the three pounds' ransom for Joan le Scrope did you demand?" I asked.

"What? You accuse me of taking the child?"

"Nay. I accuse you of profiting from the felony. 'Tis known that Howes and his band seized the lass, and that he is protected. As he resides in your manor and your cousin is a judge before whom he might stand were he charged with such a felony, you are his likely protector. You would not do so except you received a part of the loot."

"Bah! You accuse falsely. Gaston has two yardlands in his tenancy. Diligent, is Gaston. He need do no felonies to prosper."

"Most men do not need to do the felonies they undertake," I replied. "Three pounds is a significant sum. So you, your cousin, and Howes will need time to collect the coins and repay Sir Thomas."

"What?"

"Do not assume the guise of an injured man. Your guilt is

known from here to Abingdon. Now, we will investigate this house and see what may be learned. Has Howes a wife?"

"Aye."

"Smite the door and call to her."

Sir John did so. He struck the door three times and called out, "Avina... 'tis Sir John."

A moment later the door swung open upon iron hinges. A plump matron, questions in her eyes, stood in the doorway. Two children of perhaps five and eight years stood behind her, clutching the folds of her cotehardie. This garment was of fine wool and near new, not worn with age and use as might be expected of a tenant of a minor knight.

"Where has your husband gone?" I said.

"Gaston?"

"Have you other husbands?"

"I don't know where 'e went. Osbert come to kitchen door an' spoke somethin'. Next I knew Gaston was off."

"Where is he bound?"

"I don't know, do I? 'E said nothin' to me."

"We will inspect your house," I said, and pushed past the woman. She protested but I paid her no heed. I told Sir Jaket to keep watch over Sir John while I investigated the house, then I prowled through the place.

The structure was much like other tenants' homes. It had two bays: one for cooking and storage, the other for sleeping and shelter. There was a hearthstone in each bay, but the one in the sleeping bay was swept clean. No need for a blaze there in summer.

Aside the bed was a crude chest, which I opened. It had no lock. Various items of clothing were folded in the chest and I plucked them out to learn what Howes and his wife had acquired. Avina looked on with a scowl. I seemed to have produced that expression often this day.

Toward the bottom of the chest I saw a black garment. I drew it out. 'Twas a priest's robe. I held it before the woman and asked how it was that such a garment might be found in her chest.

"Milo give it to me... in 'is will. Two years past."

"Who is – was – Milo?"

"Clerk to Father 'Enry at All Saints' Church."

"All Saints'? In Didcot?"

"Aye, that's right."

"Why would a clerk leave you his robe?"

"'E was me uncle."

I decided that upon returning to Didcot I would visit All Saints' Church to learn from the priest if a clerk named Milo had died two years past. And even if the garment was fairly come by it might yet have been worn in the night upon Badbury Hill.

Above the chest and bed was a loft. I saw two pallets upon the floor beside the bed, so assumed that the children of the house slept there. What was the loft for? No ladder was visible. I asked its whereabouts.

"We don't 'ave one," the woman said.

"You have no access to your own loft?"

"Nay. Helen ain't old enough to sleep up there alone."

I might have accepted this explanation and considered my search of the house at an end. But the thought nagged me that even if the oldest lass was not of an age to be left to sleep alone in a loft, some use would be found for the space.

I closed the lid to the chest, dragged it under the lip of the loft, then tipped the chest on end. If I stood on the upended chest I could easily reach the loft, pull myself up, and swing a leg over the edge.

So I did.

Little light illuminated the loft. I saw nothing upon the rough boards; no chest, no bench, no pallet. It seemed the woman spoke true. The loft was unused.

But as I turned to drop down to the upended chest I noticed an anomaly. The end wall of the loft seemed closer to its edge than the end wall of the ground floor below. And there was no vent visible under the eave whereby smoke from the hearthstone might escape the dwelling. I cast my eyes in the other direction and saw there a vent at the other end of the room. But with only one vent hole there would be no cross-draft to expel the smoke. Such an arrangement made no sense. Unless the hearthstone in this bay was never used. And it was swept clean.

I turned from the lip of the loft and approached the end wall. As I came close I saw a door, which in the dark had escaped me when I first set foot in the loft. This door was short, so that it could only be passed in a crouch, and was barred. On the outside. What might be beyond the door which must not be allowed to escape? Lady Philippa? Milicent? If so, why did they not cry out when they heard voices below? There are herbs which will stupefy. I use them when I must cause pain in surgery. Given enough of a dose in a cup of ale, women might sleep through the Lord Christ's return.

I lifted the plank which barred the door and pulled it open. I hoped to see a woman, or two, asleep upon a pallet. I was disappointed. But there was a ragged pallet upon the boards. This I could see, but little more. I needed a cresset.

I returned to the edge of the loft and called down to Avina that I required a cresset. The woman seemed reluctant to comply. She looked to Sir John as if he might countermand my request. Likely she had heard me remove the board which barred the door and knew what dark place I wished to illuminate.

"A cresset, or a candle, please," I said again. Sir John said nothing. I saw him shrug his shoulders. Perhaps he knew nothing of the loft and so saw no danger in exposing it to the light. Unlikely.

The woman passed through the doorway to her kitchen and out of my sight. She returned a moment later with a cresset, which Sir Jaket took from her and, standing upon the chest, handed to me.

A single flame will not bathe a dark closet in light. But some light is better than none at all. The threadbare pallet I had seen dimly was thinly stuffed with straw. No feathers for whoso had slept here.

I held the flame to the walls and rafters, seeking I knew not what. In one corner of this tiny chamber I saw a chipped ceramic pot. As my nostrils came close I identified its purpose, although what contents remained were dried. No one had recently put the vessel to use.

At the peak of the roof was a place where a vent hole had been plugged. The beams and rafters about this closed opening were dark with years of soot. So when the light from the cresset flame fell upon the marks engraved in the soot they stood out clearly.

Pale scratches in the grimy rafter resolved themselves into rough letters when I brought the flame near. "Joan," they spelled, in an unskilled hand. The name was likely worked into the soot with a fingernail, so 'twas no wonder the work seemed crude.

Here the lass Joan le Scrope had been confined while her captors awaited payment of her ransom. Why did the lass not cry out for aid? She might have heard folk passing her prison on the street. Mayhap she had been threatened to keep silence. Or she was carried to the house blindfolded so she knew not that she was in a place where others might hear her screams.

I know of herbs which may dull the senses and produce a somnolent state. Perhaps Gaston knew of these also. Was Joan le Scrope given a dose of crushed hemp seeds in her ale? Or did she clamor to no avail, Gaston's neighbors unhearing or intimidated to silence? Did Howes beat his wife? Mayhap if villagers who lived near heard the lass screeching, they thought 'twas some domestic discord with which they would prefer not to become embroiled.

If the same men had seized Lady Philippa, then where was the lady? Had she been held here, then moved to some other place? Or was she never confined in this place? I moved the cresset about, seeking another name cut into the soot. I found nothing.

I was about to depart the closet when from below I heard a shout, the sound of a scuffle, and then silence. I dove through the chamber's tiny door and snuffed out the cresset. At the edge of the loft I looked down into the room below and saw only Avina Howes. Sir John and Sir Jaket were gone, the door open. I heard from a distance the sound of running feet.

I leaped from loft to chest, discarded the cresset, and ran through the open door. Fifty or so paces to the southeast I saw Sir Jaket in pursuit of Sir John. Sir Jaket is a youthful knight, risen from squire but two years past. Sir John is much older. But perhaps no wiser. 'Tis foolish for an older knight, carrying a well-developed paunch, to think he may outrun a slender youth. I set off at a run after the two knights but had taken no more than four or five strides when I saw Sir Jaket overtake his quarry and tackle him.

The men rolled in the dirt of the road, and when their motion ceased 'twas Sir Jaket uppermost, his hands encircling Sir John's throat.

I shouted for Sir Jaket to spare his adversary. I don't much care if felons are slain while about their nefarious practices, but a dead man could tell me nothing of Joan le Scrope, Gaston Howes, or Lady Philippa Molyns.

Desperation might cause a man to thoughtlessly flee. Where did Sir John believe he could go where he might escape me, Lord Gilbert, and the consequences of his felonies? Thoughtless deeds can no more be undone than thoughtless words unsaid.

While Sir John had rolled in the dust of the road with Sir Jaket, his purse had come loose from his belt and spilled some of its contents. I gathered the purse and the coins which had escaped from it and examined the money. Sir John, tight in Sir Jaket's grasp, looked on while I studied the coins. I found none that were marred. If Gaston Howes or some other of Sir John's men had collected Lady Philippa's ransom, he had not yet received his portion of the loot. Or it was safely hidden in some secure place in his manor house.

With Sir Jaket grasping one arm and I the other we hoisted Sir John to his feet and hauled him back to his manor house, where his retainers and Lord Gilbert's men stood yet, facing each other, waiting. Was Sir John embarrassed to be so unceremoniously dragged through the street of his own manor? I hoped so. May the Lord Christ forgive my uncharitable thought.

I had in mind to question the knight closely as to where Gaston Howes might be found, but thought he might be discomfited enough that the interrogation be best done privily.

"Take Sir John to his hall," I said to Sir Jaket. Then, to his men and Lord Gilbert's I said, "Remain here... but for Arthur." I nodded in the direction of the open door and Arthur followed me, Sir John, and Sir Jaket into the hall.

Arthur knows well the part he is to play in such encounters. He folded his thick arms, scowled, and gave indication that he would enjoy tearing Sir John limb from limb. Perhaps he would, and 'twas no artifice.

I pointed to a bench and bade Sir John sit. His expression told that he resented being instructed in his own house as to what he must do. But he understood that Lord Gilbert, my protector, was greater than his cousin judge. And a quick glance to Sir Jaket's hand upon the hilt of his sword, and Arthur's frown, persuaded the man that he should do as required. His attitude had greatly altered in the past hour.

"Sir Aymer told me that his father and yours were at Crécy. He said they had differing views of the battle and became enemies. Did you take Sir Aymer's wife as revenge against the son of your father's enemy?"

"My father's enemy – not mine," Sir John muttered.

"Where will I now find Gaston Howes?" I said. "I know he held Joan le Scrope in his loft. If Lady Philippa Molyns was also held there, she is no longer. Mayhap I'll find her where he has gone."

"He did not take the lady," Sir John said.

"Who did? Another of your retainers?"

"Nay."

"When I find Howes, I will know if you speak true. He will learn from Osbert why I am here, and likely will seek the lady, perhaps to move her to some more secure place. Where he is, Lady Philippa may also be."

"Last I saw, he was running to the wood beyond the hayfield. You saw him too."

"Aye. But he'd not keep a lady in a wood, nor would he remain there himself. When he seized the lass he had others with him. Now he is likely with one or more of them, and perhaps Lady Philippa also. Who are those who travel with him when he works his felonies? There will not be many, I think. He must share his loot with you and your cousin. He'd not wish to divide it in too many ways. Perhaps when you foolishly ran from Sir Jaket you intended to join Howes where he now is."

Sir John considered this, probably pondering how little he might say yet satisfy my question. Sir Jaket's sword and Arthur's folded arms again worked here to good effect. He understood that he was caught out in felonies and likely wondered how he could deflect guilt from himself to others. And deflect consequences, as well.

"If Gaston took the lady Philippa he did so without my knowledge," Sir John finally said.

"So when he and his band seized Joan le Scrope it was with your knowledge?"

"Thomas le Scrope will not miss three pounds," the man replied.

"Who are you to decide how much money another man might miss? But you speak true. When you and Gaston and your cousin the judge have repaid Sir Thomas, he will no longer miss his three pounds.

"Now, once more, where has Gaston likely fled with your man Osbert? How many have banded together with him? What are their names, and where will I find them?"

Silence was my only answer. I began to understand why. Sir John was lord of Coscote but the manor's ruler was Gaston Howes. Sir John was the intermediary between Howes and a judge of the King's Eyre. Sir Thomas le Scrope's barns might burn if he sought to punish Howes for taking his daughter. Sir John's barns may burn if he were to tell me what I asked. But a man held in Oxford Castle dungeon will burn no other's barns.

"When I find Gaston I will take him and his companions in felony to the Sheriff of Oxford," I said. "You will hear no more of him until you learn that the King's Eyre has sent him to a scaffold."

"Do not underestimate Gaston," Sir John said.

"Your cousin, should he be called to Gaston's case, will be pleased to silence him. As for you and Sir William, you should be pleased to escape with but repayment of Sir Thomas's pounds."

Another period of silence followed. Options. Sir John considered his. I had tried to make one seem more profitable to him than others. If he agreed and told me where I might find Howes, I thought it possible I might also find Lady Philippa.

"Gaston will likely seek Thomas Mowrey or Randall Attewell."

"Where do these fellows reside? Here, in Coscote?"

"Nay. Southbourne."

"Who is lord of the manor there?"

"'Tis a possession of Godstow Abbey."

I knew of Godstow Abbey, although I'd never visited the place. 'Tis at the north edge of Oxford, a place where women of noble and gentle families escape the cares of this world and prepare for the next. Would the abbess allow felons to reside in her holding? When a student at Balliol College I had heard rumors that Godstow Abbey was strapped for funds, the sisters there, most from prosperous families, being accustomed to living beyond their means. Did Gaston and Thomas and Randall have the protection of an abbess as well as a judge of the King's Eyre?

"And how far from Coscote is Southbourne?" I asked.

"A mile, perhaps a little more."

If Gaston and Osbert were fit they would already be at the village. Then it would take but a few minutes to move Lady Philippa to some more secure place. But why secrete her in Southbourne when Joan le Scrope had been successfully hidden here, in Coscote?

And the lass was released when her father paid the ransom. Why, then, continue to hold Lady Philippa when her ransom was paid? Had the felons argued about the lady's value to her husband, some demanding that more coin be required of Sir Aymer?

"Which is the road to Southbourne?" I asked.

Sir John pointed to the east. "Come," I said to Sir Jaket and Arthur. "We must make haste." Then, to Sir John, I said, "If you all of a sudden remember information which will lead me to Lady Philippa, Lord Gilbert and the Sheriff of Oxford might be persuaded to reduce any penalties they at first consider for your perfidy. But not the three pounds."

We hurried from the house. I called to Sir Ralph, Sir Humphrey, and the others of our cohort to mount their beasts and follow. Moments later the hooves of eleven horses raised a cloud of dust as we set off at a gallop for Southbourne.

There is no village in the realm untouched by plague. Nearly half the houses of Southbourne were between disrepair and collapse. As the village had been small even before the dying, it was now near to disappearing completely. But the place would have a reeve, if no bailiff. The man would likely inhabit the most prosperous house, and would know where I could find Thomas and Randall. I scanned the single street, selected a house little better than the others but featuring a well-tended vegetable garden in the toft, and dismounted before it. My companions did likewise. I approached the door and rapped upon it. If anyone was within I expected a prompt reply, as they would have heard the thunder of our beasts as we galloped into the village.

A woman of middle years opened the door, and from behind her a puff of smoke wafted through the door, surrounding her head like a halo. The thatching was old and collapsing over the vent holes in the eaves. As if to prove this conjecture the woman coughed, then, noticing my garb, bowed.

"I seek the reeve of this village," I said. "Is this his house?"

"Aye, but 'e ain't 'ere. 'E's out a-haying." As she spoke she glanced over a shoulder and I saw in the distance four men swinging scythes and three small boys turning the hay.

"Which house is Thomas Mowrey's?" I asked.

The woman looked at me with wide eyes. "You seek my 'usband, but you don't know 'is name?"

"Thomas is your husband?"

"That's right."

"And he is haying in yon field? Who else is at the haying with him?"

The question puzzled the woman, but she saw no reason to withhold the names.

"John, Alfred, an' Randall."

159

"Randall Attewell?"

"Aye. You know 'im?"

"Nay. I've heard his name."

"And my 'usband's. You not bein' from 'ere, 'ow is it you seek men you don't know?"

"I serve Lord Gilbert Talbot. I am on the Baron's business. Attewell's name and your husband's were provided me."

"What business does my 'usband 'ave with some lord?" The woman frowned with worry. When a great lord takes notice of a tenant or villein it usually portends no good thing. For the tenant.

"Perhaps nothing," I replied.

Would Thomas and Randall be swinging scythes in a hayfield if Gaston had been here and told them that a man who knew of their felonies would soon visit them? Not likely. Then where did Gaston go, and if he sought the place where Lady Philippa was held, where was that? And who besides Thomas and Randall were involved in this business? Was there a name, or names, that Sir John had neglected to mention?

And when Gaston Howes and his companions had swept down upon the Didcot Candlemas procession and carried off Joan le Scrope, whose horses did they ride? No lord of this manor would have beasts. There was no lord. Only Sir John Willoughby could provide horses. I had not pressed him about this. When we returned to Coscote I would remedy the fault.

But first I would cross the stubble and have words with Thomas and Randall. Not alone. A solitary man should not ask unwelcome questions of men wielding scythes. I called Sir Jaket, Sir Ralph, and Sir Humphrey to follow me.

The approach of four gentlemen, three with swords slung from their belts, will arrest the attention of most men. The four haymakers and three boys stopped their work and watched our approach. I sought a worried face among the men, or some indication of concern. I saw only dust and sweat-covered brows.

"Thomas Mowrey?" I said.

"That's me."

"I give you good day. When did you last see Gaston Howes?"

"Don't know the man. Though I've 'eard of 'im."

"What have you heard?"

"Nothin' much. Prosperous. Has two yardlands of Sir John."

"What have you heard of his felonies?"

"Felonies? Gaston? I've 'eard nothin' of felonies."

"If you see the fellow you may tell him that Sir Hugh de Singleton, serving Lord Gilbert Talbot, seeks him – and the rogues who accompany him. They seized a maid in Didcot for three pounds' ransom. They will pay for this felony upon a scaffold. They believe a judge of the King's Eyre will protect them, but this is no longer so. If one of the scoundrels who have done this evil send me to Howes it may be the Sheriff of Oxford will spare him."

I said no more, but watched the reeve. He blinked, then glanced to another of the mowers. Here was Randall Attewell, I thought. I also cast my gaze upon the man. He would not meet my eyes, but looked away to some distant object which seemed to have seized his attention.

"I am bailiff to Lord Gilbert at his manor of Bampton. It has come to Lord Gilbert's attention that a lady has been taken and is now held for ransom, much like the maid of Didcot. Gaston Howes may be the rogue who took this lady, as he did the lass. Have you heard of such knavery?"

The four men looked to each other, then to me, and shook their heads.

"If such a felony comes to your ears I have told you where to find me. Those who took the lady will surely do the sheriff's dance when they are found out, but might escape such an end if they give up their leader."

'Twas apparent that wherever Gaston and Osbert had run to, it was not here. Their companions in villainy would not be calmly mowing a hayfield was it so. Was Lady Philippa hidden away somewhere in Southbourne? Unlikely. If so, her captors seemed little concerned that she would be discovered. Was Gaston somewhere near, perhaps peering out from some hiding place, watching as I offered his companions a way to escape the wrath of insulted law?

"Your names," I said, "were given me by Sir John Willoughby, who is at this moment beginning to rue the day that he shared the ransom of the maiden Joan le Scrope. Why would he name you as among those who consort with Gaston Howes, whom all men know guilty of seizing the lass?"

"It wasn't us," one of the other haymakers said in a shaky voice. "Me an' John 'ave naught to do with Gaston Howes. 'E's asked often enough. Knew 'e'd come to a bad end, 'im an' them as has dealin's with 'im."

"Like Thomas and Randall?" I said.

The man did not reply, but I saw him and the fourth man, whom I took to be John, quietly taking small steps back to separate themselves from Thomas and Randall. Thomas, meanwhile, glared at the fellow. There would be hard feelings in this hamlet, I thought, and perhaps a wound or two after I had departed. Still, John and the haymaker who protested that he'd kept a distance between himself and Gaston Howes seemed brawny fellows and able to defend themselves. And my hope was that, given a day or two to consider a scaffold awaiting him in Oxford, Thomas or Randall might seek me with information of where I might find Gaston Howes. And perhaps Lady Philippa.

A day was not required.

I had bidden the haymakers "Good day," and with a last glance at Thomas and Randall stalked back toward the village. Sir Jaket, Sir Ralph, and Sir Humphrey came after. I did not expect to be followed, so did not look back over my shoulder to learn if I was – which proved to be the case.

As we four approached Arthur, Uctred, and the grooms attending our return by the reeve's house I heard a voice cry, "Wait!" 'Twas Randall.

When I first saw him he was red in the face from exertion and sun. Now he was pale. The thought of a noose placed about his neck will do that to a man.

"I know where Gaston might be," the man said. "You'll not tell 'im I said?"

162

"Do you fear him?" I asked.

"You've not met Gaston?"

"Nay."

"I thought not. If you 'ad you'd not ask such a question."

"Do you fear a scaffold more than Gaston?"

"'E told us the sheriff would not trouble us. Sir John's cousin would see to it."

"When you took the lass at Candlemas?"

"Aye."

"Did he assure you likewise about Lady Philippa Molyns?"

"I don't know about 'er. Gaston didn't ask our 'elp takin' 'er."

"Who aided him, then?"

"I don't know. But it wasn't us – not me an' Thomas."

"Howes and Sir John's groom Osbert fled Coscote. You said you might know where they now are. Might they have a lady hid away there?"

"Not likely. Gaston's got a hut in the forest, near to Coscote, an' a shed close by Didcot."

"He hides there to escape pursuit?" I said.

"Aye. 'E told us as help 'im that we'd naught to fear from the hue an' cry, but 'e'd got 'imself a hide anyway."

"Just in case?"

"Aye," Randall agreed. "Just in case."

"Can you take us there?"

"Me?" the man said with alarm. "Gaston would know who set you on 'im."

"If I arrest him and take him to the Sheriff of Oxford, why should you fear him?"

"Gaston's got friends in 'igh places what've gained from 'is thievery. What if 'e don't hang? What'll become of me then? If 'e learns I've told you even this much I'm a dead man."

"He'll not learn it from me. Where should I seek this hut? The last I saw of the man, he and Osbert were running from his house, across a new-mown hayfield, to a wood. Is that the forest where he has made his hide?"

"Aye."

"And the shed?"

"Behind the priest's house in Didcot."

Chapter 14

ere was interesting news. The clerk to Didcot's priest had been uncle to Gaston Howes' wife, and Randall said Howes was known to conceal himself in a shed upon the priest's glebe lands.

I turned from Randall to mount my palfrey.

"You'll not tell Gaston of me?"

"Nay. But you'd best convince Thomas and the others to hold their tongues also. How much did the fellow pay you to help seize the maiden?"

"Two shillings."

"You will be required to repay, I think."

"Two shillings! Where am I to get two shillings?"

I shrugged. "Same place you spent the loot, perhaps. This village is much reduced because of plague. Could you not rent more land of Godstow Abbey and increase your prosperity honestly? The abbess would not wish to see her lands go to waste. Surely she would be pleased for you and others who survive to work the strips of those who have perished."

"Rents is fixed. The law says 'ow much I must pay, an' abbess won't bargain."

Evidently the abbess of Godstow Abbey would rather see her lands earn for her no profit than a small profit. For this is the result for those landowners who refuse to transgress the Statute of Laborers and reduce the rents their tenants must pay.

The sun slanted across the road as we returned to Coscote. Much of the forest behind Gaston's house would be in shadow but I was resolved to prowl the wood and find the rogue if he was there. He was not; nor Osbert.

But before I entered the wood it occurred to me that, although Sir John's purse held no dented coins, Gaston Howes' might. I rapped upon the door of his house and called for his wife. When she appeared I demanded she produce her husband's purse. She might have claimed that he had it with him, but evidently did not think of this. I assured her I was not about to steal from her coins, and she reluctantly entered the house, returning a moment later with a small leather pouch. It contained no dented coins. This was, I admit, a disappointment. The absence of such coins did not mean Howes was not guilty of taking Lady Philippa, though the presence of them could have indicated that he was – which I had hoped to discover.

Our party returned to Sir John's manor house and I told the knight we'd be his guests for the night. He was to see to our beasts, stable and feed them, and arrange for straw and pallets to be spread upon the floor of his hall. We would explore more thoroughly the wood seeking Howes, then return for loaves and ale. Sir John was not pleased, but did as I asked. I believe he did not wish to further anger Lord Gilbert, which he assumed would be the result if I reported his intransigence to my employer.

Sir Humphrey, Sir Jaket, and Sir Ralph led our party across the stubble of the mown hayfield, then divided the grooms amongst us so we had four groups. We spaced ourselves twenty or so paces apart and planned to reorganize when we left the far side of the wood if we found nothing. This proved unnecessary.

Nearly halfway through the wood Sir Ralph shouted that Gaston's hut was found. The other three groups converged on the sound of the knight's voice, and we found a structure so cunningly fashioned of branches and shrubbery that 'twas wondrous we discovered the place at all. Indeed, Roger, who stumbled upon it, thought at first the hut was an obstacle he must struggle through to continue his part in the search.

A door of sticks woven together with vines closed the entrance to the shelter. This gate was fastened with hinges of vines. I swung it open and peered into the gloomy interior. The thick lacing of brush and twigs combined with the lengthening shadows to make the enclosure so dark that I explored it by feel more than sight. I found no pallet, and no lady. I did not expect to find either. No woman, no matter how frail, could be confined against her will in such a place unless she was bound hand and foot.

'Twas too late in the day to travel to All Saints' Church in Didcot and inspect the priest's shed. Perhaps, if Howes was there with Lady Philippa, he would, before morn, discover I had learned of the place and move on elsewhere. 'Twas not to be helped. Men and beasts were exhausted after such a day.

Sir John's ale and loaves were stale. If he had better 'twas not offered to us. Here was no surprise. I had told him he would surely be required to repay his share of the three pounds' ransom for Joan le Scrope. Likely he had decided to tighten his belt.

We broke our fast next morning with more stale loaves and watered ale. I told Sir John that, as Gaston Howes' protector, he would be held liable for any new predations for which the man was responsible. Would he? That would depend more upon the Sheriff of Oxford and Lord Gilbert than me. Perhaps even his cousin the judge and, as a last resort, Prince Edward. But Lord Gilbert's encouraging reassurance that Prince Edward would remember my good service gave me confidence that my words were not merely empty threats.

Half an hour later our band approached All Saints' Church. The priest was about to enter the porch for mass, when he saw us approach and hesitated. Was he curious about a band of mounted travelers, or did he guess we sought him?

I did not seek the priest, but rather his shed, which was clearly visible behind the priest's house. I pointed to the structure and we rode past the church while the priest gazed at us, open-mouthed.

The priest peered round the corner of the porch as we dismounted beyond the churchyard wall. I instructed the grooms to remain with our beasts, then we four knights quietly approached the shed, which I judged large enough to serve as a small tithe barn. Before we dismounted I had seen three sides of the building. There were no windows on two of the sides. The fourth side was part of the churchyard wall. Unlikely there would be a window there. The three sides I had seen were of wattle and daub, so a man imprisoned within it might batter his way out if he cared not for the noise he would make. Could a lady do so as well?

It is unwise to choose a place of concealment which has but

one exit, and particularly when that opening is also the entrance. But if felons were wise they would not be felons. The shed door was closed with an iron bar fitted to a hasp. Through a slot in the bar and another in the hasp a lock the size of my hand was fitted.

"Wait here," I said, and hurried to the porch. The nose of the priest was no longer visible, nor any other part of him.

I entered the church through the porch door as his clerk began to swing the censor. I dislike interfering with Divine Office, but thought the Lord Christ would understand if the ceremony honoring Him was delayed so justice could be done for one of His creatures. I thought it possible Lady Philippa, if not Gaston and Osbert, might be found within the shed.

I had taken only a few steps toward the altar when through the open door of the porch behind me I heard a man shout, "Halt!" Immediately there followed a cacophony of voices raised in anger. I turned and ran back through the porch. As I did so I saw the head and shoulders of a large man running beyond the churchyard wall, Sir Jaket in pursuit.

I ran for the lych gate to cut off the fleeing man. I assumed that if Sir Jaket wished to apprehend the fellow so did I.

I do not believe Gaston – for that's who Sir Jaket was chasing – looked over the churchyard wall to see me sprinting on a converging course. I ran through the lych gate as Howes came to it and there we collided. Kate's cookery has added some to my bulk, but still the man outweighed me by two or three stone. I, however, had the advantage of seeing the impact coming so was somewhat prepared. I raised an arm to ward off the blow, and the point of my elbow caught Howes aside his jaw. We tumbled to the grass in a tangle of arms and legs. By the time we unsorted our injured limbs Sir Jaket was above us, the point of his sword at Gaston's neck. To my surprise I had finally apprehended the man, though there must be less painful ways to capture a felon.

Sir Jaket's sword proved unnecessary. My elbow – which remained quite tender for a day or two – had rendered the scoundrel witless. He lay half-stunned upon the ground whilst I and Sir Jaket stood above him, dagger and sword in hand.

"Bind him," I said to Sir Jaket, then hurried to the shed. Some of the grooms of our band had followed Sir Jaket, others remained at the open shed door. How, I wondered, had a barred and locked door come open?

Arthur and Uctred stood among the grooms clustered around the open door. As I approached I saw them inspecting bar, hasp, and lock.

"Look here," Arthur exclaimed. A hole had been drilled through the door beneath the hasp, and a pin inserted from inside the shed. Pressure against the pin would raise the hasp and when a man pulled against the door, the hasp and bar would slide away from the jamb. This could not be done from outside the shed, for the pin was nearly invisible from the exterior, and could not be grasped even if it was seen.

"No man wants to be trapped in a locked barn," Uctred said as we examined the intricate mechanism. "But we 'ad a surprise when that door come open an' the fellow ran out."

"No doubt," I said. "Still, there were two men who ran across the hayfield. Perhaps one is yet lurking within this shed?"

I kept my dagger gripped firmly. Arthur, Uctred, and another groom drew theirs and we cautiously entered the shed.

Sunlight through the now wide-open door illuminated the shed interior well enough for us to see any other man attempting to conceal himself within. We prodded sacks of barley, oats, and rye – but with our fingers, not with our swords. Grain was scarce enough in the hungry months of lean times. We looked behind the sacks and peered into dim corners. No other man hid there, nor any lady. Osbert and Gaston had separated. Perhaps Gaston would know where his companion had fled.

If he did, he would not say. I had told Sir Jaket to bind Howes, but without cords this could not be done and Sir Jaket had none. As I departed the shed, blinking in the sun, Sir Jaket and Sir Ralph brought Howes at sword point to the open door. Howes had recovered from our collision but did not seem eager to attempt another escape. Two swords leveled at his belly will marvelously influence a man's conduct.

Nevertheless I wished Gaston's wrists tied tight, so I told Arthur to return to the shed and fetch one of the ropes hung neatly coiled on nails in the wall. Moments later he appeared with a length of hempen cord. Sir Jaket sliced off a segment and securely bound Howes' wrists. I know the cord was tight for I saw Gaston grimace as Sir Jaket made the rope taut.

The priest chose this moment to appear from the church porch. Two parishioners, elderly folk bent with age, followed. His congregation. The priest hurried to us, his robe flapping about his ankles.

He saw Sir Jaket completing the binding of Gaston's wrists and said, "Release this man. Who are you to seize a man who has sought sanctuary?"

"I am Sir Hugh de Singleton, bailiff to Lord Gilbert, Third Baron Talbot. This fellow has taken a lass for ransom, and may also have seized a lady."

"He has sought sanctuary. Release him."

"In a tithe barn? Sanctuary must be within the church."

"I am priest here. If I declare sanctuary for Gaston then it is so."

"You know him? He is not of your parish."

"Nay, he is not. But I serve all men."

"Especially if they cross your palm with a shilling or two. How much of Joan le Scrope's ransom did you receive?" I asked.

The priest became red in the face, but did not answer. I turned to Howes. "Did this priest offer you safety without payment?" Silence followed. No answer was an answer, though incomplete. Coins had surely changed hands, even if I would not learn how many.

"I am going to take this man to the Sheriff of Oxford," I said. "If you wish to complain that sanctuary has been violated, seek the sheriff and protest to him."

Joan le Scrope and her family were of this priest's parish, yet he had connived with those who seized the lass. Here was a priest who served himself rather than the folk of his parish. This priest would soon seek another post, for when Sir Thomas learned of this priest's perfidy – and he would learn, for I would tell him – he'd see that a new shepherd was found for the flock at Didcot.

Howes now stood quietly, his wrists bound tight behind him.

"Where is Lady Philippa?" I asked.

"Who?" he replied.

"Lady Philippa Molyns. You collected three pounds' ransom for Joan le Scrope, so decided to seize a lady upon the road near to Clanfield."

"I've never been near Clanfield."

"You, or mayhap men you sent, found the two pounds Sir Aymer Molyns left as ransom for his wife upon Badbury Hill. But you have not returned the lady. Do you intend to demand a greater ransom?"

"Where's Badbury Hill?" Howes replied.

"You take a lass at Candlemas, hold her for ransom, but when another is taken in much like manner you claim innocence. Why should you be believed? Where is Osbert? Did you send him to move Lady Philippa to some new location?"

"I don't know where Osbert went. 'E didn't want to come 'ere. Said 'e'd find 'is own way."

"If the lady is without food or drink she will surely die."

"That's as may be, but I don't know who she is or where she is or who's got 'er."

"Mayhap the sheriff's serjeants will persuade you to tell more," I threatened.

"I can't tell what I don't know. An' Sir John's cousin, 'im what's judge of the King's Eyre, will 'ave a chat with the sheriff."

Howes said this with a smirk. He had experience of felonies committed and pardoned in the past, so saw his capture as a minor impediment to continued knavery.

We had no beast for Gaston Howes. I thought to require the fellow to walk to Oxford, but this I quickly dismissed. 'Tis more than ten miles from Didcot to Oxford. I wished to travel more rapidly than Howes could – or would – walk.

Walter, one of Lord Gilbert's grooms, is a small man. I told him Gaston would ride his palfrey in the saddle before him. This did not please the fellow, nor likely did it please Howes. The decisions a bailiff must make are often offensive to others. Even Walter's palfrey was likely offended.

Arthur and Sir Ralph lifted Gaston to the saddle before Walter. "You are violating sanctuary," the priest said as I set my palfrey to motion. "Bishop Wykefield will hear of this."

"A man caught running outside the lych gate has himself forfeited sanctuary," I replied. "As for the bishop, I trust you will tell him all. If you do not tell him of the perfidious events about Didcot and Coscote, I will."

The priest seemed taken aback by these words. The more power a man has, the less effective are any threats made against him. Arthur is nearly immune to threat. At least from one man, or even two. My powers are of another sort. Lord Gilbert provides the authority behind my deeds and voice. Perhaps the priest considered this, for he said no more but watched silently as our band set off on the road to Abingdon and Oxford.

I had hoped to return this day to Bampton, either with Lady Philippa or with the knowledge of where she was kept. I would not do either. At Oxford Castle I turned Gaston Howes over to the hands of Sir Roger de Elmerugg, then, without Lady Philippa and without information of her whereabouts, I led our band across Bookbinders' Bridge and set off for Eynsham Abbey. There we might find succor – for our band had enjoyed no dinner this day and we had broken our fast with but stale loaves and watered ale – and beds for the night.

We found beds, and Abbot Gerleys required of his guest master that a capon be found for us to flavor the plain pottage which was the monks' supper. But I found little rest. I had, perhaps, ended the villainies of Gaston Howes, but I had not found Lady Philippa. And there was at least one felon at large near Didcot and Coscote. Mayhap Osbert knew where the lady was held, and was either making sure of the security of her confinement, or moving her to another location of which even Gaston would have no knowledge. So even if the sheriff's serjeants extracted a fingernail or two,

Gaston could not tell them where to find Lady Philippa, but only where she had been.

We broke our fast with maslin loaves fresh from the abbey oven and new-brewed ale. I told Sir Jaket, Sir Ralph, and Sir Humphrey to return to Bampton with the grooms – all but Arthur and Uctred – and report to Lord Gilbert the events of the past few days.

In the night I had resolved to return to Didcot with Arthur and Uctred, and seek Osbert. If he believed me to be away, and to have taken Gaston, I thought he might have returned to Coscote. If he had, I thought it likely Lady Philippa would not be far from the village. I thought this because I had not the shrewdness to imagine any other fate for the lady.

Sir Jaket would not hear of leaving the pursuit of the felons who had Lady Philippa. He insisted on returning to Coscote with me. I did not overrule his decision. I had come to appreciate his wit and valor.

As Sir Ralph, Sir Humphrey, and the returning grooms were mounting their beasts, another thought occurred to me. What if more ransom had been demanded, Sir Aymer had paid it, and the lady was returned to Coleshill? I had had no discourse with Sir Aymer for many days. Much may have happened since I was last in his presence.

I told Sir Ralph to inquire of Lord Gilbert if a report had come to Bampton regarding Lady Philippa's abduction. If so, I charged him to get a fresh horse from the castle marshalsea and seek me immediately in Coscote with the information. If Lord Gilbert had no tidings of the lady, he should mount the fresh horse and make for Coleshill, there to inquire of Sir Aymer if Lady Philippa had been returned. If she had, he must then seek me at Coscote with the discovery.

Sir John was not pleased to see me when, two hours later, we four stopped at his manor house door. Few folk are pleased to see a bailiff arrive unbidden at their door. A groom answered my rapping and Sir John was summoned. He offered no greeting, did not wish me "Good day." He likely wished my day would be dreadful and was no doubt willing to do what he could to make it so.

"Has your groom, Osbert, returned?" I began.

"Nay. I've not seen him since he ran off with Gaston."

"Howes is now the guest of the Sheriff of Oxford. Where might Osbert be? Has he family nearby where he might seek to be hidden?"

"Osbert has no wife," Sir John replied.

"Brothers? Sisters? Cousins, perhaps?"

"A brother and two sisters."

"Have they tenancy of you?"

"Aye. But you will not find Osbert with them."

"Why not?"

"Osbert does not get on well with his kin."

"Does he hold lands from you? Where is his house?"

"He didn't inherit. His father and him were at odds, so he left Osbert nothing. All went to the man's brother and sisters. Osbert sleeps in the stables and cares for my horses."

"So most folk dislike Osbert?"

"Aye."

"Why, then, has he found a home with you?"

"He does what I tell him and makes no complaints."

"Even if what you command is to assist Gaston Howes in his felonies?"

"What Osbert does with Gaston is his own business."

"But you make it yours if they require protection, and you demand payment of them."

Sir John said no more. He did not deny the accusation. Why would he? I already knew his role in the abduction of Joan le Scrope. Was this the only felony Gaston and Osbert and their companions had done? Not likely. If the rogues had done other evils it seemed likely that Sir John and his cousin, perhaps even the priest of Didcot, had been rewarded often for looking the other way.

We had already searched the crude hut in the forest and discovered no man, or woman, there. That did not mean that no man would be there now. Mayhap Osbert knew I had already found and examined the place, and therefore thought himself safe from discovery if he now sought shelter there. Why would I inspect the hut twice?

Why? Because I had no other thought as to where the man might be, could think of no one who might tell me his whereabouts, and if I could not find Osbert I was certain I would not find Lady Philippa. The lady would not be hidden away alone in the hut, unless bound securely. 'Twould be far too easy for her to break free of the flimsy structure. Where Osbert was, there would be Lady Philippa. So I thought.

We departed Sir John's presence and rode across the stubble of the hayfield to the wood. I told Uctred to remain with our beasts, then Sir Jaket, Arthur, and I entered the wood. I urged my companions to silence. If Osbert was within the hut with Lady Philippa I did not want him to hear our approach. Although if he did and fled without the lady, my purpose would be served. And if he fled with her, we would surely hear them stumbling through the brush and fallen branches, and overtake them.

I knew the location of the hut but it was so much one with the forest that we were nearly upon it before I saw it. I held a finger to my lips, motioned Arthur and Sir Jaket to remain still, then approached the pile of sticks and branches and vines.

I hesitated before the opening, listening. I heard no voices, no sound at all, but for a jackdaw which gave me a proper scolding. I quietly removed the vines which held closed the door of the hut and slowly drew it open.

I saw the feet first. They were close to the crude opening so the light filtering through leaves illuminated the calloused extremities. The body attached to these appendages lay in dark shadow, garbed in a brown cotehardie. 'Twas a dead man, face down upon the forest floor. I thought I knew who this might be.

Sir Jaket peered over one shoulder and Arthur the other, each wondering, I suppose, why I hesitated to enter the hut after dragging open the woven twigs and vines which served as a door.

"Osbert," Arthur said.

"Likely," I replied. "Let's have him out."

I bent low to enter the hut, grasped the corpse's shoulders, and with Arthur at the feet we hauled the fellow out to the mottled light of the wood. Most of what I had seen of Osbert had been at a distance. Only when I had confronted Sir John before his manor house did I look the man in the face, and that briefly and before I knew his name.

I brushed leaves and moss from the dead man's face and regarded his features.

"This is one of 'em what attacked me an' Uctred upon the road Monday," Arthur said.

"You're sure?"

"Well, not so sure as I'd wager ten shillings on it, but sure enough."

"'Tis Osbert," I replied. "Slain. See the gash in his cotehardie?"

Arthur and Sir Jaket peered down at the corpse. A small, blood-spattered slash appeared directly over his heart. The man must have died immediately, for little blood stained the cut in the fabric. He was not long dead. I touched the stain at the edge of the cut in his cotehardie and my finger came away tinged with red.

I re-entered the hut to learn if there might be any sign another soul – a lady – had been recently within. I cannot say what I thought I might find. Perhaps a fragment of fine wool or linen, or even a bit of silk ribbon. Or perhaps a long hair.

On hands and knees I inspected the hut, and even threw off some of the interlaced foliage the better to illuminate the place. I found nothing to tell me a woman had recently been within.

Who had slain Osbert? Did the killer seize Lady Philippa from him so as to keep for himself any greater ransom which might be demanded of Sir Aymer? Possession of the lady might make a man a target for some other knave, as would possession of a sack full of groats. Or was he slain to close his mouth, so others involved in the lady's abduction might remain unknown? How many others could there be? Four men swooped down upon the Candlemas procession to seize Joan le Scrope. Gaston, Osbert, Randall, and Thomas made four. Would more than four men be required to take Lady Philippa and her maid from their wagon on the Clanfield road? Only if the felons intended combat, if necessary, to snatch her. If stealth was intended, then four would be enough. Perhaps four would be too many for a covert deed.

Might Lady Philippa have found a dagger and at an opportune moment slain her captor? To do such a thing would require courage. Was Lady Philippa such a woman? If felons abducted my Kate, and she was required to slay one of them in order to return to her babes, would she do so? Mayhap most mothers would. But Lady Philippa had no children. Would she risk her own wounding or death to return to a husband who had upon occasion mistreated her? I am a man. How can I know what a lady would do? My Kate will have an opinion.

We slung Osbert's corpse across Arthur's beast and all four walked across the hayfield, leading the horses, to Sir John's door.

He seemed remarkably calm when presented with a dead groom. Had he known Osbert's fate before he saw the corpse? Did he, or a retainer, slay the groom? Why? To silence him? What more could Osbert tell me about this cabal of felons and their protectors which I did not already know? The whereabouts of Lady Philippa?

If Sir John had not done this murder, or commanded it, then the murderer must likely be Thomas Mowrey or Randall Attewell, for to my knowledge Osbert had no coin or chattels worth stealing, and what could he tell but the place where Lady Philippa was held?

Did Thomas and Randall now have Lady Philippa? Or one of these? Randall had seemed frightened when he disclosed to me his role in Gaston Howes' felonies. I found it difficult to imagine he would slay Osbert and risk a noose. Of course, risk of a noose he had already undertaken.

"You have brought trouble and now death to Coscote," Sir John complained. "Did you slay Osbert because he would not cooperate with your nonsense?"

"Trouble may frequently follow truth," I replied. "Truth has many enemies and often few friends. I suppose you will continue to tell me that you know nothing of the taking of Lady Philippa Molyns or her whereabouts. Or whoso has slain your groom. Dead grooms can tell no one of the evil deeds of their masters. Osbert can now tell me nothing of your part in the taking of Joan le Scrope or any other felonies. I would much prefer the man alive than dead."

"Osbert had nothing to tell of my deeds," Sir John growled. "So I'd no cause to see him a corpse."

"Hah! Someone did. What is your opinion? If you had nothing to do with Osbert's death, who do you believe may have? Had he enemies in Coscote?"

"No more than most men," Sir John shrugged. "None who'd risk a noose to be rid of him."

"Mayhap the murderer had already done evils which would bring him to a scaffold were they known. Thomas or Randall, for example."

"They faced no scaffold," Sir John said. "Sir Thomas's lass was returned to him."

He might have added that his cousin would see to their immunity and earn his fee.

"But Lady Philippa has not been returned to her husband, so far as I know. Perhaps she attempted escape from her captors and was slain."

"Nothing I'd know of," Sir John said. "If Gaston or Osbert or Thomas or Randall had aught to do with the lady's disappearance, they did not speak of it to me."

Should I believe the man? He was a felon. He had admitted so. Would a man guilty of one felony lie to escape the consequences of another crime? Will the sun rise tomorrow?

A visit to Southbourne and Randall Attewell might be a waste of time, but time spent in conversation with Sir John Willoughby was also ill-used. And Thomas Mowrey seemed likely less amenable to questions delivered with threats – real or implied – and black looks.

Sir John and his valets and grooms outnumbered us this day, but the knight was sufficiently daunted to give no sign he wished his retainers to do us violence. The name of a baron of the realm has such an effect on most men. The mention of Lord Gilbert Talbot has prevented me much grief, I am sure. Even so I bear scars for my service to Lord Gilbert. My Kate prays daily there will be no more. As do I.

We four mounted our beasts and were shortly in Southbourne. I knew which house was Thomas Mowrey's and as there were but four others in the village which appeared occupied, I halted before one of these and rapped upon the flimsy door. An underfed matron opened it.

"I seek Randall Attewell," I said. "Which house is his?"

The woman's eyes were wide in her sallow face. When a strange gentleman seeks a poor villager, the cause or result is likely to mean trouble for the commoner. She assumed Randall was in trouble. She was correct.

"Just there," she pointed. "House near to the well."

Of course. How else did the man receive his name? Probably his father and grandfather before him had resided within the same house, or upon the same plot of land. I thanked the woman and bade her "Good day." From her gaunt appearance I thought she enjoyed few good days. Perhaps she was a widow, trying to survive working the few acres her husband had left her, delving and planting with her children, hoping from one harvest to the next to endure for another year.

Or perhaps she had a husband. A cotter, and he was employed this day upon some other man's lands. Or mayhap he was away thieving to keep body and soul one for himself and family. If caught at a felony he would die for the crime. Perchance he would die if he did not commit some theft. And his wife and children, also, if such there were within the dim, smoky house.

We led our beasts from the woman's hovel to the house she had identified. Before I could approach the door Randall appeared from behind the house, making for his toft and its rows of onions and cabbages. He caught a glimpse of us and stopped, holding the hoe before him as if it could be a defense against four armed men.

"Have you seen Osbert this day?" I began. "Or yesterday?"

"Nay. You said 'e was with Gaston."

"No longer. Gaston is in the Oxford Castle gaol. Osbert is in a shroud."

"Shroud? Dead? Who...?"

Randall peered at his feet as his voice faded.

"Who slew him?" I said. "Likely some companion in villainy."

"Not me," the fellow said vehemently. "He was fine when I..."

"When you what?" I said.

Randall's response was silence.

"When you saw him last? When was that? Yesterday? This morning?"

"I didn't slay 'im!"

"He was well when you last saw him? Did he seek you, or did you seek him?"

"'E come 'ere last night. After dark. Gave me a start, poundin' on the door. What honest man goes about in the night?"

"Indeed. What did Osbert want of you?"

"'E wanted to know why 'e'd not been taken along with us when we seized that lady you been seekin'."

"He wanted to know of Lady Philippa's taking?" I found it difficult to contain the surprise in my voice.

"Aye. 'E wanted a share of 'er ransom. So I told 'im we'd not seized the lady."

"He thought you intended to cut him out of her ransom?"

"Aye. 'E sounded right bitter about it. 'E wouldn't believe me when I told 'im Gaston an' Thomas an' me wasn't them what took the lady."

My theory of Lady Philippa Molyns' abduction dissolved. Osbert did not have the lady. He had never had her. He had not known where she was. Randall could be lying about this conversation with Osbert, but I thought not. His fear of the noose had made him truthful in the past.

"If he believed he was being denied his share of the loot, did you convince him otherwise?"

"I doubt it. Said he'd seek Thomas. They was always mates."

"He was hale and hearty, then, you claim, when he left you?"

"As fit as you be."

It must be, I thought, that when Osbert found Thomas the two fell out over Osbert's assertion that he had been cheated of a share in Lady Philippa's ransom, which he mistakenly assumed Gaston, Randall, and Thomas had hidden from him. I had planted this seed of suspicion in his mind. I had been wrong. Osbert thought I knew what I was about. Did this cause his death?

I bade Randall "Good day," and led Arthur, Uctred, and Sir Jaket to Thomas Mowrey's house. My companions had heard Randall's words and now knew as well as I that Osbert did not have Lady Philippa, nor had he to do with her abduction. Nor, apparently, did Gaston, Randall, or Thomas. Then who did? Who came to Badbury Hill in the night and collected the two pounds?

Thomas Mowrey's wife again answered the door when I rapped upon it. Thomas, she said, was hoeing weeds from a field of dredge. I would find him behind the house, near the hayfield. We followed her directions and found the fellow. He had discarded his cotehardie and worked in chauces and a sweat-stained kirtle. He saw our approach and leaned upon his hoe, perhaps pleased to be required to halt his labor for a time.

I bade the fellow "Good day," and before I could ask of Osbert he spoke.

"I know why you're 'ere," he said. "I seen you come from Randall."

"Osbert accused you, Randall, and Gaston of cheating him of a share of a lady's ransom," I said.

"That's right. I tried to tell 'im we'd naught to do with the lady – like I tried to tell you."

"Did he believe you?"

"I don't know." Thomas shook his head. "I think so."

"In his anger did he attack you?"

"Osbert? Nay! 'E'd not assail me. We been mates too long."

"Where did he go when he left you?"

"'E didn't say, did 'e? Back to Coscote, I s'pose. They'd need him. 'E cares for Sir John's beasts an' sleeps in stable, does Osbert."

"No longer," I said.

Thomas scowled. "Has Sir John give the job to another?"

"He will, for Osbert is dead, slain. A dagger was thrust through his heart."

"What? 'E was set upon along the road to Coscote?"

"Nay. You and Gaston, Randall, and Osbert had a hut in the forest near to Coscote where you might hide if trouble came to your doorstep. I found him there a short time ago, slain."

Thomas shook his head again, as if in so doing he could reject this knowledge.

"Why would he be murdered soon after speaking to you and Randall?" I said.

"I cannot say. I don't know."

I believed him. For a few minutes.

"Osbert had nothing worth taking. What did he know that some other man wished him to take to his grave unshared? What other felonies have you and he, Randall, and Gaston committed? I know you seized Joan le Scrope at Candlemas. It's become common knowledge. He was not slain to keep him from telling me of that felony."

Thomas was silent. So was I. I have learned that men with guilty consciences are oft best left to consider their sins without further questions from me.

"'E said Sir Thomas offered 'im coin."

"Sir Thomas – le Scrope?"

"Aye. Now that Gaston's in Oxford Castle gaol, Sir Thomas 'as little to fear of 'im – or of us. 'E said if Osbert would testify before the King's Eyre of what Gaston and Sir John 'ad done, 'e'd pay 'im ten pence an' see to it 'e come to no 'arm. Osbert told me if 'e didn't get a share of the lady's ransom, 'e'd do as Sir Thomas asked, and me an' Randall could 'ang along with Gaston, if Sir John's cousin couldn't save us."

"When he left you last night was he yet convinced he had been cheated of a share in the lady's ransom?"

"Mayhap. I told 'im 'twasn't so."

"Perhaps he went from here to Coscote to confront Sir John?" I suggested.

Thomas shrugged. "'E'd get no different answer than from me an' Randall. Unless Gaston took the lady without us, an' Sir John knows of it."

Such a deed on Gaston's part seemed unlikely. The man had not worked his evils alone in the past. But the thought could not be entirely disregarded. Yet how would one man overwhelm Lady Philippa and her maid without creating a din which others in Sir Aymer's party would hear? Even John Cely, blind as he is and as deaf as he may be, could have heard, if not seen, such a clamor. The thought took me back to Coleshill and the last time I had seen the aged groom. Arthur's suspicions that John heard more than he let on had proved well founded. Exactly how sharp was his hearing, I wondered? Was it even impaired at all? And why, if Gaston Howes or some such rogue took Lady Philippa, would Cely not tell what he might know of the felony? Had he been paid to close the eyes already of small use to him, and feign a deafness beyond his real state?

If Gaston indeed took Lady Philippa, acting alone, where was she now? Hidden away where only Gaston knew her location? He protested no involvement with her abduction. If he spoke falsely, the lady might be without sustenance and perhaps dead by now. Nay, for Gaston took a lass or lady only for the profit such wickedness might bring. He had no intention of doing murder. Dead captives cannot be ransomed.

Unless the victim is thought to be alive.

I could see little more was to be learned of Thomas Mowrey. Likely there was much more I would care to know, but aside from stretching his limbs upon the rack – a tactic reserved to the sheriff and his serjeants – I knew of no way to force truth from the man.

Chapter 15

I bade Mowrey "Good day," with a reminder that he would soon be required to repay Sir Thomas le Scrope his share of the ransom collected for the lass, Joan. I was uncertain if this threat of mine could be carried out. If Lord Gilbert or Prince Edward would not compel the scoundrels to repay Sir Thomas, there would be little I could do to enforce forfeiture. Sir Thomas might recoup some coin from Gaston, Thomas, Randall, and perhaps even the priest of Didcot. Would Sir John and his scurrilous cousin, the judge, be required to return their portion of the ransom? I had my doubts, despite Lord Gilbert Talbot's encouragement and reassurance.

If Sir John wished to know who had slain his groom, he had his own bailiff to whom he could assign the matter. I had already a duty beyond my own bailiwick. I desired no other. We rode past Sir John's manor house, left Coscote behind, and turned our beasts toward Bampton. When we arrived, Sir Jaket, Arthur, and Uctred continued to the castle with my exhausted palfrey while I dismounted at Church View Street and made my way to Galen House. I was pleased to walk. And I did not want to rest my rump in a saddle again for many days. Lord Gilbert had other thoughts.

I always feel some apprehension when I approach Galen House after an absence. Will I find my Kate and babes well? I have seen so much of untimely death, whether through accident, violence, or the plagues that stalk the land. I long to see both my children grow to maturity unharmed.

A year and more past, Robert Caxton was on the verge of starvation, his stationer's shop in Oxford near bankrupt from theft and loss of custom after plague had taken so many scholars. With some difficulty I had persuaded my father-in-law to remove to Bampton. He had not wished to burden me and Kate, but when I at last convinced him that we needed his aid in the many times Lord Gilbert's business called me away, he agreed to come to Bampton.

Caxton greeted me when I entered the house. I thought his voice seemed reedy, but when Kate heard our words, left her kitchen, and greeted me with a kiss I forgot my father-in-law's quiet welcome.

I was becoming accustomed to missing my dinner. Nearly. My nose caught the scent of supper. Perhaps Kate saw my twitching nostrils, for she announced that she had held back some of the meal in anticipation of my return.

"There is a dish of beans yfryed," she said, "and chewits of herring." In reply to this announcement my stomach growled loudly. Bessie heard, and laughed. I am a fortunate man that within my house hunger causes laughter, not sorrow.

My Kate was willing to see me fed before interrogating me regarding the journey to Didcot.

"Will Uctred's ear be restored?" – her first question. No doubt she remembered Sir Simon Trillowe and his misshapen ear. I was not responsible for the blow which nearly severed the knight's ear from his skull, but I was responsible for the crude attempt to stitch the appendage back to the place God intended. 'Tis onerous work to sew an ear to its proper location, and not taught in the year I spent studying surgery at the University of Paris. An ear is tough, constructed of oddly shaped gristle, and difficult to penetrate with a needle. So when I had finished with Sir Simon's ear it protruded from his head so that ever after he wore his cap with the liripipe covering the unappealing sight. For this he blamed me. He also blamed me for wedding Kate. He had had intentions toward her himself, although I am sure marriage had not been among his designs. So when his ear healed badly I was not much chagrined for my untidy work. May the Lord Christ forgive me, for we are to do good to those who use us badly. Well, I did my best for Sir Simon. The practice I gained may help Uctred's ear to heal less objectionably.

"You believe justice will be done in the matter of the lass whose father ransomed her?" my father-in-law said when I had told the tale of capturing Gaston Howes and delivering him to the Sheriff of Oxford.

"Who can predict," I replied, "what a judge will decide? It may be Sir William Willoughby will sentence the fellow to hang so as to silence him, or mayhap he will feel loyalty to a man who has contributed coins to his purse, and set the rogue free."

"Especially if the felon has a few more coins he can send to the judge," Kate offered. "If the rogue is freed he may then continue his wickedness, and the evils will then continue to profit Sir John and his cousin judge. Would a corrupt judge cut off such a flow of pence and shillings?"

"If he thinks Lord Gilbert and Prince Edward have taken an interest in the matter, he might."

"Have they?" Caxton said. He spoke so softly that I could scarcely hear him.

"Lord Gilbert has. And if I bring the matter to the prince's attention I believe he will require that justice be done. He is disturbed about the condition of the realm."

"'Twould be a marvel," Kate sighed, "to see justice done in England."

I agreed with Kate, but silently. Bessie is of an age where she repeats much of what she hears. I prefer that Lord Gilbert not know of my concern for the state of the kingdom. Bessie would not speak of the criticism to Lord Gilbert, but words spoken in darkness will oft travel to the light. The old king, once a great warrior and leader of men, is now infirm. Some – silently for fear of being thought traitorous – wish the man would abdicate for his son. Or die. But I have seen Prince Edward's weakness. Were he to become king in his current condition, the realm would have no more energetic a ruler than now. What then? The boy, Richard, Prince Edward's surviving son, become a child king? Avaricious counselors would surround him. Could Queen Joan fend them off, particularly Prince John, and protect her son? A woman would govern England. Could the land be worse administered than now? If justice is done anywhere in England it is left to sheriffs and local knights to see to it. Sheriff of Oxford, Sir Roger de Elmerugg, is known to be a fair man, as is my employer. I must thank the Lord Christ that I live and work in Bampton, and not in some troubled shire or village where malefactors hold sway.

"Is Lady Philippa lost?" Kate said, breaking in upon my thoughts. "If you cannot find her, who will? You have never yet failed when Lord Gilbert asked you to bring light to some dark evil."

"Mayhap this matter will be the first," I said. "Indeed, my mind is empty of thoughts concerning the lady. She has vanished and I can discover neither the place she is held nor who has her. But defeat is often temporary. Only surrender is permanent."

"Then you will continue the search?" Kate asked. "*Someone* has the lady – and Sir Aymer's two pounds, as well."

"Perhaps more than two pounds now. I sent Sir Ralph to Coleshill to learn if Lady Philippa had been freed. He was to seek me at Coscote if she was. He did not, so tomorrow I will go to the castle and ask him of Sir Aymer and what, if anything, he learned in Coleshill."

As Kate and I spoke I saw my father-in-law's head drop to his chin. He slept. But the movement brought him jerking to wakefulness. Kate also saw, and gently suggested that he seek his bed. He needed no urging. He swayed to his feet, gathered himself, then tottered off to his chamber. This was upon the ground floor, a room I had previously used for storage, and as a surgery when folk came to my door after doing themselves some injury – or having it visited upon them by some other. 'Twas well Caxton's chamber was not in the upper storey. As I watched him depart the kitchen I thought it unlikely he could manage to ascend a flight of stairs.

Kate sat silently watching her father's laborious progress toward his accommodation. When she heard the door close behind him she spoke.

"He is ill – to death, I fear."

"What is his complaint? I have been away and have not observed him."

"He does not eat. When he does he has great unease, and belches foul breaths. Yet his belly grows apace and is as round as a pig's bladder."

When I did not immediately respond she spoke again. "Your silence betrays you. He will not live long, will he?"

"I cannot tell. Mayhap there is a cancer in his belly."

"Are there no herbs which will cure such a thing?"

"Nay, none."

"He is sometimes in pain, I think. I have seen him clutch at his stomach and bend over. But if he knows I have seen this he will force himself erect and pretend all is well."

"He does not wish to worry you," I said.

"No doubt. But he does. If 'tis indeed a cancer he will soon go to St. Beornwald's churchyard."

"Aye, he will," I agreed.

"I am prepared," Kate said softly, and glanced to a basket in the corner of her kitchen. It was filled with oak galls.

John cried from his crib for an evening meal, which ended, for a time, our conversation. Kate climbed the stairs to our bedchamber whence came the wails and I went out through the rear door to the toft, where Bessie was playing with the doll her grandfather had made for her from scraps of fabric and a broken tree branch.

The lass has become old enough that she can carry her part of a conversation. Indeed, she insists upon doing so.

Bessie has named the doll Agnes. How the name came to her I cannot tell. I know no woman of that name. None in Bampton. I asked of Agnes's health.

"She is not well," Bessie reported.

"What is her illness?"

"Her stomach is sore. She will not eat her dinner."

"Ah. That is troubling. Perhaps some thin broth might help her recover."

"I will ask Ma. You think thin broth would help Grandfather?"

"Perhaps."

Bessie had seen her grandfather's illness and the malady had registered with her. How, I wondered, should I prepare the lass for her grandfather's death? If not soon, as I expected, Caxton would eventually die. Would Bessie decide that Agnes must also perish?

Who can know the mind of a child?

My daughter had also heard the reason for my frequent absences in the past several days. "Did you find the lady?" she asked.

"Nay, not yet."

"You will, Mother says. But what if she doesn't want to be found?"

"Then finding her will be more difficult."

And it would be more difficult to return her to her husband. I did not say this to Bessie, but the thought had troubled me since discovering Osbert's corpse. I had been persuaded that rogues had carried Lady Philippa away, and the ransom demand brought credence to the theory. Would Lady Philippa demand two pounds of Sir Aymer to finance escape from a tyrannical husband?

Two men had collected the ransom. If the lady had chosen to escape her husband it was with the aid of men. I was back to Martyn de Wenlock. Why had the scholar fled Oxford, then suddenly returned? And the groom John Cely? Deaf and near blind. Was he so? Blind, aye, the milky appearance of his pupils made this obvious. But so deaf that he would not hear his lady and her maid spirited away? Arthur thought the man may have heard my estimate of his condition. I thought so also. Was he paid to neither see nor hear Lady Philippa's disappearance? If so, by whom? Martyn de Wenlock? Where would a poor scholar find the coins to do such a thing? Perhaps he was not so poor as I had thought. Would Cely risk his employment for a few coins? Were he a party to the disappearance, when found out he would lose his position. Where, then, would he go? Who would employ a man so infirm?

I began to notice a change in my thoughts. To this day I had considered Lady Philippa's disappearance an abduction. The ransom demand made it seem so. Now I began to think of the matter as her disappearance. Not her abduction. This would not explain the ransom. Or would it? Starting a new life with a scholar, poor or not, would require a subsidy. Sir Aymer would be a near source of pence and groats. Where would Lady Philippa or Martyn find another?

I came back to the present to find Bessie staring at me, Agnes clutched to her chest. The kitchen door swung open on squealing hinges and Kate called Bessie to come to bed. Tomorrow I must grease the hinges. For tonight I would draw from my father-in-law's chamber the half-barrel I use to bathe.

Many years past I had found the old cask discarded. I cut the barrel in half with a borrowed saw, paid a smith sixpence to secure an iron band about the open top, and then smeared pine pitch between the staves to make the container watertight.

I wished to soak away the sweat and dust of the roads I had recently traveled. Kate has two large pots: one of iron, the other of bronze. I placed wood upon the hearth, filled the pots, set them upon the embers, then took our pail to the village well. 'Twas near dark, and past curfew, but Edwin, Bampton's beadle, would not trouble me.

Three pails full I emptied into the barrel, and the two pots of heated water. With a cake of Kate's Castile soap I washed away the grime I had accumulated. After putting Bessie to her bed Kate heard my preparations and decided to join my ablutions. She placed the iron pot back to the fire to warm more water and when I had scrubbed myself clean she bade me leave her, added the heated water from her iron pot to the barrel, and prepared to immerse herself. I would have stayed but she laughed and chased me away.

Saturday dawned as grey as my mood, which had nothing to do with being chased from the kitchen the evening before. Why is it that failures are more likely to possess our thoughts than success? Perhaps other men are unlike me, and are able to dismiss their defeats and think on their accomplishments. I have enjoyed no little success in past investigations for Lord Gilbert, but these seem to fade before a more recent frustration.

I broke my fast with half a maslin loaf and ale, then set off for the castle. I needed to speak to Sir Ralph about his visit to Coleshill. He had not sought me yesterday, so I assumed Lady Philippa was yet absent from her home. And I must relate to Lord Gilbert the tale of my fruitless visits to Didcot and Coscote. Not completely fruitless. Gaston Howes awaits the King's Eyre in Oxford Castle gaol. It may be that justice will be done for Joan le Scrope and her father.

As I passed under the castle gatehouse I thought I saw Sir Ralph enter the stables. I followed, and found him with a stable page inspecting his horse's hoof. He turned to see who had blocked the light, saw 'twas me, and spoke.

"Good day, Sir Hugh. My mare came up lame yesterday upon my return as I neared Radcot Bridge. I had to walk and lead her. I could see nothing in her hoof, and 'twas too dark last night for a close examination. I can find nothing yet this morning, but there's got to be something troubling the old girl."

I moved away from the stable door to permit Andrew and Sir Ralph more light. This was still insufficient, so Andrew led the beast to the stable yard where the morning, albeit cloudy, would allow better visibility.

Sir Ralph kneeled and raised the mare's hoof to rest it upon his knee. "Look... what is there?" he said, and pointed to the hoof. Andrew bent low to inspect the hoof.

"'Tis an abscess," the stable boy said.

"What is to be done? The mare is my finest ambler," Sir Ralph said.

Andrew did not reply, but stared at the hoof as if in deep contemplation. "I seen an abscessed hoof once," he finally said.

"How was it dealt with?"

"It wasn't. Nothin' to be done. The beast died. She ended as food for the hounds."

Sir Ralph looked to me. I had been an observer, waiting to speak to the knight when he had concluded his business with Andrew.

"I should hate to see this horse founder," Sir Ralph said to me. "Have you dealt with abscesses in men?"

"I have."

"Successfully?"

"Aye, but for one."

"Can you do for this beast what you did for men you treated?"

I bent low to see the afflicted hoof. The abscess was not large, but oozed a grey pus and when I put a finger to the injury the mare drew her hoof away from the touch.

"The wound must be opened and allowed to drain," I said, "and then packed with herbs which will soothe and heal the injury."

"You have the proper herbs?"

"I do. Oil of lavender soaked in goosegrass."

"Have you other matters to attend to, or can you deal with the abscess today?"

"I came here to speak to you about your journey to Coleshill, and to discuss matters with Lord Gilbert. 'Twill not take long to deal with the mare's hoof. You can tell me of Coleshill while I do. Then there will be time enough to seek Lord Gilbert. I will need to return to Galen House for a scalpel and the herbs. Wait here with your beast. I will not be long."

I hurried to Galen House and trotted back to the castle with my herbs and scalpel. I asked Sir Ralph to again raise the mare's hoof, and told Andrew to search the marshalsea for a discarded sack and a short length of cord.

The mare was gentle and patient. She did not object to having her tender hoof once again lifted but when I drew the scalpel across the abscess she kicked, and the blow sent Sir Ralph sprawling. The knight picked himself up and grinned sheepishly. "Didn't much like that, did she? Must you cut away more?"

"Nay, I think not. I needed to slice an opening for pus to escape. In a few minutes, when it has done so, I will pack the lavender oil and chopped goosegrass into the cut."

"She'll not like that much, either."

"Not likely. I will try to be gentle."

Andrew returned with a piece of coarse hempen sacking and cord. I told the lad to stand ready, then asked Sir Ralph to again raise the mare's hoof. He approached the task gingerly, but the beast cooperated. So long as no man touched her aching hoof she was complacent. But I was about to touch it.

At Galen House I had placed the chopped goosegrass and lavender oil in a vial, stopped with a cork. When Sir Ralph had the hoof again upon his knee I removed the cork and poured the mixture from the vial into my cupped palm. As gently as I could I pushed the compound into the laceration my scalpel had made. To my surprise and gratification the mare did not object. No doubt Sir Ralph was also gratified. I placed the hempen sacking over the hoof, drew it up above the fetlock, then tied the cord so the sacking would, if the mare allowed, remain over the hoof and protect it from the filth of the stable.

I had been too intent upon the mare and her sore hoof to question Sir Ralph, but when the work was done and Andrew led the beast back to her stall I remembered why I had sought the castle and the knight.

"He believes she's dead," Sir Ralph said when I asked of any information Sir Aymer might have provided regarding his wife. "He said he thinks she tried to escape her captors and was slain. That's why she's not been returned even though the ransom was paid. He said, was she yet living the rogues who took her would either set her free or demand more coin for her release. They've done neither, so Sir Aymer believes she is slain."

There was logic in Sir Aymer's view of the matter. 'Twas indeed a puzzle why Lady Philippa had not been released, or no greater ransom had been demanded.

"Sir Aymer's squire," Sir Ralph continued, "believes the knight is about to seek Bishop de Brantyngham to have Lady Philippa declared dead."

"Surely he will not do so when the lady has been missing not three weeks," I replied.

"Squire said that Sir Aymer is gathering coin to influence the bishop."

"How much?"

"He didn't say. Probably doesn't know. Mayhap even Sir Aymer doesn't know how much the bishop will require – or if he will declare Lady Philippa dead for any amount."

I do not know any bishops, but their reputations, like that of bailiffs, precede them. I felt sure the Bishop of Exeter would accede to Sir Aymer's request, and also sure the cost of his decree would come near to bankrupting the knight. But Sir Aymer desires an heir, regardless of the cost. If he weds another, and the lady does produce a child, the lad or lass will inherit an estate much reduced, the wealth having gone to provide pleasing items of gold and silver and precious jewels for the bishop's palace.

Lady Philippa had not been returned to her husband, but neither had a greater ransom been demanded. Felons would hold her, I thought, only if it were profitable to do so. Keeping the lady, but not requiring a greater ransom, would be foolish for such scoundrels. Even rogues would have wit enough to understand that so long as they possessed Lady Philippa the chances of discovery would increase. If she was released, her husband would have less reason to search for her, and in the quest find her captors.

Then where was the lady? If she was released, did she refuse to return to Sir Aymer? Squire Giles had said her life in Coleshill was difficult, Sir Aymer dealing harshly with her because she could not give him an heir. Would she take the opportunity, if those who seized her had let her go after collecting the ransom, to seek Martyn de Wenlock? The youth had abruptly departed Oxford, then as suddenly returned.

I left Sir Ralph to deal with his mare and sought Lord Gilbert. John Chamberlain directed me to the solar, where I found my employer with his son. Richard is sprouting and will soon be as tall as his father, although he has the slender appearance of his mother. Does he remember her, I wonder? She perished five years past. Surely he is old enough to have her image fixed in his mind.

The two were sharing cheese and a wheaten loaf with ale – well watered for Richard. Would Lord Gilbert seek another wife, I wondered? He is yet a vigorous man. Perhaps his mind's eye is yet clouded with visions of Lady Petronilla so that other ladies are obscured.

"What news, Hugh? Is Lady Philippa found?"

I told him "Nay," and reviewed my visits to Didcot and Coscote, and Sir Ralph's conversation with Squire Giles.

"So you have not found the lady, but you have discovered where she is not," Lord Gilbert said. "Then you are now closer to finding where she is, and who took her, having eliminated Didcot and the felons who took the lass at Candlemas."

"Aye, I suppose. There are yet too many places she may be hidden, and too many knaves who may be responsible."

"Sir Aymer has given up finding his wife alive, the squire thinks?"

"So he told Sir Ralph. Do you believe the Bishop of Exeter will grant Sir Aymer's request to declare him a widower so he may wed again?"

"I don't know the bishop well, but most of them can be bought for any purpose if the price be high enough. What think you, Hugh? In your opinion does the lady yet live?"

"Why would her captors slay her?"

"Hmmm. Mayhap she could identify them," Lord Gilbert said, "and the place she was held."

"Possible, I suppose. But the captors would have been careless to allow the lady to see them unmasked or the place she was taken. The men who took Joan le Scrope sequestered her in a tiny, windowless closet in a loft, and no doubt she was taken there blindfolded."

"This matter frustrates you."

"Aye, it does. You have told me that I may leave the mystery to others, and there are moments I am willing to do so."

"But you are too stubborn to give the matter over."

"Me? Stubborn? Nay, I am a model of pliancy."

"Hah! Lady Katherine will tell you what I have said is so. A wife knows her husband. I suspect your tenacity is one reason she was willing to be joined to you. Most women, I think, wish for a husband who determines a course and then adheres to it."

"Even when the path leads him where neither he nor she wishes him to go?"

"Where we wish to go and where we must go are oft different places."

"Aye," I agreed. "Surely the Lord Christ did not wish to go to a cross, but He knew He must, else where would we poor sinners be?"

"Amen to that! So, you intend to continue to seek Lady Philippa? Where?"

"Martyn de Wenlock's behavior puzzles me."

"The suitor passed over for Sir Aymer?"

"The same. He could not have taken her, if his landlord spoke true, but his friends might have, or even if not she may be with him now."

"If her captors released her and she went her own way?"

"Aye."

"What do you intend?"

"I will go to Oxford, in the guise of a scholar, and try to follow de Wenlock. He has seen me, and may remember the meeting. If Lady Philippa has somehow got to Oxford and the fellow knows it, he will seek her as often as may be."

"You intend to do this alone?"

"Aye. Neither Arthur nor Uctred would be believable disguised as scholars."

"On the road they would not need to be. As you follow de Wenlock they might follow you. You have already enough scars in my service. I wish for you to add no more."

"I have no objection to them attending me, but they may be reluctant. Uctred's ear is yet tender and Arthur's ribs bring forth a wheeze now and then."

"You will not need to require them," Lord Gilbert smiled. "They have served me many years and Uctred my father before me. I know them well. They will not allow you to risk the road alone. When they know of your scheme they will wish to be a part of it."

They did.

I told Arthur we would travel to Oxford on Monday. We would

rest on Sunday, which was God's purpose for men – one day of the week with no labor – and allow our saddle-sore rumps to recover. And Uctred's ear and Arthur's ribs, also.

When Kate and I walked from Galen House to St. Beornwald's Church on Sunday morning her father did not accompany us. He had always risen with the sun, but for the past week or so had remained in his bed 'til long after the morning Angelus Bell sounded. This day he attempted to rise but his legs failed him, and Kate, from the kitchen, heard him tumble to the floor. The rushes broke his fall, but he was sorely injured.

Kate cried out when she found him prone upon the rushes. I had just drawn on my cotehardie, and hastened down the stairs to learn what had caused her shriek. I found her bent over her father, attempting to ask him of his hurt. He could not reply, but gasped something incomprehensible.

Together we lifted Caxton to his bed, but not without a groan of pain.

"He has injured himself falling from his bed," Kate said.

"Aye... or did the injury cause the fall?"

"What do you mean?"

"I fear he has broken his hip."

Kate's face lost color at these words.

"Mayhap his hip broke when he stood from his bed," I said, "or the fall caused the fracture."

"It makes no difference, does it?" Kate replied. "He will soon die."

"Likely."

"Is there nothing to be done to ease him?"

"His breathing will be easier if I raise the head of his bed. Perhaps Philip Carpenter will have some scrap I may place under the bedposts."

He did, and but a few minutes later I had raised the head of my father-in-law's bed the length of my hand. When the aged cannot leave their beds their lungs fill and they soon perish. If their heads be raised above their feet this does not happen so soon. But it will happen.

Kate brought part of a loaf and a cup of ale to her father but he took scarcely a mouthful of the loaf and would have no more. Most of the ale dribbled down his whiskers and onto his kirtle.

"You go to the church for mass," Kate said. "I wish to remain with my father."

Caxton heard, and had enough strength to reply. "Nay. You must pray for my soul."

We left Caxton to rest upon his bed and with Bessie and John walked Church View Street to St. Beornwald's. Kate was silent until we came to the lych gate. The structure reminded her of its purpose. "Shall we send for Father Thomas soon?" she said.

"Aye. Soon."

"Today?"

"When the mass is finished we will see how your father fares."

He did not fare well. Each breath seemed it might be his last. Kate had prepared to make a leach lombard for our dinner but her mind was upon other matters. Adela did not attend her work on Sunday, to assist with our dinner, so I told Kate we would make our dinner of maslin loaves and ale, and there was a small portion of honeyed butter which pleased Bessie. And me.

After the brief meal I went again to my father-in-law's chamber. I found him asleep, his breathing shallow. More so than an hour past. It was time to send for Father Thomas.

I told Kate I was off to the priest's house. I found the priest at his dinner, licking the grease of a roasted capon from his fingers. When I told him of my mission he stood, called for his clerk, then went to a closet where he withdrew surplice and stole, and a small box containing the blessed sacrament.

The clerk led the way when we departed the priest's house, ringing a small bell. All who heard it peered from open doors along our path, and knew what the procession portended.

Father Thomas attempted to ask the seven interrogations but Caxton was insensible. The priest drew a small vial from a pouch fixed to his belt and from it took a drop of oil with which he anointed the dying man. He next took a wafer, placed it upon Caxton's tongue, and spoke the paternoster.

There was no more to be done, but to wait.

"I will send Odo to ring the passing bell," Father Thomas said.

The clerk bowed, acknowledging his obligation, and the priest and clerk departed. Minutes later I heard the bell of St. Beornwald's Church toll three times. Then a pause. Then the bell sounded three times again.

Chapter 16

There would be no journey to Oxford on Monday. If I traveled there, 'twas in my mind to remain as many days as would be needed to find and follow Martyn de Wenlock as he went about his business. I felt certain that if Lady Philippa was in or near to Oxford, and the scholar knew of it, seeing her would be part of that business.

But I could not leave my Kate to deal alone with her dying father. I told her that I must visit the castle but would return anon.

I did not return so swiftly as I might have. I found Arthur and Uctred and told them our journey to Oxford would be delayed, and why. Ribs and ear would have a few more days to mend. Then, upon my return to Galen House I stopped on the bridge over Shill Brook to study the flowing stream.

A leaf passed under my gaze, drifting south with the current. How many hours or days would pass, I wondered, 'til the leaf joined the Thames? And how many more days 'til it passed under London Bridge? If it did not sink first.

What would happen while the leaf continued its journey? Would my father-in-law die? Likely. Would I find Lady Philippa? If the past points the way to the future that seemed unlikely. I had wasted many days prowling about Coscote and Didcot. How many more days would I squander in a quest for a lady who could not be found?

When I returned to Galen House I found Kate tending her largest iron pot upon the hearth. She was stirring the contents with a stick long enough that she could stand away from the heat, but her face was beaded with perspiration. I came close and did not need to ask her work. The pot was two-thirds filled with a black liquid and a bundle of cloth. Linen, I thought. Kate had pounded the oak galls fine and was now boiling a shroud in the black solution produced when galls are soaked in water. Here was Robert Caxton's funeral shroud.

Kate glanced toward me as I entered and I saw that the moisture upon her face was not all due to the heat of her work. Tears had left tracks upon her reddened cheeks. As I watched she used the stick to wind the black-stained cloth to a bundle, then lifted it from the pot. She allowed it to drain, then with Adela, who had learned from the passing bell that her aid might be needed, quickly took the bundle out through the kitchen door to the toft. There she and the maid stretched the cloth upon a bush to dry.

Adela busied herself in the kitchen, emptying the pot of oak gall solution, while Kate washed as much of the black stain from her fingers as she could, then gathered up John and went to sit by her father's bedside. I had drawn a bench to the chamber and 'twas large enough for two. Or three. Bessie had watched this day's activities with wide eyes. Now she crawled between us and sat silently. Her usual exuberance had vanished.

Adela prepared a dish of pease pottage for our supper, and as Kate and I had consumed only a loaf for our dinner, and not much of that, we ate with more enthusiasm than was reflected in our faces. Kate was eager to return to her father, so gobbled her bowl of pottage and returned to his chamber. She would be there, she said, if he awoke. He must not find himself alone upon his deathbed.

Adela took Bessie and John to their beds, then bade us "Good night" and departed for her parents' house in the Weald while there was yet enough light for her to see her way.

When darkness came to Galen House I lit a cresset and placed it upon a stand in Caxton's chamber. Kate and I sat silently in the dim room, listening to her father's breathing. In the silence of the night there was no other sound. It seemed to me that the breaths were becoming farther apart. I was about to mention this to Kate when the sound stopped and although I waited for Caxton's breathing to resume, it did not.

Kate's head fell upon my shoulder and I felt and heard her sobs.

"He is with the Lord Christ now," I said.

"What of purgatory?" she said through her tears.

I had been reluctant to share my views of purgatory with Kate, or anyone else for that matter, for fear of outraging priests and archdeacons and bishops, as I once did. If no such place awaits those who die in faith then there is no reason for those who survive the dead to pay clerics to pray for their souls and release the dead sooner from such a terrible place. I did not believe Kate would speak intentionally to others of my views, but a word spoken carelessly could create much trouble. A man who questions purgatory might reduce a bishop's income. So far as the bishop would be concerned, such a man would be a heretic. Although nowhere in Holy Writ is such a place as purgatory mentioned.

Perhaps I should not write such words. Well, no matter. I do not put thoughts to parchment for the entertainment of others. When I complete the tale of Lady Philippa Molyns – if I ever do – I will lock the parchment away in my chest. Mayhap Bessie or John will someday read of my views. I pray that, if they agree with their father, they will also be silent.

I left my Kate and walked the short distance to Father Thomas's vicarage. The house was dark, but after a few minutes of pounding upon the door the clerk opened to me. I told him my father-in-law was dead and he should ring the passing bell again. Shortly after I returned to Galen House I heard the bell of St. Beornwald's Church ring out over Bampton's sleeping rooftops.

Kate had dried her tears and composed herself when I returned. I led her from the corpse and chamber, and told her she must seek our bed.

"Tomorrow and the next day will be busy," I said. "You must rest."

She said nothing, but did not resist when I took her arm and led her to the stairs. We went to our bed but sleep did not come soon to Kate. I know this because I lay awake and knew she was likewise unable to find Morpheus. 'Twas near dawn, a faint light at the windows, before Kate's breathing became steady and told me she slept. I must then also have fallen to sleep, for the next thing I remember was John wailing to break his fast, the windows glowing softly with the light of a new day.

Adela helped Kate wash Caxton's corpse and stitch it into the shroud, which was now dry. Adela prepared a roasted capon for our dinner. I was pleased to see Kate consume a reasonable portion, along with half a barley loaf.

Robert Grosseteste has said that drunkenness and merriment at a wake are disrespectful of the dead. I agree, as does Kate. So from Matilda Hugill, one of Bampton's alewives, I purchased but four ewers of ale, and from the baker I collected five of his best wheaten loaves. We had at Galen House a fair supply of parsley butter.

Perhaps some who gathered that evening at Galen House for Robert Caxton's wake thought me parsimonious. They received slices of wheaten loaf with parsley butter and ale. Most, when they saw there would be no foolishness attending the death, stayed only long enough to commiserate with Kate, then made their way home through darkening streets. John Fothergill was the only participant to overindulge with Matilda's ale, but made no complaint when I gently steered him through Galen House's front door and set him reeling off toward his home on Bushy Row.

The funeral was Tuesday morning. I had hired Arthur, Uctred, and two other of Lord Gilbert's grooms to carry the pallet upon which the earthly remains of Robert Caxton would be conveyed to St. Beornwald's Church. Bampton's three priests, Fathers Thomas, Simon, and Ralph, arrived to lead the brief procession from Galen House to the church, and many of Kate's friends were milling about before the door.

A moment later I saw Lord Gilbert stride from the corner of Bridge Street. He had chosen to honor Kate by being present at her father's funeral. Even though she is now Lady Katherine, old habits remain and she curtsied as he drew near.

Father Simon motioned to the bearers, they lifted the pallet, and as we set off up Church View Street Kate's friends set up a terrible wail. Some folk hire mourners for such a display, but so well regarded in the village is my Kate that we had not needed to pay any to bawl out in sorrow. Nevertheless, when the funeral was done, I gave a ha'penny to each of the women.

The priests stopped at the lych gate, where the corpse was set down while Father Simon spoke a prayer for Caxton's departed soul. When this was done the priests led the way to the porch and into the church. From the corner of my eye I saw three men leaning upon shovels, ready to dig a grave when the funeral mass was done.

The day had dawned cloudy, but when we emerged from the church the sun was breaking through, illuminating the south side of the church, where Robert Caxton would await the Lord Christ's return. Father Ralph led the way to the site chosen for my father-in-law's grave and sprinkled holy water upon the grass. The gravediggers moved to the place and bent to their work. These were men who knew what they were about, and soon a grave was opened to a depth of four feet. The grave could go no deeper, for the gravediggers came upon a set of bones from a previous burial. My father-in-law would have a companion as he awaited the return of the Lord Christ.

The priests scratched their heads and muttered amongst themselves as to whose grave had been disturbed, but none could remember a burial at that location. Men and women have been put into the ground in Bampton's churchyard for five hundred years. As someday I will be. 'Tis no wonder the place is filled with those waiting. How much longer, I wondered, would their wait be?

The grave was soon filled and the mourners, with last words of condolence to Kate, bade us farewell and departed the churchyard. Lord Gilbert waited until most were away, then approached me.

"You are off for Oxford tomorrow, with Arthur and Uctred? Or will you delay?"

"I think Thursday will be soon enough," I replied. "I dislike leaving Kate alone so soon after her father's death. If I would be away but for a day or two I might think differently."

"You believe many days will be required?"

"Aye. To find and follow de Wenlock, perhaps a week."

"I do not begrudge your service to Sir Aymer," Lord Gilbert

said, but then continued. "But I employ you to attend me, not him."

So he did grudge the time I had spent seeking – unsuccessfully – for Lady Philippa. He added, "If after a week in Oxford you have not found the lady, you must inform Sir Aymer that your labor on his behalf is at an end."

I agreed I would do so, then walked with Kate, Bessie, and Adela to Galen House. Our dinner was a simple meal of stockfish in bruit with maslin loaves and what little remained of our parsley butter and ale. The noon Angelus rang from St. Beornwald's Church as I crossed Shill Brook. At the castle I told Arthur and Uctred to be ready upon Thursday morning to journey to Oxford. They were.

Our palfreys were well rested. We departed Bampton before the second hour and crossed Bookbinders' Bridge before the noon Angelus pealed forth from Oxford's many churches. We made our dinner at The Fox and Hounds, a meal of battered eggs and maslin loaves, then sought Master Wycliffe at his lodgings at Queen's College. For what I intended, I would need his aid.

Wycliffe had just concluded his own dinner when I rapped upon his chamber door. His repast was not so grand as mine. His meal was a loaf and ale, but he seemed content – and pleased to see me again.

"The missing lady... have you found her?" he began.

"Nay. I am yet searching. I have been given one more week to find her."

"So you have come to me at Queen's. You must believe I may assist."

"Aye. I need lodging in a vacant chamber, and also for my men. I need also a scholar's gown so that I may go about the town unremarked."

"I can accommodate you on both scores. There is an empty chamber off the hall, and above the refectory is an unused storage room. A bit dusty, I'd think, but I'll have my man put it right. You may lodge together there. A week, you say?"

"Aye. If I have not found the lady or discovered some hint as to her whereabouts, I am to quit the search. We will take our beasts to the stables upon Catte Street and return. Can you have the gown ready?"

"Oh, aye, 'tis in my chest. There'll be a moth hole or two, mayhap."

"All the better. 'Twill lend me credence as a poor scholar. But I think I must visit a barber and shave my beard. The grey whiskers which have appeared will cause folk to doubt my vocation."

"Why so? Claim to be a graduate Master of Arts, now seeking the awarding of a Bachelor of Theology, as I am. I am older than you, and my beard greyer. No man will think twice at such a tale. There are men of forty years seeking a degree as Bachelor of Theology."

This was true, I knew, and so decided to cast away the thought of shaving my beard. When I returned to Master Wycliffe from the stables, he had the gown ready. Moths had indeed feasted upon the cloth, but it would suit my purpose. Many students wear similar attire.

I left Arthur and Uctred at Queen's College and prowled Oxford's streets. I went first to Little Bailey Street and the Red Dragon, where Martyn de Wenlock had taken a room.

I spent the afternoon walking past the inn, first one way, then the other, and watched as many scholars entered and departed the place. De Wenlock was not among them.

I hesitated to ask the proprietor if the scholar yet resided there for fear that, if he did, his landlord would tell de Wenlock that some other scholar sought him. I did not want the fellow to have even a hint that another man was asking of him.

'Twas near dark when I gave up prowling Little Bailey Street and returned to Queen's College. Arthur and Uctred were pleased to see me, as 'twas many hours since our dinner. A few steps from the entrance to Queen's was an inn, the White Boar, where we found pease pottage and barley loaves for our supper.

Next day, shortly after I rose from my bed, Master Wycliffe found me and enquired if I had met with any success the day before, seeking Martyn de Wenlock. When I told him the search had proved so far a failure he suggested I ask Eustace le Scrope of the fellow's whereabouts.

"He knows Martyn well, I think, and may know if he has changed his lodgings."

He had.

Wycliffe accompanied me to Balliol College where he inquired of le Scrope. The scholar was soon found, and readily explained de Wenlock's absence from Little Bailey Street.

"He has taken a chamber here, at Balliol, and studies here now. Meanwhile he is laboring as a copyist for a stationer on High Street."

I seemed to remember several stationers' shops along the High Street. "Which one?" I asked.

"Adam Huckett," le Scrope replied. "Shall I show you? Martyn will be there by this hour."

"Nay, I'll find the place. And please do not mention to de Wenlock, if you meet him, that I asked for him."

I received a puzzled expression in reply.

"Sir Hugh yet seeks the missing lady we first spoke of some two weeks past," Wycliffe explained.

"She was not taken by the scoundrels from Didcot?" Le Scrope looked surprised.

"Nay. Scoundrels they are, but they did not seize her."

"You think Martyn might have done so?"

"Mayhap, but if so, 'twas possibly with the lady's connivance. And he will know where she now is, and visit her when he may."

"If the lady is not near to Oxford, and Martyn does not seek her, what then?"

"Then I am absolved of further obligation in this business and Sir Aymer may seek his wife without my help."

"Do you suppose those who took her might have slain her?"

"Possibly. Her husband believes it may be so, and is prepared to seek another wife."

Master John and I returned to Queen's and found Arthur and Uctred, who were roaming about, raising their eyebrows, wondering where I had gone. We sought a loaf and ale at the White Boar, and they walked with me to High Street and Adam Huckett's shop.

"Here, or somewhere near on the street, is where I may be found," I said. "Unless de Wenlock has left the place and I am following."

"We've nothing to do," Arthur said. "Whilst you follow the fellow, we'll follow you."

"Don't get too close," I replied. "The scholar may remember you."

I dared not enter the shop for fear de Wenlock would remember me if he saw my face at close range. At a distance I would appear as any other scholar, and if he noticed me walking along behind him, there would likely be others garbed in black abroad on the same streets, as likely behind as before.

I thought it possible the man might leave his toil and seek dinner at some nearby inn, so I hung about close to the shop as noon approached. My hunch proved true. Moments after the noon Angelus rang out, my quarry departed the shop and strode to the corner of Cornmarket Street. I followed and watched as he entered an inn. I glanced behind me and saw Arthur and Uctred cautiously peering around the corner to see where de Wenlock and I had disappeared to.

My stomach took that moment to growl. How could I watch for de Wenlock's departure from the inn and yet see to my own empty belly? I trotted back to the corner, withdrew a few pennies from my purse, and told Uctred to enter the inn and purchase loaves and a ewer of ale – for de Wenlock knew Arthur, but not Uctred.

He returned before de Wenlock had finished his meal, so when the scholar set out and I followed I did not need to do so upon an empty stomach.

De Wenlock did not return to his pen. From the corner of Cornmarket Street and High Street he continued north. Was he going to lead me to Lady Philippa, or return to his lodging at Balliol College? A quick glance back over my shoulder reassured me of Arthur and Uctred coming after, Arthur yet chewing upon his loaf.

De Wenlock did not seem hurried. He sauntered well past Balliol College, toward a water meadow bordering the Thames.

Here he found a log at the riverbank, likely deposited there in some freshet, and sat, looking out upon the river. At this distance from the city wall there were few others upon the street, so I continued past de Wenlock until I found a path leading east which I hoped would lead me to the Banbury road.

Arthur and Uctred saw me stroll past the seated scholar and they likewise sauntered by. I glanced back from the path, and so far as I could tell de Wenlock paid them no heed. His gaze seemed fixed upon the stream. Behind Arthur and Uctred two more scholars walked the street. I hid myself behind a bush and watched as they also passed de Wenlock. Again, he paid no notice.

Arthur and Uctred soon caught up with me and joined me behind the shrub.

"What you s'pose 'e's about, just sittin' there watchin' the river?" Uctred said.

"Perhaps he enjoys a quiet moment," I said, "away from Oxford's noise and stink."

"Quiet enough 'ere," Arthur said. "What you going to do now?"

"I'll wait. And if I can, without being noticed, I'll follow him when he's had enough silence. You two had best follow this path 'til it comes to the Banbury road. Follow that back to Oxford. I'll join you there at Queen's College."

Every day it was the same, but for Sunday, when de Wenlock did not go to the stationer's shop but rather attended mass at St. Michael at the Northgate. But each day he took his dinner at the same inn, then walked nearly a mile north and sat upon the same log for an hour, staring at the river.

Perhaps, I thought, 'twas not the river which captures his attention, but the orchard on the west side of the stream. But why study apples so intently? And from a distance of two hundred paces? Occasionally I saw black-clad forms amongst the trees. The orchard must, I thought, be the property of some abbey. Godstow Abbey, perhaps. I knew there were several abbeys and priories and such places to the north and west of Oxford.

I followed de Wenlock for five days, becoming increasingly exasperated with the man. He never varied his routine. At the stationer's shop by the third hour. Away to the same inn at the sound of the noon Angelus, then off to the north up the Woodstock road to sit upon the exact same log, from that seat to spend a full hour intently studying the river or the orchard – whichever had so consumed his interest that he could not ignore it, even for a day. Thence returning to his labor at the stationer's shop until the light began to fail.

On Tuesday he had wit enough about him that when he sat down he swiveled about upon the log to peer behind him. He had never done so before, never taking more than a sideways glance at any of those who might have been upon the road before or behind him – and usually there were several besides me. He saw me approaching from a hundred and more paces behind, and I think 'twas then he remembered that he had seen a similar scholar appear from the same direction at the same time for the past several days. Had there been some other path leading from the road I could have turned aside to it, but there was no other and it would seem suspicious for a scholar to suddenly leave the road and wander off into the bushes.

De Wenlock stood and turned to face me. I walked on, feigning disinterest. He studied me intently as I approached, but said nothing. I touched my hood as I passed, walked on as if with purpose to the path to Banbury Road, then from the convenient bush parted a few branches and examined the log. De Wenlock was nowhere in sight, but Arthur and Uctred were. They had just then reached the log and seemed to be casting their eyes about, seeking me. I moved from behind the bush and called softly to them.

"That fellow took off back toward town in a tearin' 'urry," Arthur said. "'E looked us over good as we passed by, too."

This exercise had been futile. Whatever his purpose in his daily jaunts, 'twas not to have chat with Lady Philippa. I had followed de Wenlock once too often, and now he had seen my face clearly I could no longer trail him without being identified as one who had been taking a great interest in his life.

I missed my Kate. She was alone with her sorrow, but for the children and Adela. I told Arthur and Uctred that our visit to Oxford was at an end. We would return the worn scholar's gown to Master Wycliffe, take a quick dinner at the White Boar, retrieve our palfreys from the Catte Street stable, and set off for Bampton. I had failed to find Lady Philippa and was willing to admit it.

Chapter 17

We could not travel all the way to Bampton before dark. As I have done many times in the past, shortly after we splashed across the Thames at Swinford we halted before the gatehouse to Eynsham Abbey.

The abbey entrance looked crowded, and from the back of a horse I could see why. The almoner was passing loaves to poor folk, food left after the monks had enjoyed their supper. Most days monks have but one meal each day, but in the long days of summer, when the hours of labor are extended with the hours of the light, they will partake of a simple supper.

The porter recognized me, as well he might, for I have visited the place often. He sent his assistant to fetch the guest master. Our palfreys were soon ensconced in the abbey stables, and we three in the guest house, where we were told that bowls of pease pottage and loaves would be brought for our supper.

The novice who served our meal bowed and said that, when I had eaten, Abbot Gerleys waited on me to attend him. I had done the abbey some service a few years past, discovering who had slain a novice attached to the abbey. At the time Brother Gerleys had been the novice master. In the process of finding a murderer I had learned that the prior, whom all thought would supplant the aged abbot, was a heretic. So when Abbot Thurstan died, it was Brother Gerleys whom the community elected as their abbot. I have never been quite sure if he is pleased with the advancement.

I needed no guide to lead me to the abbot's chamber. I had visited the place many times. His door stood open, and when he saw me he lifted his eyes from the book upon his desk and bade me enter. He held in one hand a round glassy object fixed to what appeared to be a bone handle – a glass just like Master Wycliffe used.

Abbot Gerleys saw me glance inquisitively at the object, held it up before me, and explained: "'Tis a glass which will enlarge the words upon a page. My eyes serve me less well for reading and study than when I was young. This is a great help. Come, see for yourself."

He took the book he had been examining, lifted it around so that it faced me, then offered the glass. The apparatus was slightly larger than the palm of my hand, and 'twas exactly as the abbot said. The delicate letters and columns of numbers upon the page were startlingly enlarged. The exact cost of five gatherings of vellum leaped forth from its surroundings to gain my attention. Even a man near blind, I thought, could read using this glass.

"Spectacles help many," Abbot Gerleys said. "Brother Simon and Brother Andrew of this abbey use them. But I find this glass of greater help. Tomorrow, when the sun has risen, before you travel, I will show you an amazing thing this glass can do.

"When I heard you and your men had stopped to ask our hospitality I sent for you. When you travel to Oxford 'tis usually because some mystery must be untangled or some evil put right, or both. Which is it this time? Life in an abbey can be dull. I would have you enliven my day."

"Have you heard of Sir Aymer Molyns, of Coleshill?" I asked.

"Sir Aymer?" The abbot pursed his lips and finally admitted ignorance of the name and man.

"He was traveling from Coleshill, with his wife, her servant, and his retainers, to another of his estates. He intended to interrupt the journey at Bampton and enjoy Lord Gilbert's hospitality for a day or two."

"Intended?"

"Aye. Lady Philippa and her maid traveled in a wagon, closed against dust and sun. When Sir Aymer's party reached Bampton Castle the wagon was found empty."

"The lady had vanished?"

"Aye, she had. And is yet missing."

For the next half-hour I recounted my fruitless efforts to find Lady Philippa. Abbot Gerleys listened intently, his chin resting upon his fists, elbows upon the table. I spoke of Martyn de Wenlock's curious behavior of the past days and concluded the tale. We looked at one another.

"You've decided to give up the search?"

"Aye. I can think of no other path which might lead to the lady."

"Sir Aymer has lost a wife and two pounds."

"So it seems."

"Well, that's odd," Abbot Gerleys said, turning the book to himself again and picking up the glass. "Here is an entry for two pounds."

"You examine the accounts of the abbey?"

"An account ledger, true enough, but not for Eynsham Abbey. For Godstow Abbey."

My puzzled expression drew forth an explanation. "Godstow Abbey is nearly bankrupt. The nuns there have no sense of responsibility. Most are daughters of knights and bannerets and an occasional earl, and they've never in their lives needed to restrict their expenses. So the bishop has made me keeper of Godstow Abbey. The abbess doesn't much like it, but I've put my foot down. There are twenty in orders there now, and I've made it a rule they may have one servant and one chaplain each, no more."

"You spoke of an entry of two pounds to the abbey's account," I said. "How long ago was this entered?"

"Three weeks ago. When you mentioned the ransom I remembered seeing an entry for exactly that sum just before you came to my chamber. Our sacristan has a head for figures and keeps the entries up to date, but I review the ledger every week or so."

"When a woman, or a man, enters into a vocation," I said, "are they expected to make a contribution to the house to pay for their keeping?"

"They are."

"Does Godstow Abbey have an orchard?" I asked.

"Aye."

"Is it close along the river?"

"It is. Fertile soil. An excellent garden, as well, and the river provides water for fishponds. There's no reason the sisters should be so penniless but for their extravagances."

For several days I had watched Martyn de Wenlock study that very orchard. I recalled to my mind's eye that beyond the orchard, just visible through the trees, arose a wall, and beyond that the peak of a church roof. And occasionally I had seen black-clad figures walking under the trees of the orchard. Nuns of Godstow Abbey, surely. Although from where I had walked 'twas too far to make out if those who roamed the orchard were male or female.

Did Martyn de Wenlock walk north from Oxford each day hoping for a glimpse of Lady Philippa? Did she connive at her own disappearance? Was the two pounds entered into Abbot Gerleys' ledger the ransom I had carried to Badbury Hill?

If so, 'twas no wonder I had been unable to find the lady. She was safely hidden behind an abbey wall. She could not have put herself there alone. John Cely, her loyal man, must have turned his blind eyes and deaf ears from the wagon when she left it. Perhaps Maurice and Brom were given a few coins to ride ahead of the wagon as it slowed upon the hill, and a servant and chaplain of Godstow Abbey came to Badbury Hill to collect Sir Aymer's ransom. A hill they had not likely visited, but was described to them by a lady who knew it well. She knew, furthermore, that those who lived nearby would not be persuaded to deliver a ransom to the place for fear of the spirits thought to dwell there at night, and that the ransom exchange would not likely, therefore, be interrupted.

I explained to Abbot Gerleys the pattern I had before thought unlikely but now believed to be the solution to this mystery: Lady Philippa had conspired in her own disappearance.

"Who is abbess of Godstow Abbey?" I asked.

"Agnes de Stretely."

"If I travel there tomorrow will she see me?"

Abbot Gerleys scratched at his chin. "If she knows, or guesses, why you've come, likely not."

I was silent for a moment. I had entertained many thoughts as to who might have taken Lady Philippa and where she might now be, but all of these had proven false. Now here was a new possibility. But without access to Godstow Abbey and the cooperation of the abbess, how could I know if the lady had sought refuge under holy orders?

"What are you thinking?" Abbot Gerleys said, breaking in upon my thoughts.

"May a married woman take holy orders without her husband's knowledge or approval?"

"Nay."

"So Lady Philippa could not legitimately be of Godstow Abbey now, even though there is evidence that it may be so?"

"If Abbess Agnes decided to ignore the rule, and she is one who would do so, your lady may be there."

"If 'twas known that Lady Philippa had gone off to an abbey, and was yet alive and well, Sir Aymer would not be free to wed another," I thought aloud.

"Unless he could have his marriage vows annulled," the abbot said.

"And that would cost him a few shillings," I said.

"Shillings? Hah. A few pounds, more likely."

"The knight is already proclaiming his belief that felons took his wife, and she is slain. He intends to ask Bishop de Brantyngham to pronounce it so and grant him permission to wed again."

"Three pounds," Abbot Gerleys said.

"What?"

"I know the Bishop of Exeter well. He will require at least three pounds of the knight."

"If I seek Godstow's abbess tomorrow, you believe she will avoid me?"

"Probably. Especially if the lady is within and Agnes guesses your mission."

"Why would she?"

"You have been seeking the lady for four weeks. Do you suppose knowledge of your search has remained confidential?"

"I suppose not. What would you suggest?"

"I will journey to Godstow with you tomorrow. Agnes will not turn me away. I hold her purse strings, and can draw them tight if I wish. I probably should, anyway, whether Agnes will cooperate or not. The woman is much too profligate."

From Eynsham to Godstow is but five miles or so. After breaking our fast with wheaten loaves and ale Arthur, Uctred, and I met Abbot Gerleys and two of the abbey monks before the gatehouse. Both abbot and monks were mounted upon mules – a symbol of humility, I suppose.

We traveled through Wytham and by the third hour arrived before the gate of Godstow Abbey. I was surprised to see it standing open, no porter in sight, with men entering and leaving the environs freely. Abbot Gerleys saw my astonishment.

"Visitors and merchants come and go here as they please. The abbess will not control this, and I cannot be here each day to do so," he said.

"The nuns are permitted visitors?"

"With some limits. And they are often seen upon Oxford's streets."

"Not Lady Philippa, if she is here. Someone would eventually recognize her."

"Just so. Well, let us seek the abbess and learn if she has a new novice."

I saw none of the sisters about the gatehouse, but chaplains and friars apparently attached to the abbey were present. Several of these glanced toward Abbot Gerleys and their expressions indicated neither surprise at his presence nor ignorance of his identity.

No man came to greet us or offer to see to our palfreys and mules, so the two monks, along with Arthur and Uctred, took the beasts in hand and led them to a shady corner behind the church.

"The abbess's chamber is there." Abbot Gerleys pointed and led the way to the door.

The chamber was sited as it would be in any monastery, with an inner door which would open eventually to the cloister, and an outer door where visitors could gain entry without disturbing monks or nuns in the cloister. There was no man at the abbess's door, nor woman, either. No one to announce us. Abbot Gerleys wore a thin-lipped expression. He was not pleased, I think, with this welcome.

He pounded upon the chamber door, none too gently. The response was nearly instant with his last strike. The heavy oaken door swung open and a young woman, surely a novice of the house, stared at us with wide eyes.

"I am here to speak to Abbess Agnes." Abbot Gerleys did not need to introduce himself. The woman knew who he was.

The young woman turned to look back over her shoulder. She surely knew of Abbot Gerleys' authority over Godstow Abbey and perhaps thought her abbess would prefer to avoid the conversation.

If Abbess Agnes was within she must have heard Abbot Gerleys announce his presence. She was, and she had. The novice looked back to us, bowed, and stepped aside, conveying her superior's invitation to enter.

A plump woman sat behind a desk, her cheeks red and bulging out from her wimple. "I give you good day, Abbot Gerleys," the abbess said, and he returned the greeting. The abbess was smiling, but her smile seemed contrived, as if she struggled to overcome some other, more natural inclination.

"Who is your companion?" the abbess said.

"Here is Sir Hugh de Singleton, bailiff to Lord Gilbert Talbot at Bampton, and recently knighted by Prince Edward for services to the prince. He wishes to speak to you upon an urgent matter."

The abbess turned to me, the smile yet fixed to her face, as a plaster I might place upon a broken arm. She waited, silent.

"I wish to speak to Lady Philippa Molyns," I said.

"There is no one at Godstow by that name," was her calm reply. The smile was yet rigid upon her face.

No, there would not be. Lady Philippa would surely have taken another name. Many monks and nuns do.

"What she is now called is of no consequence to me. But I must speak to the woman who came to Godstow bearing that name when she arrived a few weeks past."

As I spoke I saw the abbess's jaw work, her eyes grew wide, she swallowed, and the smile faded. When I had demanded to see Lady Philippa, I was yet unsure she was at Godstow. But the abbess's reaction to my request told me she was. Unless I am a failure at reading the expressions of women. Which is always possible.

Abbot Gerleys had been silent during this conversation. Now he spoke. "Send your novice to the lady." He said this softly, but in a tone which told the abbess he would brook no resistance.

The abbess was silent for some moments, then turned to the inner door of her chamber and called out, "Amecia."

The young woman who had greeted us at the outer door appeared. "Fetch Sister Heloise," Abbess Agnes said. An appropriate name to choose for one whose love could not be, I thought.

The abbess turned to me, her smile gone. A look of sorrow had replaced it. Not anger. She did not speak, nor did Abbot Gerleys. We waited.

It seemed an hour had passed, but surely not, when I heard light footsteps upon the flags outside the abbess's chamber. A slender black-clad form swept through the open door and said, "You sent for me?"

Sister Heloise saw me and Abbot Gerleys as she spoke, and her words trailed off to a whisper.

Did she know who I was and why I had come? Perhaps she guessed.

"I am Sir Hugh de Singleton, surgeon, and bailiff to Lord Gilbert at his manor of Bampton. When your wagon was discovered empty there a search was begun. I have been from one place to another, and men have suffered blows while seeking you. One man is dead. Although his death cannot be solely attributed to you, it came about because of our search," I said.

The woman looked down to her hands, which she was clasping and unclasping.

"I am sorry to have troubled you so," she whispered.

"And what of your husband? You have troubled him, and cost him two pounds."

The woman looked up sharply and her demeanor changed. "What of my husband? I have earned his two pounds many times over with his cruelty and his shaming because I did not bear him a son."

"Will you not return to him? You have taken holy orders, or soon will, without his permission."

I turned to the abbess. "Will you countenance such a thing?"

The abbess did not reply, which was reply enough.

"You said men suffered blows seeking me. What of the blows I have suffered?" Lady Philippa looked at me steadily. I had no answer.

"I beg of you that you do not tell Sir Aymer where you have found me. Those who aided my escape will suffer, as well as I, if you do."

"John Cely?"

"Aye. And Brom and Maurice."

"How much did you pay for their silence?"

"John would accept nothing. I gave a shilling each to Brom and Maurice."

"What of Milicent Dyer?"

"She is here, with me."

"She will also join the abbey?"

"Nay. She will continue as my servant for a year or two. Meanwhile we will send a message to Giles that Milicent will be his, but he must wait for her. When he no longer serves my husband, she will be free to join him wherever he might be."

"When you fled the wagon, who was there with a cart upon the Burford road, awaiting you?"

"Friar Geoffrey and Gospatric."

In reply to my blank expression the abbess said, "Friar Geoffrey is my confessor, and Gospatric cares for the abbey fishponds."

"They brought you and Milicent here? Did they then return to Coleshill with the ransom demand, and again to collect the coins?"

"Aye. I could not enter the abbey without payment."

"Who wrote the ransom note?" I asked.

"I did," the abbess said. I now understood why the demand was written upon a fragment of a Gospel, and in what we judged to be a woman's hand. "What do you intend?" the abbess continued.

"Aye," Abbot Gerleys looked at me. "What now will you do?"

My mind was awhirl. Must I send word to Sir Aymer where his wife was? Should I send word? And what would happen if I did? Lady Philippa must then return to a life of misery and beatings. Because of me. Or might Sir Aymer understand his behavior nearly cost him his wife, and amend his ways? Could I be sure of that when he had already supplied his bed with another woman?

Nay. But if I departed Godstow Abbey leaving Lady Philippa in peace to be forever Sister Heloise, I must return to Bampton a failure in men's eyes. Are there things worse than being considered a failure? Aye; succeeding in some evil.

What would I say when asked if I had found Lady Philippa? Had I? Or had I found a woman named Sister Heloise? Did Lady Philippa Molyns still exist? I might say, "Nay, she is no more," but would this be true? The woman who once was Lady Philippa Molyns lives and breathes as before, regardless of any new name. And yet, when anyone is in Christ the old has passed away; there is a new creation.

Would the Lord Christ punish my lie if I said I had failed to find Lady Philippa? Upon one occasion in Holy Writ God rewarded a lie. Pharaoh told the Hebrew midwives to slay all their male infants, but the midwives did not, and told the king that Hebrew women gave birth so quickly that a child was born before the midwife could attend. For this lie, saving male babes, God rewarded the midwives. If I was silent, would the Lord Christ reward me for saving a woman from the wrath of an angry husband, or would He punish me for being false to Sir Aymer, Lord Gilbert, even my Kate? For if I were to keep this secret I must take it to my grave. And what of the sanctity of marriage? Had it been undone by Sir Aymer's own adulteries?

Nay. I have no secrets from my Kate. I had to tell her of this business, no matter what I decided.

"What of Martyn de Wenlock?" I asked at last.

"You know of Martyn?" Lady Philippa said, and her eyes brightened.

"He walks each day north of Oxford and sits upon a log gazing over the Thames toward the orchard and the abbey beyond. Did you know of this?"

"Nay," she replied.

"Why does he do so? Does he know you are here?"

"Aye, he does."

"Then he must hope to catch a glimpse of you from across the river," I said.

A tear welled up in Lady Philippa's eye. Was it due to thoughts of Martyn de Wenlock and his devotion, or to a fear that I would tell Sir Aymer where he might find her?

What if I told the knight where his wife had fled and when he arrived at Godstow to claim her she refused to leave the abbey? Would Abbess Agnes support her? Would Abbot Gerleys, as keeper of Godstow Abbey, permit the woman to defy her husband? I was sorely troubled by the decision before me.

Abbot Gerleys had been silent, listening to the discourse between me and Lady Philippa. Now he spoke.

"You said Sir Aymer believes his wife slain. Or he says he believes it so. He wishes to wed another who might provide an heir, but cannot do so while yet wed to this lady. He must convince the bishop that she is no more. Does Lady Philippa Molyns yet live? Or is this woman, who stands before us, Sister Heloise? By what name does the Lord Christ now know her?"

"How is a man to know the mind of the Lord Christ?" I asked. "If He stood here, in my place, what would He do?"

"That is what you must ask yourself, and when you find the answer you must have the courage to do the same."

"As in all things," I replied.

I looked to Lady Philippa, and my Kate appeared in my mind's eye. Would I tell her that I had sent Sir Aymer's wife back to his harsh treatment, or would she hear that Lady Philippa will spend her days in communion with the Lord Christ, not with an earthly husband? At that moment I knew what I must do, for I know my Kate, and I know what her choice would be.

"Sister Heloise, I bid you good day, and you also, Mother Abbess. M'lord abbot, if we leave now we may return to Eynsham in time for your dinner."

"But will you tell Sir Aymer where you have found me?" Lady Philippa cried.

"I have not found Lady Philippa Molyns," I said. "I failed."

We did return to Eynsham Abbey in time for dinner. I was eager to be on my way after the meal, but Abbot Gerleys asked me to wait briefly. He sent a novice to his chamber with a request that the lad return with the glass.

When the youth appeared, the abbot bade me follow to a grassy place near the wall, bent low, and held the glass above the turf. I saw a bright spot centered upon the grass and immediately a wisp of smoke curled above the dry vegetation. A heartbeat later a tiny flame emerged.

Abbot Gerleys stood, gave me a triumphant look, and spoke. "Amazing, is it not? The sun can be so focused as to start a blaze."

I watched astounded, resolving that upon my next journey to Oxford I would own one of these marvelous instruments.

We entered Bampton before the sun dropped behind the forest to the west of Bampton Castle. As before, I left my palfrey with Arthur and Uctred, telling them to inform Lord Gilbert I would call at the castle in the morning, then I walked the length of Church View Street to Galen House. From Godstow Abbey to Eynsham, and from Eynsham to Bampton, I had said nothing more about the search for Lady Philippa to Arthur or Uctred.

"When I tell Lord Gilbert we've returned," Arthur said, "an' that you'll seek 'im tomorrow, 'e'll likely ask what you learned in Oxford. What'll I tell 'im?"

"Tell him the search has failed, and I will explain on the morrow."

Bessie ran to greet me when I opened the door to Galen House, and my Kate was not far behind with John in her arms. Bessie grasped my knees and Kate my shoulders. I was embraced from top to bottom, and for a moment understood Sir Aymer's sorrow.

"What news?" Kate asked.

"I will tell all after we have eaten and our lass has been put to bed."

Bessie was old enough that she understood she was to be excluded from her parents' conversation, and a pout shaped her lips. But the lass does not hold grudges for long and by the time we sat before a pottage of whelks, and barley loaves she had forgotten her pique.

I moved our bench to the toft while Adela took Bessie to bed and Kate gave John his late supper. When Adela had departed for the Weald and our babes were abed, Kate joined me in the toft and I explained all to her. I could not help but remember that the last time we sat in this place we were three. Someday, many years hence, I pray, we three will be gathered together again, awaiting the Lord Christ's return.

"So, in men's eyes," I concluded, "I have failed."

"But not in mine," Kate said.

"If you regard me well I am content."

"What of Lord Gilbert?" Kate said.

"He has already told me I must quit the search for Lady Philippa, as the matter is not of my bailiwick."

"But did he mean it?"

"I will learn tomorrow."

He did. I made my way to Bampton Castle at the third hour, stopping only at the bridge over Shill Brook to collect my thoughts whilst gazing into the stream.

I found Lord Gilbert with his chaplain, in the solar, reading from his Book of Hours. He dismissed the priest and spoke.

"Arthur told me your journey to Oxford bore no fruit," he began.

"Aye. I spent five days following Martyn de Wenlock about the town. Never did he visit any woman. On the fifth day he recognized me as one whom he had seen on previous days and I realized that 'twas no longer possible to catch him out attending upon Lady Philippa."

"Arthur said that yesterday morn you visited some abbey, along with the abbot of Eynsham."

"Aye. Many times when I followed de Wenlock he walked north, then sat upon a log by the Thames and would gaze at the orchard of Godstow Abbey, across the river. I thought perhaps Lady Philippa was within the abbey, and that drew his interest."

"She was not there?"

"The abbess said no one of the name Lady Philippa Molyns was within."

I waited for Lord Gilbert to ask the question which would require me to lie. He did not. Did the question not occur to him, or did he wish to save me the embarrassment? He did not ask if Lady Philippa Molyns had ever been within Godstow Abbey.

"If Sir Aymer sends a man to ask of his wife I will tell him you have failed to find her and I charged you to be about my business, not his," Lord Gilbert said. "And that business includes seeing to Peter Alderson, who yesterday fell from a rafter while erecting a barn in his toft. His leg is broken, I am told."

"He resides on Bushy Row?"

"Aye, he does."

"I will see to him immediately," I said, and rose from my bench.

"A broken leg," Lord Gilbert said with a smile, "is easier to deal with than a missing lady, eh?"

He looked at me and raised an eyebrow as I departed his presence.

A fortnight later I traveled with Arthur to Oxford to purchase more gatherings upon which to complete this tale, and to purchase a glass such as Abbot Gerleys had. While in the town I visited the castle to learn of Gaston Howes' fate.

"Sentenced to hang," the sheriff said. "But King Edward has offered clemency to any felon who will join his army. He intends to go to France next year and regain his lost lands in Limousin, and for this he needs more archers. Gaston has been reprieved."

I never learned if Sir Thomas le Scrope recovered the three pounds' ransom he paid for his daughter. Some evils are unlikely ever to be righted. In this life.

Afterword

Badbury Hill was an iron-age hill fort located just west of Faringdon. The site now belongs to the National Trust and is popular for nature walks.

Great Coxwell barn was built in about 1292 for the Cistercian Beaulieu Abbey. It is now in the care of the National Trust. The barn is 152 feet long, 43 feet wide, and 48 feet high. A small car park serves visitors, and Badbury Hill is visible from the barn.

Numerous criminal gangs operated in medieval England. They were generally composed of family units. Some of the best known were the Folvilles, the Coterels, and the Bradburns. These criminals were often protected by local authorities – for a price – even including sheriffs and abbots.

Many readers of the chronicles of Hugh de Singleton have asked about medieval remains in the Bampton area. St Mary's Church is little changed from the fourteenth century. The May Bank Holiday is a good time to visit Bampton. The village is a Morris dancing center, and on that day hosts a day-long Morris dancing festival.

Village scenes in the popular television series *Downton Abbey* were filmed on Church View Street in Bampton, and St Mary's Church appeared in several episodes.

Bampton Castle was, in the fourteenth century, one of the largest castles in England in terms of the area enclosed within the curtain wall. Little remains of the castle but for the gatehouse and a small part of the curtain wall, which form a part of Ham Court, a farmhouse in private hands. The current owners are doing extensive restoration work. Gilbert Talbot was indeed the lord of the manor of Bampton in the late fourteenth century.

Mel Starr

The Easter Sepulcher

An extract from the thirteenth chronicle of
Hugh de Singleton, surgeon

Chapter 1

John was feverish and so was my Kate, so I attended the Maundy Thursday mass with only Bessie to keep me company. The new year had begun but a few days before, and the calendar said that spring was to be in the air. The calendar lied. A low sky spat frozen rain upon my fur coat as Bessie and I hurried to St. Beornwald's Church.

Father Simon placed the host into the pyx as the service concluded, and Bessie and I scurried home to escape the hard pellets of ice which stung our cheeks. The year of our Lord 1374 had begun badly. It was sure to improve. I have been wrong before.

I returned to the church alone for vespers on Good Friday. Bessie and John regularly pass coughs and dripping noses back and forth. This time 'twas John's turn to send a flush to Bessie's cheeks and redness to her nose.

When the mass was completed Father Thomas took the host from the pyx, wrapped it in a linen cloth, and placed it, along with a crucifix, within the Easter Sepulcher where, like the Lord Christ, it would remain buried 'til Easter morn.

The Easter Sepulcher at St. Beornwald's Church is unlike that of St. Anne's Church in Little Singleton, where I was born. The church there is small and plain, as is the Easter Sepulcher. 'Tis but a wooden frame which is covered with a linen cloth, as a burial shroud, whereas the Easter Sepulcher at St. Beornwald's Church is a niche in the north wall of the chancel. Inside the niche is the wooden structure where host and crucifix may be placed, then the whole covered by a cloth cunningly embroidered with scenes of our Lord Christ's passion.

John Younge, St. Beornwald's sexton, moved to the chancel as Father Ralph and Father Simon joined Father Thomas at the Easter Sepulcher to light candles. The chancel was soon glowing.

'Twas John Younge's duty, along with the priests' clerks, to keep watch over the Easter Sepulcher 'til Easter morn. This was a great honor, he had told me a few days earlier. Alone in the church, the nave and aisles dark but the chancel bathed in candlelight, a man might inspect his soul for the betterment of the days remaining to him. Younge would serve the first watch of the night. I saw him from the porch as I departed the church, standing squarely before the Easter Sepulcher, arms folded across his chest, determined in his duty.

Kate's rooster woke me at dawn on Saturday, as he does each morn, competing for the honor with the Angelus Bell ringing from the tower of St. Beornwald's Church. Had he not, the pounding upon Galen House's door moments later would have. I crawled from our warm bed, my joints complaining – they never used to – drew on chauces and cotehardie, and stumbled down the stairs.

'Twas Father Thomas who had bruised his knuckles upon my door. When I opened it he said abruptly, without a greeting, "Odo's gone missing. We've searched the church, but he's not to be found."

"Your clerk?" I said stupidly. So far as I know no other Odo resides in Bampton or the Weald.

"Aye... Odo."

"Was he not one of the watchers at the Easter Sepulcher?"

"Aye. He was to attend to the duty after John."

"He did not do so?"

"He did. Peter said Odo arrived to take up his post in good time, but when Ernaud went to ring the dawn Angelus and replace Odo, my clerk was not there."

"Perhaps he left his duty early, when he heard Ernaud ring the Angelus Bell. He would know that his replacement was present within the church."

"Nay. Ernaud saw from the base of the tower that Odo was not where he should be before he rang for the Angelus devotional. Father Simon arrived moments later to conduct the Angelus devotional and together they called out for him, Ernaud said, but there was no reply."

"'Twas a cold night," I said. "Perhaps he became chilled and sought his bed."

"So I thought, and went to his chamber to reprimand him. If the Lord Christ could die for Odo's sins the fellow could withstand a cold night for but a few hours to do honor to his savior. But he was not there. His bed was cold."

Here was a puzzle. 'Tis an honor to stand guard at the Easter Sepulcher, and one that John Younge and Peter Bouchard, Ernaud le Tourneur, and Odo Fuller – sexton and clerks – defend vigorously. Others of Bampton, good men and true, have volunteered to watch, but these four will not share the honor.

"You have begun to search for Odo?" I said.

"Aye. Ernaud and Father Simon came to me and Father Ralph. I combed the church and when 'twas light enough examined the churchyard. He is not there. Where might he be?"

"Where indeed?" I replied.

My wits were gradually returning after being roused from my bed so precipitously, but not so much that I could devise a response to Father Thomas's question.

I stood in the doorway, scratching my head, which was empty of intelligent thought, when Kate came down the stairs behind me.

"Might he have visited the tithe barn?" she said. She had heard our conversation and offered a solution. "Did he need to replenish stores at your vicarage?"

Father Thomas stroked his beard and spoke. "Mayhap. Alan, my cook, cares for that usually. But I will question him. He may have asked Odo to do an errand for him."

"But you think not," I said.

Alan had not done so, and as with all others we spoke to that morning had no thought as to where Odo might be.

By the third hour the church, churchyard, tithe barn, and vicarages had been searched over and again. Odo was not found. I told Father Thomas that I intended to return to Galen House, break my fast with a loaf and ale, then seek the castle and bring back with me some of Lord Gilbert's grooms so as to widen the search.

I am Hugh de Singleton – Sir Hugh, since Prince Edward saw

fit to offer me a knighthood for services I rendered to him – surgeon and bailiff to Lord Gilbert, Third Baron Talbot. Lord Gilbert had returned to Bampton Castle but a fortnight past, after spending the winter at Godrich, another of his possessions.

When I walked under the castle portcullis I saw Lord Gilbert striding toward the castle marshalsea. He has skilled pages, grooms, and farriers to care for his horses, but as with most of his class considers himself an expert judge of beasts, their care, and their ailments. No doubt he intended to peer over some stable groom's shoulder.

I hailed my employer and hastened to where he stood awaiting me. If I intended to take half a dozen or so of his grooms from the castle to seek Odo Fuller I should tell him why.

"Father Thomas's clerk, you say?" Lord Gilbert said when I told him of the missing man. "Has he ever shirked his duty in the past?"

"Not that I've heard. Father Thomas is a friend, and has confided in me in the past, but has never complained of Odo's work or his loyalty. Indeed, if the clerk had given him reason to do so the priest would have sent him packing and Odo would be seeking other employment."

"True enough. Father Thomas is not one to suffer incompetence," Lord Gilbert agreed. "Well, take whom you need, and inform me when you find the fellow. Must be somewhere near."

With that conclusion he bade me "Good day" and continued toward the stables. I sought Arthur Wagge, a groom in Lord Gilbert's service who had proven himself useful to me in seeking felons and suchlike rogues in the past, and Uctred, another groom who had also been of assistance. I found Arthur with two other grooms at the castle sawpit where the three of them were sawing planks for an addition to the castle larder. No doubt they were pleased to be released from this arduous labor. I told Arthur to find Uctred and two more grooms, then the six of them were to proceed posthaste to St. Beornwald's Church. And I told him why. Arthur tugged a forelock and set off to find Uctred. I hastened from the castle, crossed the bridge over Shill Brook without stopping to gaze into the stream – a thing I often do – and went to the church.

Priests, clerks, and sexton were milling about the porch, exchanging suggestions as to where Odo might be and why he would be there. When I came near I told them that six of Lord Gilbert's grooms would soon arrive and we must organize a search which would see the entire village examined.

When Arthur, Uctred, and four others appeared, I sent the searchers out in pairs – what one man might disregard the other might see. With Father Thomas I divided Bampton amongst the searchers so that no place would be overlooked while some other street or house or barn might be examined twice. The searchers were told to assemble at the church with their reports when the noon Angelus sounded.

Peter rang the noon Angelus as Arthur and I walked under the lych gate. Father Simon and Father Ralph and their clerks had preceded us, and Uctred and the other three of Lord Gilbert's grooms soon appeared. No trace of Odo had been found, no inhabitants of Bampton or the Weald had seen the clerk since Friday.

"Has Odo enemies?" I asked Father Thomas. "Mayhap he has not gone away, but some other has done him harm."

"What enemies would a clerk make?" the priest replied, shaking his head. "Odo was honest with me and, so far as I know, with all men."

"Honesty is known to cause trouble," I replied. "There are men who prefer deceit. Has Odo had reason to consort with deceitful folk, either willingly or unwillingly, so that they might despise his truthfulness?"

"Not that I know of. He'd have spoken of it to me, I think, had he done so. His life was this church and service to it, and to me. How would such a life bring Odo into conflict with evil men? That is your thinking, is it not? That Odo has not gone off of his own choice, but some other man has done away with him? Was it so, would we, or some other of Bampton folk, not have found his corpse?"

"Unless it was well hid," I said.

"And if some rogue did injure or slay Odo, would there not be some sign of the evil in the chancel? He was there, we know, when he took Peter's place at the Easter Sepulcher. He would not have departed the chancel and ignored his duty for some light reason."

"We have not sought any sign that harm came to Odo while he stood guard," I said. "Such a thought did not occur to me, or to you, I think. Why should it? What mischief could come to a lowly clerk as he stood watch at the Easter Sepulcher? Mayhap it is time we considered that possibility."

Father Thomas span on his heels and entered the porch, but I grasped his arm and said, "Wait. Many men have already stood about the chancel and before the Easter Sepulcher. If more of us do so, whatever sign of evil done to Odo may be obscured, if 'tis not already."

"What do you intend?" Father Thomas said.

"I would like to examine the chancel alone. The sky is beginning to lighten, and the candles also provide light. Windows and flames may permit discovery of things not seen or expected this morning."

"Very well. I see your point. I and Father Ralph and Father Simon will observe from the rood screen while you search the chancel."

They did, as did Arthur, Uctred, and the other grooms. These fellows felt themselves a part of the mystery and were interested now in seeing the matter to its conclusion.

I walked past the rood screen and cautiously peered at the flags before my feet. Stone does not preserve footprints. I cannot say what I thought I might discover there on the floor of the chancel, but whatever it might have been I did not at first find it.

As I slowly walked past the Easter Sepulcher I saw, between the sepulcher and the high altar, a tiny dark dot upon the flags before the altar. The speck was about the size of the nail upon my little finger. 'Twas no wonder neither I nor any other had taken note of it in the dim light of early morn. Even the flames of a dozen or so candles would not make the spot plain to a casual observer.

I kneeled for a closer look and from the rood screen Father Thomas said, "What have you found?"

"I am unsure," I replied. As I spoke I remembered that in Galen House I had a tool which might allow me to better examine the spot before my eyes. I stood, walked to the rood screen, and spoke to those who stood near it.

"I must go to Galen House, but will return anon. Please allow no man to enter the chancel. There is a mark upon the flags which is suspicious and I have at Galen House an instrument which may help me learn what is there."

The speck was dark brown and I feared it was a dried drop of blood. The past summer I had seen Master John Wycliffe and Abbot Gerleys of Eynsham Abbey using a glass which enlarged the letters upon a page. I had purchased one of these lenses, and now it occurred to me that the instrument might allow me to better identify the stain I had found.

"Have you found the clerk?" Kate asked as I entered my home.

"Nay, and I fear we may not."

"You may not? Why so?"

"I may have found a drop of dried blood near to where Odo would have stood while watching over the Easter Sepulcher last night."

"You may have? How will you know?"

"I have come for the glass I bought last summer. It may tell me what my eyes alone cannot."

The glass was within my chest in our chamber. I hurried up the stairs, withdrew the glass, and clattered back down again. Kate was where I had left her, at the door, a worried expression upon her face. Perhaps she was anxious that I would do myself some injury if I did not take more care upon the stairs.

"Will you return soon for your dinner?" Kate asked. "I have prepared stewed herring and rice moyle."

Until Kate spoke of it I had not thought of my empty stomach, being too much involved with the matter of Odo Fuller's disappearance.

"I will not be long," I said, and I wasn't.

At the church I produced my glass and Father Thomas spoke. "I've heard of such things, but I've never seen one before."

"The work of the devil," Father Ralph said. "Making of things what they are not."

"Nonsense," Father Thomas replied. "The words on a page are not made other than what they are by being enlarged so that men of great years may yet read them. I wear shoes so as to protect my feet and make them more useful. Are shoes the devil's work also? I warm myself at the fire. Shoes and fire are man's creation. God did not light these candles the better that we may see. Men did. You suggest that what men can create is the work of Satan?"

Father Ralph sniffed in reply but said no more.

I passed the rood screen and bent to find the speck upon the flags. 'Twas not readily visible, but after a moment's searching I saw it, dropped to my knees, and held the glass over the spot. With a fingernail I cautiously scratched at the dried matter and watched through the glass as some of it flaked away. Here was a reddish-brown drop of dried blood, I was sure of it. The glass helped make clear what I had suspected.

One drop of blood. If Odo was slain here, why so little gore? Certainly he was not stabbed. Had this been so he would have left his blood spattered about. Strangled? Then there would have been no bloodstain at all. Struck upon his head? Aye, that would answer. A blow upon a man's skull might slay him and cause little bleeding. If Odo was knocked upon his head, what was the weapon? A felon might take his club with him after his evil deed, and that would likely mean he had entered the church intent upon striking Odo down, and so brought the weapon to the church with him. I glanced about the chancel and high altar, peering into dim recesses, and even opened the door to the vestry. But that chamber had already been searched in the morning and I found nothing new.

My eyes were drawn to the altar, and the two great candlesticks there. They were silver, heavy, and costly, a gift to the

Church of St. Beornwald by Sir Aymer de Valence many years past. The candles upon these candlesticks were lit, providing light as I approached them. A blow from one of these could propel a man into the next world. They were as long and thick through as my arm.

"What do you see?" Father Thomas asked.

"There is a speck of blood upon the chancel flags."

"Then some evil has happened here."

A glance at the candlesticks told me nothing. To more closely examine them I must extinguish the candles so that I could handle and turn the candlesticks in the light of the windows and other candles illuminating the chancel. I did so, and at the base of the first candlestick I lifted I found another brown smudge, and a hair.

"Come," I said to Father Thomas. "Odo has been struck down."

The priest hurried to where I stood at the high altar. "Look here." I pointed to the base of the candlestick. This is blood. And Odo is fair-haired, is he not?"

"Aye, he is."

"Do you see the hair caught in the blood? 'Tis not dark."

"It is difficult to know," Father Thomas said, "from just one hair. But it does seem the hue of Odo's hair. What has happened here?"

"Some man struck Odo down whilst he stood watch at the Easter Sepulcher," I said.

"But where then is he? Did his assailant drag him away? Was he not smitten unconscious, but forced to accompany his attacker? Or was he slain? If so, where is his corpse?"

These were all laudable questions, for which I had no answers.

"Here is another question," I said. "How would some man enter the chancel, filled with light as it is from the candles, and seize a heavy candlestick with which he could then strike Odo? The clerk would surely have seen the man enter."

Father Thomas glanced about him, as if to reassure himself that what I said was so.

"It must be," the priest finally said, "that whoso attacked Odo – if this is truly what happened – was known to him."

"I agree, unless Odo was dozing and did not see or hear his attacker enter. Odo is a small man, and not accustomed to labor or combat. A large man might overwhelm him, I think."

"Aye," Father Thomas agreed. "And even if Odo thought himself in danger he would not forsake his duty to stand guard at the Easter Sepulcher. He was not a man to shirk an obligation, especially an obligation to the Lord Christ."

"Was not a man? Already we speak of him in the past," I said.

"The blood upon the floor and candlestick cause me to believe his life is ended," the priest said. "If I am wrong, why can we not find him? If he lives, why has he not shown himself? Would some man bludgeon him over the head, then drag him away and keep him hidden, but alive?"

"I can think of no reason for doing so," I said.

"Neither can I," Father Thomas agreed.

We spent the remainder of the day – but for the two other clerks and John Younge, who returned to watching over the Easter Sepulcher and occasionally glancing over their shoulders – searching for Odo Fuller. I did not expect to find him, and we did not. We might have not troubled ourselves. Odo was found the next day, Easter. But unlike the Lord Christ he had not risen from the dead.